Flyte or Fancy

You Decide

—

Flyte or Fancy

You Decide

Evelyn Waugh Meets
Harry Clifton On
The Road To Brideshead

By

David Slattery-Christy

First published 2023
The right of David Slattery-Christy to be identified as the Author of this work has been
asserted in accordance with the Copyright, Designs and Patents Act 1988.
This is a work of Fiction.

British Library Cataloguing in Publication Data.
A catalogue record for this book is available from the British Library.
Published By Christyplays
ISBN: 9781838136567
November 2023
www.christyplays.co.uk
Typesetting and origination by Christyplays Publications.
Printed in Great Britain.

Please Note:

This book is a fictional dramatization. For dramatic and narrative purposes the book contains
fictionalized scenes, composite and representative characters and dialogue. Some events have
been imagined and space and time have been rearranged. The views, opinions and events
depicted are those of the characters only and do not represent or reflect the events or the
views and opinions held by the individuals on which the characters are based.

Cover Design by **Ed Christiano** of Deeper Blue Design
Evelyn Waugh image courtesy of Alarmy Stock Images.

Grateful thanks to **Mathew Rajat Bose,** who played Harry Clifton in the short film 'Flyte of
Fancy', for which the author of this book wrote the screenplay, for allowing the use his image
on the cover.

—

Author's Note

For some years now I have found myself more and more fascinated with the history of Lytham Hall and the stories surrounding the Clifton family, who once owned most of the land between Blackpool and Lytham for hundreds of years. Now Lytham Hall is open to the public again, since being purchased by the trust that now runs it, and the rich history is once again being examined and brought back to life, and the hall itself reborn as a living museum for visitors to enjoy.

When I started researching the life of Harry Clifton I became aware that Evelyn Waugh had also visited Lytham Hall in the 1930s and that Harry and Evelyn both went up to Oxford and both were sent down without degrees in the 1920s! So they had that in common. Harry was at Christ Church and of course this was where Waugh's famous character Sebastian Flyte had rooms in Brideshead Revisited. Interestingly, Waugh continued haunting Oxford, probably in the hope that his tutor, with whom he had a feud, would relent and let him graduate; but of course his tutor never did. The original Hypocrites Club, a private members club set up by students, became so notorious that by 1925/6 the original lessee had relinquished the club to appease the university. However, the club was taken over by another lessee and continued as a 'private drinking club' that was still The Hypocrites in all but name, until it finally closed for good in 1929. Evelyn Waugh continued to go to the club when visiting Oxford as late as 1928.

As Harry Clifton was such a spoilt and eccentric heir to his family's estates, and was no stranger to fine champagnes and a pampered life, it wasn't long before I began to wonder if the speculation, voiced by his mother in 1945, that he could have in some way inspired the Sebastian Flyte character in Brideshead. He would have been attracted to the excesses of the private drinking club, and had the money to indulge himself, so it is more than possible that Oxford is where he and Waugh first encountered one another. There are other contenders, especially Waugh's lover at the time Alistair Graham, but I would imagine that Flyte was actually based on more than one person – if not several – that Waugh encountered along the way.

—

With that in mind a story started to develop in my mind and I decided to create it. There is a lot of fact in this story, especially the exploits of Harry Clifton and his odd behaviour, also that of his family members, and Evelyn Waugh also visited Lytham Hall as a guest in the 1930s. He wrote to Lady Asquith and told her the Clifton's were "all tearing mad" but indulged him in the finest food and champagne. He was also very complimentary about the fine Georgian manor that is Lytham Hall.

There is also fiction as I have had to imagine possible situations and conversations, and for the purposes of the story to add a pinch of artistic license to the mix. That said I have remained as true to some facts as I possibly could. One area I allowed myself real artistic license was with Harry's teddy bear that he doesn't name until he gets to Oxford. After visiting St Aloysius Catholic Church, on the Woodstock Road, he decides to call him…well; I will let you guess that one! Interestingly St Aloysius used to have an infant and junior school attached to the Catholic Church and that was my first school. The school and church would have been known to Waugh, so I did wonder if that is where the idea came from for Aloysius. The Cliftons' were Catholics and Evelyn Waugh converted to Catholicism in the 1930s, so they also had that in common.

The story covers the period from 1923 to 1939 and takes us on a journey through the end of the roaring 20s to the new era that was the hedonistic 1930s, until it all came tumbling down with the outbreak of WW2.

I hope this story will give you, if nothing else, an introduction to the fascinating history of the Cliftons' of Lytham Hall and Evelyn Waugh's novels. Please visit Lytham Hall, you will not be disappointed and read the novels if you haven't – they shine a light on a past that is rich in eccentric characters, a lost world, and they are also very funny too.

David Slattery-Christy
July 2023

Chapters:

Images: With grateful thanks to Lytham Hall, who kindly gave me permission to use various images of the Clifton family for this book. All images subject to copyright of Lytham Hall (LH); David Slattery-Christy (DSC); Royal Collection (RC).

1. Harry Clifton – pages 27 & 288 (LH)
2. Evelyn Waugh – page 280 (Alamy)
3. Clifton Family: John Talbot, Easter Daffodil, Violet, Michael, Harry – page 11 (LH)
4. Lillie Langtry – page 100 (RC)
5. John Talbot Clifton – page 296 (LH)
6. Violet Clifton – page 295 (LH)
7. Lilian Clifton – page 287 (LH)
8. Avia & Daffodil Clifton – page 297 (LH)
9. Grand Duke Michael Romanov – page 294 (RC)
10. Daffodil & husband Gerald Baird (LH)
11. David Slattery-Christy & Rajat Mathew Bose – page 8 (DSC)
12. Ritz Hotel Restaurant – page 299 (DSC)
13. Renaissance & Rosebud Eggs – page 300 & 301 (Faberge Museum)
14. Austin Car & David Slattery-Christy – page 302 (DSC)

David Slattery-Christy and Mathew Rajat Bose who played Harry Clifton in the short film 'Flyte of Fancy' whilst filming at Lytham Hall in 2022.

'Flyte of Fancy' was a short film with a screenplay by David Slattery-Christy.

Once Upon A Time

*These young things were
more brittle than bright…*

—

———

L to R : John Talbot de vere Clifton, Easter Daffodil de vere Clifton (standing), Violet de vere Clifton, Michael de vere Clifton (standing) and Henry Talbot de vere Clifton (known as Harry).

Taken at Lytham Hall in 1925

With Thanks

Christ Church, Oxford

Peter Anthony, Paul Lomax and the trustees of Lytham Hall

Mathew Rajat Bose
Ed Christiano
David Brown
Dr. Robin Darwall-Smith
Islay Tourism Office
Ritz Hotel
Faberge Discoveries

Jane Cross for proof reading and editing the manuscripts

Robert Smith Literary Agent

———

Prologue

Emery's Hotel – Brighton – 1979

The screeching of seagulls reverberated through the squalid room. The bottom sash window, with broken and cracked glass in the corner, and chipped paintwork, was devoid of its cords so was propped open by a discarded bottle. Beyond the grime of the glass, the blue sky could be seen, with Brighton's rooftops sweeping away towards the domes of the pavilion and the sea beyond. The gulls circled on the look out for food that could be stolen or scavenged; they cried to each other shrilly and created a cacophony of sound almost unbearable.

Inside the room, in the fleeting moments of silence, the heartbeat of the elderly man could be heard. His actual age was difficult to guess but he was physically thin and frail and his grey goatee beard was unkempt. To anyone who had known him in his prime, the shadow of the man that was left would be unrecognisable. His breathing was laboured and raspy as he lay across the bed. His head turned and his eyes closed.

The room was grimy and dull, the furniture, once fashionable and sought after, was battered and made cheap with use, the carpets worn and made threadbare by countless feet over countless decades. The floorboards would creak and groan as if protesting at yet more stress inflicted onto the aged, worm eaten, dry Georgian timbers. Dust seemed to hang constantly in the air illuminated by the sudden ruthless shards of sunlight streaking through the window.

Opening his eyes the man seemed to struggle to comprehend where he was and what he was doing in this room. Slowly comprehension once again filled his sad eyes and he listened intently to his own heart beat and remembered. This was his friend's hotel, his favourite psychic and soothsayer, his money had probably bought it for her, but he couldn't remember. The sound of his heart seemed to fill his ears and become louder and louder as his anxiety grew. He turned over and then breathlessly heaved himself upright and swung his legs off the bed and put his feet to the floor. He stared at them as if they belonged to someone else; he marvelled at the dingy, stained carpet and thought of nothing apart from breathing. He was relieved the sound of his heart beat had diminished.

Looking around the room he fixated on the dank, peeling wallpaper. The once vibrant pink and red climbing dog roses were now faded and lifeless on their printed trellis. Damp and stains of goodness knows what defiled their beauty. Tears formed in his eyes and he suddenly felt overwhelmed by the travesty of it all; why did everything have to fade and lose its lustre? Life held no thrill anymore for him. He struggled to breathe and do any normal activity. Excess had caught up with him.

He slowly pushed himself up into a standing position. This simple act made him gasp for breath so he stood trying to catch his breath enough to continue his journey to the dressing table where a carafe of water and a glass stood on an old battered tray. Stumbling to it with all the will he could muster he crossed the room and sat heavily onto the rickety stool.

As he did a cloud of dust escaped and whooshed up around him as the gulls screamed and the harsh winter sun shone through the murky window glass. With a shaking hand he poured some water into the glass and took a few desperate sips to alleviate the dryness in his mouth and throat. It made him choke and splutter because he had swallowed too quickly; he gasped for air again and clutched at his chest the pain in his arm returning. He felt the beads of cold sweat on his brow and the sting of tears in his eyes and suddenly, with energy he didn't know he had, he brushed away the tears and the sweat defiantly with the back of his hand. Catching his breath he gazed into the mirror and sighed loudly at what he saw.

The woman's face stared out at him from the mirror and she looked concerned and angry as she nervously fumbled with her rosary beads. She focused on him as if wanting to be sure it was him. Then his father appeared behind her and looked out staring at him intently.

"What do you want, mother?" The man said with sarcasm in his voice. "Thank you for bringing father to admonish me too," he spluttered, "to hell with you both and your damn bells and smells!" He yelled at them and then instantly gasped for breath he could not find.

"Repent your sins, son, it's not too late!" She implored, "Your father is furious with you but if God can forgive you so will he," she pleaded, "repent your sins…repent, son, please!" With that they faded away and were gone.

The man folded his arms onto the dressing table and lay his head down on them. Tears were in his eyes; but this time tears of anger. "Leave me alone," he sobbed, "leave me alone."

Suddenly he heard the sound of distant jazz music – a saxophone and a piano dominated the mix. He knew this music, remembered this music, where was it? He then recalled it was Oxford, the Hypocrites Club in the 1920's. "I was so happy at Oxford," he cried softly to himself, "so very happy with Bertie and Evelyn." He lifted his weary head and again tried to focus his eyes in the mirror. At first it seemed smoky and hazy but then it began to clear and the music became louder. He saw his younger naked self cavorting and dancing with his friends. Their youth and beauty visible now more than it ever was in the moment. Then, in that past, they took it all for granted, believing they would live forever as they laughed and loved with abandon.

"We were so bright, so young," he whispered, "but it's all gone, everything," he then cried out with a vigour he thought he no longer possessed, "where are they now? Will I see them again those friends I loved so much?" His head collapsed into his arms and he sobbed for what was, for what might have been and for a different ending to his life. His cries of anguish and regret, before his last gasp of breath, went unheard as the screeching of the gulls fighting over some scraps beyond the window drowned them out. But then, nothing mattered anymore; not for him anyway.

Chapter One

Destiny - 1923

Henry Talbot de vere Clifton:

Being me is never easy and never has been. I'm sixteen years old, the perfect age to finally discover one's own self and have independent thoughts. The public me is Henry de vere Clifton the heir apparent to my family's lands, titles and wealth on the grounds that I was the first born son. The private me is Harry Clifton, a less formal name and preferable to me but not my parents or the legions of staff, estate managers or my father's solicitor. As a result my relationship with my mother, Violet, and father, John Talbot Clifton is strained to say the very least. I fear they would have chosen another kind of son, one that happily conformed and did his duty without complaint. Alas they were as stuck with me as I am with them. As my favourite author Edgar Allan Poe put it: "Years of love have been forgot, in the hatred of a minute."

The 'minute' in question was the moment my father realised I would stubbornly stride along my own path in life and would not be bullied, coerced or threatened into following meekly in his footsteps and continuing what had always been. I could never understand why people wanted to reaffirm what had "always been." Why not have something new, it might even be better. Hypocrisy was evident to me but alas not to them. Like the fable of 'The Emperors New Clothes' they blithely continued with their blinkered and Victorian existence. I was determined to be my own man and live fully in the 20th Century and damn them all. Life was indeed for living. I relished the opportunities.

There was just one small problem. My father controlled the money, so at this early stage in my life I had no choice but to try and create a middle ground where we could all hang on to our hopes and dreams without them being totally dashed into the mud.

My mother bravely did her best to keep the peace between us and must have been exhausted in the process at times. I admired her and despised her in equal measure. I am sure the feeling was mutual at times. Oddly, I was actually more like her than my father so maybe she recoiled at my thoughts and actions sometimes because she recognised them as her own. However, being a good, obedient, Victorian wife she would have never gone against my father or any other male figure for that matter. She obediently followed what had always been and was loyal in spite of her own thoughts and feelings – whatever they might be. In many ways they still lived a Victorian existence even though the era had long passed through the Edwardian to the new Georgian in which we now lived with King George V and Queen Mary. They too seemed of a bygone era, stolid and stoic and dependable. Three qualities I hoped never to define me!

I often wondered if my mother loved me in the real sense, or indeed any of her children, or were they just the result of her duty to my father to produce an heir and a spare so the traditions could continue uninterrupted into some far flung future we had not yet met. My sisters were inconveniences along the way in pursuit of male heirs. Families are ever complicated. Mine more than most and navigating my way to find myself and my own spirit and desires had been treacherous indeed.

Lytham Hall, that fine Georgian manor, was our family home and a splendid one it was too. The family had been the squires of this and vast acres of Lancashire along the Fylde Coast since the 16th Century. Indeed parts of the original Tudor manor were incorporated into the upper floor of the Georgian house; mainly paneling that was dark and rather gloomy at times but creating a more warm and cosy atmosphere in winter with a roaring log fire.

Alas the servants had to drag themselves up to the highest part of the manor with baskets of logs, to keep the home fires burning in this and many other rooms occupied by family and visiting friends. I'm sure they preferred when we used the formal ground floor and first floor drawing rooms as it was so much easier. That said, and to my shame when I think of it, we tended to not see the poor staff scuttling about ensuring our every need was catered for. To us vile children they were invisible and we certainly never engaged them in any kind of conversation. Even less knew their names. Thinking of this now appalled me. How could we have been so beastly and indifferent to their existence? Now I could see that and feel some shame, I declared I would never be so remote again from those I encountered daily.

My sisters were seen by my father as trinkets or attractive adornments to the family as they had no use beyond that for the dynasty. My self and my younger brother were the requisite heir and spare.

My sisters Hermione and Avia were rather distant at times and always wrapped up in prayer, or some other kind of charity work with the poor of the parish. They had moments of exuberance and could be great fun but this was soon tempered by father and mother who found such displays of frivolity slightly irritating and a little shocking. Girls were to be seen when required but not heard and they were sadly rarely encouraged to have any kind of opinion of their own. I was far too self absorbed and selfish to understand and I had that arrogance of the first born son who would as a right one day inherit everything. How utterly vile I must have seemed to them with my strutting self importance. Little wonder they sought the comfort of religious retreats at the earliest opportunity – and then husbands; but only suitable ones! It was their way to escape beyond the control of father. Mother was happy as long as father was, I so wanted her to rage against things and stand up to him but she never did. She was deeply loyal and knew her place in the marriage. She had a talent for writing but she would only develop this fully in later years.

My father dominated with his personality and always had. My younger sister Easter Daffodil declared that she missed him, "beasting about the place" when he was off at a hunt or another of his hideous blood sport adventures. She was always good at summing things up with a few words and she got him perfectly with "beasting." Daffodil was the exception in regard to sisters. She made me laugh and I noticed often how she seemed older and wiser than her years considering the limited education she had received.

That mischievous twinkle in her eye was something that could never be taught! However, she did not let a lack of formal education hold her back, and took to reading books avidly – taking advantage of the dusty tomes filling the library at Kildalton Castle on Islay, our home in Scotland, or Lytham Hall. Often she could be heard laughing out loud at some passage that had amused her. Her face would light up as she explained the latest adventure she had immersed herself into.

My parents turned a blind eye to this eccentric behaviour believing she would eventually grow out of it. They hoped in vain, and for one I am glad she did not. Secretly I admired her panache and bright, eager face full of wonder and interest in life. Sometimes I sensed she saw right through me and realised that beneath all the conditioning, I was a little daunted at the position my birth demanded of me. As she was born on Easter Monday, my father thought it amusing to call her Easter Daffodil. She suited it perfectly, in spite of it being a ridiculous set of names, whenever she entered a room it lit up like spring sunshine and she positively glowed. In my heart I felt I had some love for Daffodil, my preference was to call her that, I could find nothing resembling it for my other two sisters or, to be honest, for my brother Michael. Certainly not my parents. Oh, dear. Merely having that thought fills me with a sadness I find hard to analyse. Love is an odd thing, isn't it?

Alas, my father was a brute. Emotionless at the best of times and especially when killing on a hunt. I never could bear the thought of killing anything.

Daffodil was right, he was indeed a beast! Catholic High Church religious too, as was my mother, with her endlessly fumbled rosary beads, and the religion was enforced upon us children. "Hail Mary Mother of God. Forgive them for they know not what they do."

This resonates deeply with me and it's why I gradually found a space in my mind that was just my own. A space where I could nurture an alternative to what had 'always been' and map out a path in life for myself that would break down barriers fully; knowing this would infuriate my father. That was the least of my worries, my ever increasing need to be liberated from enforced duty grew silently within me from an early age and the more it developed the more determined I became. The more my father berated me for not being good enough the more I realised I was and would be superior in the way I wanted to change the world and take a different path. It was my first sense of the spiritual connection one can have with one's own being. I mattered more than hundreds of years of family history. Lytham Hall and the estates be damned!

When I was five he made me shoot a deer and then slit its throat and smeared my face with blood. I can still hear my screams and relive the horror in my dreams; the smell and feel of the still warm blood being roughly applied to my face, as the dead eye of the poor animal stared at me accusingly. My father carried me indoors and made it clear how embarrassed he was at my behaviour and from that day his one aim in life was to toughen me up. It achieved exactly the opposite. Maybe that was the 'minute' for him where he started to hate having a son who failed to share his monstrous activities? In my mind, even at that age, I could not reconcile my father killing innocent animals and then piously kneeling to pray to God. How did he do that?

My sisters Hermione and Avia were often off to the retreat for some seminar or other. They conformed of course to the demands of father and mother and to them I was a minor annoyance. My younger brother Michael was much more like father. I sensed that from an early stage they wished he was the elder and would inherit. When Michael was bloodied on his first hunt he smeared the blood on his face with glee and laughter shared with father.

Unless I died he would not inherit, but maybe father would happily shoot me to ensure his carbon copy would succeed him. The thought made me shudder. I felt it was not a thought that he hadn't had.

I was sent away to school so that gave me an escape from one kind of hell to another. Downside School near Bath in Somerset was run by Benedictine Monks and the two priorities were sport (of every kind) and general abuse of boys. I hated sports. The whole timetable was to get the academic subjects out of the way in the first two periods and then the rest of the day was devoted to rugby, football, running, tennis, cricket, athletics, long distance races. Day in and day out, winter or summer, rain or shine we were tortured thus.

Thankfully I was a little academic and literate so the library was a sanctuary, as was the sick dorm where I ended up rather frequently with a chill or cold under the supervision of a sympathetic nurse. It is where I discovered Edgar Allan Poe's works. The darkness of his writing enthralled me. My father, using his weird logic, imagined this type of school would toughen me up and make me a man. It did neither with any great success. But it opened my eyes to survival.

The Brothers could be worse than father because their brutality was physical and some boys just broke down unable to bear it. There was buggery too, along with physical punishments like the strap or the cane that would leave horrid red welts across one's skin for days. The buggery was directed more at the pretty blond boys, so being overly tall and gangly and dark I was spared that particular horror – mostly.

I couldn't wait to leave that place. The irony that on the site of Lytham Hall there once stood a Benedictine Priory in the 12th Century was not lost on me. Once I had completed my final exams, it was decided I would go up to Oxford. Sadly, I was never privy to these discussions and decisions. Father just announced the fact and I had no choice but to go along with it or else. What "or else" actually meant I'm not sure as I always acquiesced as it was easier. One day I hoped to have the courage not to. One day.

> *Gaily bedight,*
> *A gallant knight,*
> *In sunshine and in shadow,*
> *Had journeyed long,*
> *Singing a song,*
> *In search of Eldorado*
>
> *But he grew old –*
> *This knight so bold –*
> *And o'er his heart a shadow*
> *Fell as he found*
> *No spot on the ground*
> *That looked like Eldorado*
>
> *And, as his strength*
> *Failed him at length,*
> *He met a pilgrim shadow –*
> *"Shadow," said he,*

"Where can it be –
This land of Eldorado?"

"Over the Mountains
Of the Moon,
Down the Valley of the Shadow,
Ride, boldly ride,"
The shadow replied, -
"If you seek for Eldorado!"

[E.A. Poe]

Harry Clifton circa 1935

Chapter Two

Finding The Past – 2023

As I turn into the entrance of Lytham Hall the imposing and hugely dramatic gates tower above me. The tiny gate lodges seem impossibly small and I wonder if anyone ever really managed to live in them in the past. Today the huge ornamental wrought iron gates are opened and closed with electronic hydraulics, but a 100 years ago their function would have been someone's purpose of employment by the estate. For estate it was back then - a vast one.

A large chunk of the Lytham Hall parklands were sold off in the late 1970s to build a huge new housing estate that is today called South Park. Considering the history of the land it was constructed upon there is an absence of real character in the houses that are arranged oddly and somewhat soullessly.

Harry Clifton and his parents would not have recognised these streets, in their time it was still lush and abundant parkland attached to Lytham Hall. What, I wonder, would they have to say about it? Harry would probably look over it sniffily and turn his back on it; as he had done with most of reality in his own time. His mother would be horrified at the loss of parkland and also the abundance of establishments serving alcohol in Lytham itself.

The pleasures and certainties of the rich and landed gentry swept away in the name of progress. Harry's father, John Talbot de vere Clifton, would eye it all with suspicious sadness as his childhood in the area had not been a happy one. His father died when he was a boy and his mother packed him off to Eton as soon as she could.

Violet would say he spent his life trying to prove himself as a result of his mother's coldness and disapproval to him. As a new baby he had suckled her breast so hard and with such determination it injured her. Therein lay the foundation of her dislike of him. It is why he was so hard on his own children, he wanted them to be tough and survive what the world threw at them. Harry was damaged by this harshness and lack of love; as the eldest and heir he came in for the worst of his father's wrath.

Proceeding along what is now the main drive to the Georgian manor that is Lytham Hall, it snakes rather oddly at the side of the estate, and glimpses of bland, 1970's houses from the estate can be seen through the trees as if slightly embarrassed to be there at all. They are certainly at odds with the grandeur of the hall itself. Passing through a smaller, more modest and secondary set of ornamental gates, the towering trees create a shadowy effect that draws you along come summer or winter.

In summer the dappled green of the trees in leaf create an instant romantic atmosphere; whereas in winter the scrawling bare tree branches still manage to promise something unexpected if not slightly sinister in an Edgar Allan Poe fashion; whose stories and poems were so loved by Harry Clifton and his father.

Suddenly the fine Georgian manor comes into view as you break through the protective trees, its façade takes your breath away and it sits proudly in what remains of its depleted parkland. Harry Clifton would feel a wave of anxiety wash over him as his car approached the house along this route; knowing that inside his father and mother awaited him to castigate or admonish him over something he had undertaken that they disapproved of. Perhaps he wished he felt more love from them. It then occurred to me that perhaps in Harry's day the drive took a different route and had been changed when the estate was owned by Guardian Royal Exchange. Perhaps the original drive approached the house front and centre for the maximum dramatic effect? Looking at the parkland I could see a wide expanse of lawn with what looked like an entrance drive in the far distance.

This would have given the house a more imposing first impression to visitors. I wished in that moment I could have asked Harry about this but alas he was long passed from this world. However, I could imagine Evelyn Waugh approaching the house in a chauffer driven car and being immediately impressed by its towering dignity and promise of what lay within. That made me wonder if the effect of the house inspired him to revisit again and again during the 1930s and for what purpose?

Sitting on a bench overlooking the parkland by the hall, there were people coming and going and walking dogs, mothers with children and elderly couples out for a stroll. A hundred years before this would not have been possible as the house and inner grounds were private and only the estate staff and servants would have had access as part of their employment – although the outer area of the parkland was open at times for locals to promenade. Their leisure time, such as it was, would have been limited to areas of the estate where they would not have been visible to the family from the hall.

There would have been a couple of hundred staff and servants in that time. The stables and blacksmiths, with their living quarters above, those buildings still visible if you care to notice and much as they were. Nobody lives in the rooms above now. The staff quarters empty and coated with the dusts of time giving the place the air of a museum rather than and living working estate. But the sense of that past prevails. The head gardener's cottage built against the wall of the walled garden still stands proudly but instead of an army of gardeners growing and providing food year round for the family and staff, it is now a garden centre with pretty flower displays. The courtyard where staff would have managed the demands of the house now an open air café for visitors, done so cleverly the ghost of its past use still tangible.

This is still a place vibrant with life, it's just a very different kind of life lead by those who would have been employed here a century before. The remarkable thing about the hall is that it survived at all. It could so easily have been abandoned and fallen into ruin after it passed from the Clifton family ownership.

Had the charitable trust not purchased it and set about reinvigorating it and opening it to the public for the first time just a few short years ago its fate would have been very different. I could not sit here without trying to imagine the ghosts of the past. The famous visit by the Tsar of Russia's brother, The Grand Duke Michael - there is a picture of him standing with John Talbot Clifton at the side family entrance door to the hall. The occasion was a shoot and the christening of Violet and Talbot's daughter Avia in 1908. This the caliber of guests the family attracted for shooting and hunting trips. Violet Clifton looking haughty and slightly regal – she was a tall woman for the time and seems impossibly exotic with an almost masculine face.

She recalled friends saying to her " I saw a man like a Viking who walked down Bond Street as though he were breaking a trail, is your husband now in England?" And another: " I passed a man that looked like a Russian Duke, from what I have heard of him I think he must have been John Talbot." Her husband was a cut above with his bright blue eyes and masculine physique and undoubtedly made many a heart flutter. Little wonder he struck up such a friendship with the Russian Imperial family. Both John Talbot and Violet were different in nature and physicality from other landed gentry. It is borne for their love of adventure and striding about the world as if it was the perfectly natural thing to do.

Harry, their eldest son and heir, had a lot to live up to in many ways. Little wonder he never felt he had his father's approval, but always his scornful disapproval. As a small child his mother recalled her husband telling her, "not to hold the little boy's hand but to let him fall."

No warm embraces or encouragement, no molly-coddling, because the boy had to grow up tough. No wonder Harry was so determined to set his jaw against his father and their relationship so volatile. How sad people can be so cruel to the ones they should love the most.

John Talbot Clifton had purchased in 1922 his idea of a dream family home and the home from hell as far as Harry was concerned. On the Hebridean island of Islay was Kildalton Castle. For him it was a utopia, somewhere to bring his family and indulge them in the shooting, stalking and fishing opportunities. All the things his adventurous spirit adored and thrived upon.

The land that came with the house afforded long walks in the often inclement weather come winter or summer.
It replaced their esate in Ireland where, after an altercation with the IRA John Talbot had been driven off his lands as it was no longer safe. The family moved to Kildalton Castle from Lytham Hall immediately and no doubt Harry gave thanks that he was a boarder at Downside School, however unpleasant that was, and allow it to be the lesser of two horrors for him. Holidays came and of course he had no choice but to endure it the best he could in chilly Scotland.

Harry's siblings loved the place as did his mother. His father would bellow for them to get ready and embark on some God forsaken adventure in the hills about the place, in the drizzly damp conditions, accompanied by the game keeper and the piper that his father loved. The scrawl and whine of the bag pipes was the final straw for Harry and often he would lay in bed with a streaming cold perhaps brought on psychosomatically to avoid the ordeal that everyone else seemed to relish.

As these thoughts carried me away to that other time I couldn't help feeling sad for all of them. What a difference some love and kindness would have made to the family dynamic and maybe that would have changed the outcome and tragedy that was to come for the dynasty.

By 1926 Harry had left Downside School and his father had made arrangements for him to go up to Oxford. He had hoped to send him to his old alma mater at Cambridge but that wasn't to be so Christ Church, Oxford, it was. Harry, of course, had no say in the matter and was expected to just do as he was told and be grateful. He was anything but!

Chapter Three

Conforming – 1926

Harry Clifton:

We were visiting Lytham Hall so father could see to estate business. Father and I argued more and more as I got older and the less he felt he could manipulate me the worse his rages became. As a result he was on the war path again, as we had argued over a charity event, and as I was due to go to Christ Church at Oxford to read Modern History, had decided to defy him by declaring I would not go up to Oxford. Ours was a constant battle and perhaps full of many 'minutes' where love turned to hate for both of us.

I was adept at being in the right place at the right time and managed to overhear and see things by crouching underneath the drawing room window which was ajar slightly - without being noticed.

"Henry? Henry! Where are you?" My father roared like an angry lion from deep within his chest. "Where is that damn boy?"

The butler, Lomax, winced at the sound of my father's angry bellowing.

"I'll thrash some sense into him if it's the last thing I do…"

Bursting into the drawing room father sees my mother Violet sitting at her desk dealing with letters whilst Lomax attends to putting a log on the fire - as it is a cool early summer morning it was my mother's demand that a log fire be lit. My father, on seeing Lomax, bites his tongue as mother swung round on her chair to face him. After a moment he says to Lomax angrily through gritted teeth: "Find my son and tell him I want to speak to him now. Now! Do you understand?"

"Yes, sir." Lomax replies as he scurried out after getting a reassuring look from mother.

"Darling, what is the matter now?"

"That boy will be the death of me…"

"You may be right if you carry on like this! You will make yourself ill, mark my words," she smiled patiently, "You know what the doctor said…"

"Bugger the damn doctor!"

Violet shakes her head in a slightly disapproving but amused way. She then asks him calmly "What has Henry done now?"

"Cancelled the charity billiard match – or tried to – and left me a note saying he's not going up to Oxford."

"That's ridiculous; he's been accepted to study Modern History, whatever that is, at Christ Church. God will guide him."

Father banged his fist on the mantle of the fireplace. "The toe of my boot will be guiding him if he defies me over this!"

"I'll Modern History him when I get my hands on him!" Mother said scathingly and imperiously to make him laugh, mainly to take the heat out of the moment. It worked.

He suddenly couldn't help but laugh at mother's comment. It came from deep within him and resonated around the room. From my vantage point crouched under the slightly open window I had a great view.

"He's going to Oxford if I have to drag him there myself" She added to tickle him further.

Laughing heartily he crossed to mother as she stood up and looked deeply into his eyes. He gave her a bear hug as he continued to laugh. She allowed herself to be pulled into his powerful arms – a thrill it seemed to an observer like me, by the look on her face, that had never waned where father was concerned.

My mother was a skilled diplomat and knew exactly how to handle my father. I marvelled at the overtness of the love she had for him and he for her and wondered why there seemed so little, if any, left for their children.

I couldn't imagine either of them embracing me in a way that would give me any kind of comfort.

The charity event my father was annoyed about was linked to the dreaded billiards he loved to play. We had a Billiard Room at Lytham Hall with a full sized table and my father liked nothing more than retiring there after dinner with his male friends to drink a tipple, smoke horrible cigars and play billiards. The conversation at such events would be his exploits and adventures in various parts of the world – and that of his friends - all trying to out-adventure each other.

Because he wanted to toughen me up and make a man of me he could be proud of, he insisted I learn to play billiards. I did my best but it interested me not one jot. The worse I played the more he would bellow at me. He got so frustrated he declared that I would have to play until I beat him at a game. Alas, for him, it was all rather in vain as I was genuinely useless and couldn't see the point of hitting tiny balls across a green baize table with sticks. I can still see his face when I said this whilst banging down the billiard cue on the table. He looked as if he would pop or have a heart attack. I told him I would not play the charity match, and he demanded I did.

"Come on boy!" He roared, adding sneeringly, "Hit the damn ball properly."

I deliberately hit the ball badly hoping he would give up and leave me alone. On reflection I realised this was a pointless strategy as my father never gave up on anything he set his mind to and that included me. I looked at him and his rage towards me increased.

"For God's sake boy," He bellowed, "everyday you play and never once have you seized the challenge. Fortune favours the brave. Where is your determination, your will to win, your guts?"

On "guts" he poked his cue into my ribs and made me wince in pain. I looked him in the eye and found the strength not to blink. I could see he liked that sign of anger in me so I quickly looked away and declared: "Taking God's name in vain is blasphemy, according to mother…"

He threw down his cue and banged his fists onto the table with such force it genuinely frightened me. However, I stood my ground and didn't flinch even though every muscle in my body wanted to run towards the door. My father had never hit me physically but there was perhaps always a first time…

"Don't provoke me, boy. You are not too old for a thrashing." He walked towards me slowly and continued. "I will make you play billiards every day until you beat me," he picked up his cue and began to calmly chalk the end as he looked right into my eyes, "I'll make a man of you yet."

That one statement told me everything I needed to know regarding his thoughts of me. He considered me somehow lacking and less of a man than he was. I was an embarrassment of sorts, one that must be tortured to conform and be what he wanted me to be. I knew just as certainly that I could never be what he wanted me to be. Indeed, both my parents' expectations of me were futile. I was determined to follow my own path whatever hardships I would have to endure to clear my way. Financially I was totally dependent though, so that was a bitter reality I had to swallow and accept. For now, at least.

After my eavesdropping I made my way through the parkland and sat in the rose garden looking at the statue of Diana the huntress - she stood silent and erect in the centre oblivious to everything. I found myself envying her that. The early summer roses were abundant with blooms and the heady scent caught the gentle breeze and surrounded me, briefly overwhelming my senses. I felt overwhelmed in many ways but was determined I would not feel self pity. I loathed that, it was a useless emotion that led to far darker consequences of despair.

In the distance I could see the butler, Lomax, steadily making his way towards me like some special agent in a conspiracy novel. It made me smile to think how everyone trod on egg shells to keep my father from further eruptions of temper. My mother had them well trained. I felt I was in some dream watching him scampering in the shadows towards me. As he approached he stopped and corrected his clothing, then in a formal butler like way came towards me. I didn't look at him and offered no surprise to him suddenly being there. I looked around at the rose bushes and could see him doing the same – no doubt imagining my father had seen him and his mission, probably initiated by mother, was discovered and having to face her disappointment in him for failing.

"Such beauty," I said wistfully, "bedevilled by the demon that is my father." I laughed to myself and could see his discomfort although he remained expressionless and silent. "He would rather kill innocent animals and trample on the miracles of nature…"

"Sir…"

"What is it, Lomax," I sighed and turned to look at him. He shifted uncomfortably. "Well?"

"Her ladyship asked me to find you…"

"So now you have!" I said this rather impatiently but then decided to tease him a little. "Have you been sent to reprimand and shackle me?"

"No sir, that is not my place."

I looked at him and felt like bursting with laughter. Here he was looking more and more uncomfortable having to impart whatever my mother had asked him to. He must think me an odd sort to be so flippant with him. "Place?" I looked him in the eye. "Ah, yes, we all have a predestined place in this world don't we? My place is to obey, just like yours is Lomax. We are all subservient, just with different rules. These are the chains we must bear."

Indeed, sir," he muttered as he shifted from foot to foot, "but your mother…"

"It's all just an accident of birth," I replied cutting him off, "just an accident." I looked at him again and could see tiny beads of perspiration appearing on his brow. "Imagine," I added, "if I were the butler and you the heir to all this. Would you behave differently to me?"

As I said this there was the sound of a shotgun blasting in the distance. It made us both jump so engrossed were we in our own little drama. We both knew that was my father killing birds with my young brother Michael. I put my trusty teddy bear down on the ground at the side of the bench.

"Sir," Lomax said insistently, "your mother asked me to tell you that your father…"

I recoiled from him slightly in horror to emphasise my point. "My father? The murderer of innocent animals and more bestial than anything born wild?" I shuddered visibly, "Oh, to glory in blood? Imagine!"

"To tell you your father has threatened to cut off…"

I held my hand up to stop him talking and sucked in my breath with horror. He looked totally defeated and I felt rather bad for treating him so badly. Out of nowhere my mother appeared – this being a special skill she possessed that amazed me everytime she pulled it off.

"It's all right, Lomax, I will discuss this with master Henry myself," she said.

My mother looked at me disapprovingly and Lomax scurried off back to the hall. She then sat beside me on the bench. Another gunshot blast shattered the peace of the day and a flight of panicked birds fled across the parkland.

"My name is Harry, mother, you know how much I hate being called Henry."

I heard her "tut" with impatience. "Let's not go into that now," she said seriously enough to change the tone of the conversation, "Your father is furious with you."

"So, he spills the blood of innocents…"

"Don't be absurd," she said as she turned to look at me, "he loves shooting. It relaxes him."

It surprised me not that mother rationalised such cruelty in such a matter of fact way. I looked at her askance. They accepted it as normal, as a perfectly acceptable way for grown men to behave. This is why they would never understand me. I was the odd one in this world, or so it seemed.

"I feel their pain," I said, "He brutalises me too, I'm sure he would shoot me if he could get away with murder."

"You really must try to behave more rationally," she said with exasperation, "and, well, normal. You have a destiny and responsibilities."

"Normal like Michael," I countered, "A twist of fate he should be the younger. He shares father's pleasures and gruesome pastimes aged just nine."

"Your brother is not you!" She then added with a hint of regret in her voice that hurt, "More's the pity."

"Don't let father send him to Downside. That school destroyed me."

She looked at me bemused. "He's already secured a place for him. Besides, the monks gave you a good education."

"They also brutalised me and others who didn't fit in."

For a brief moment, due to the way she slowly turned to look at me again I thought there might be some compassion in her, but I was wrong. "Why," she said firmly, "do you have to make everything about you? It's so self-indulgent and tedious."

"Oh how I wish you could pity me instead of always berating me."

I looked at her steely reserve and composure and knew there would be no reassuring hugs or kindness. They had that only for each other, those parents of mine. It is like they never really see who I am and what I would be capable of if approached differently. Duty, duty, duty! Bugger everything else. How sad that made me feel, for them more than me.

"You must pull yourself together," she continued oblivious to my thoughts, "and accept your fate like, well, like…"

"Like a man?" I finished her sentence for her. "What actually is that?"

"I know it is hard for you," she soldiered on, "but you must hide your eccentricities from the world and put on a good front. You are, or will be one day, the master and relied upon. Think of all the staff and servants here and at Kildalton. It's you job to continue the Clifton dynasty."

"Good God," I exclaimed, "it's too much - and what about me?"

"Please," she said disapprovingly, "don't take God's name in vain."

"Bugger God," I gasped, "what about me, it's me you should favour and protect."

I watched as she looked shocked and genuflected.

"Really," she said haughtily, "you go too far sometimes!"

"God will understand," I shot back, " I will go up to Oxford, only because I want to be as far away from Lytham Hall, Kildalton and my father as possible."

Her attitude immediately changed back to formal every day, everything is alright and there is no conflict.

"So glad you have seen sense, your father said he would cut off your allowance if you refused to go."

"Enforced conformity," I laughed the words out bitterly, "I'm a hypocrite! Ah, well, at least it's not my head he wants to cut off."

"You are an adult now and must expect to be treated like one," she said imperiously.

Her eye wandered to my teddy bear sitting beside the bench and I heard that "tut" again followed by a long sigh.

"An adult, what does that entail I wonder?" I said this knowing it would irritate her.

"For a start," she hissed rather conspiratorially, "an adult doesn't cling on to childhood teddy bears – it really is too absurd."

I could see she was whispering because she was embarrassed by my bear. I picked him up and hugged him close. "He's my only true friend!"

The exasperation she felt flickered through her eyes as she looked at me with disapproval. But then matter-of-factly she got up and delivered her parting shot.

"Don't be late for dinner and do try and beat your father at billiards – he'll let it go then and won't torture you anymore once the charity match is over."

I watched as she strode across the garden to the hall. Her posture and purpose told me she was pleased with the outcome of our meeting and it was time to move on and give her attention to more important things.

Hugging my bear as she departed, I whispered in his ear. "Torture, did you hear that? They speak of torturing me as if it is quite, quite normal."

I hear another gunshot blast much closer and the scream of panicked birds. I can see my father and little brother Michael. My father exclaims "Good shot my boy, good shot!" He then picks up the bird my brother Michael shot and slices it open with a knife. He proceeds to wipe the still hot blood all over Michael's face to signify his first kill. Michael laughs delightedly – but he is just nine years old – I had a flash back to when my father did the same to me and the hysteria it induced in me. Hot tears came and splashed onto my hand. I hugged my bear and ran into the woodland so they wouldn't see me. There I could mourn for the bird and all the slaughter of innocents.

Chapter Four

Evelyn Waugh & Christ Church

Harry Clifton:

A young man already at Oxford but at war with his tutor, who was refusing to let him graduate because he had not completed enough weeks and terms, was a man who would cross my path, and I would curse his, in many ways. He was charming and mercurial and a notorious seducer of anyone who would let him. He didn't identify as anything and was sexually fluid as well as a beautiful, obnoxious soul who was made up of contradictions but had an aura that was hard to resist. He was a rebel and I admired that. What charisma! Love had nothing to do with him.

Evelyn Waugh:

What kind of parents gives their son a name like Evelyn? I'll tell you. My parents. All my life I get asked "Why do you have a girl's name?" or "I thought you would be a girl when they said your name was Evelyn." This is my curse and I am sure it will be for the rest of my life. I came up to New College, Oxford, to read Literature and History. I will be honest and say that if I had pursued my studies as avidly as I did the chance for a fuck I would have faired much better and had a more positive relationship with my tutor.

He hated me. Justifiably some would say as I couldn't like the man or force myself to be civil to him. Life was, I grandly declared, too short. I also suspected he was homophobic, either that or he secretly desired the "love that dare not speak its name" probably up his tight repressed backside. My guess was probably the latter but that didn't help my cause as he refused to let me graduate on tenuous grounds. The latest excuse, declaring I had not attended the required number of weeks for each academic year. Fuck! My father was rightly enraged after all the money it had cost him to support me and pay the fees. I had done my best to sort this out so I could graduate – I seemed destined to be an eternal student.

To add to my problems it was common knowledge amongst the academics that I was a founding member of the Hypocrites Club. This was true, it was also a private club for members only approved by me and my friends Bertie Pemberton-Billing and Alistair Graham. Bertie I had fucked happily until I met Alistair and my attentions had obsessed on him. Bertie didn't care as he had lots of admirers whom he happily serviced with his inimitable charms. It is true the club was an orgy of hedonism and what went on there stayed there: nudity, homosexual sex, heterosexual sex, transvestites, drag queens and everything in between. It was a cocktail of, well, mainly ardent cock to be honest. We were young and determined not to conform or be hypocrites about sex like the

Victorians and the pre war generation. Life "was for fucking" as I would say to much gasping of breath and clutching of pearls by my elders and betters.

My ambition was to become a novelist, but a novelist who broke boundaries and encompassed the sexual and liberal traits of my Oxford contemporaries. The ones they hid away and pretended weren't there – those I liked the most and couldn't wait to expose. I loved imaging them naked – stripped of their secrets and for all to see. I wanted to shock them and fuck with their heads. You can't pretend that all life is pure and lovely when you hide the urges that go on by making them illegal or ignoring their existence.

Luckily for me my father was a publisher and his firm was respected as they had been the ones who handled Charles Dickens's works until the copyright ran out. So, my thinking was, to save him more money supporting me financially, my father would happily push for a publishing deal for me. I was starting to formulate my first novel, Decline & Fall; the title alone would raise a few eyebrows. Good.

I thought I had seen it all, had it all, and experienced it all, until Bertie told me about a new undergraduate at Christ Church called Henry Talbot de vere Clifton. He was tall and very handsome. I was smitten and demanded an introduction. Oxford and my life would never be the same.

Harry Clifton:

The journey to Oxford from Lytham Hall in Lancashire was tedious to say the least. It had to be done as I was of a mind to submit to the luxury of the family Bentley rather than endure a long, uncomfortable train journey. I was feeling very anti social since I had agreed to go up to Oxford as it was, so having to make small polite chat with random strangers was not high on my list. Instead I would have the company of our chauffer Andrews, along with my possessions – thankfully the bulk of my things had gone ahead in trunks so I wasn't too overburdened. Andrews was delightful because he was happy to speak only if I wanted to; and probably glad I didn't have much inclination to on this journey if the truth be known. I was very tedious when out of sorts and nobody knew me better in that way. At times like this I realise how terribly spoilt and indulged I was and that not everyone in life is as fortunate. With that thought I immediately focussed on the passing countryside because it was a sentiment that my mother could have said – and I did not want to imagine I could be anything like her! I genuflected at the thought and then laughed at my own ridiculousness. I had tired of the bells and smells of the Catholic Church too – but that I kept to myself and played along when necessary; actually I could please myself now in that regard, which made me smile with joy.

I must have drifted off to sleep because when I awoke the countryside was much more hilly and the roads winding precariously; so unlike the Fylde in Lancashire which is very flat. Andrews looked at me using his rear view mirror.

"Is everything all right, sir?

"Yes," I replied sleepily, "just a tad uncomfortable. These leather seats make me sweat horribly."

"Yes, sir," he said and then added, "Would you like to stop and stretch your legs, sir"

"That would be heaven, Andrews. Thank you."

I was about to ask him how he was and then thought better of
it. He would not expect me to enquire after his well being and
would think me odd for doing it. So I just smiled and adjusted
my clothing to make myself more comfortable. I admired his
ability to drive for such long periods, but then I hated driving
too much myself as it was so much easier with a chauffeur.

Once we had stopped and I had taken the air, it was a fine
morning too, Andrews informed me we were just about to
enter Oxfordshire from Warwickshire, so had broken the back
of the journey. We should arrive in Oxford about mid
afternoon all being well, he said. I thanked him.

So, I thought to myself, here I am going to Oxford really
against my own wishes but it had a purpose. It allowed me to
escape my family and avoid financial penury threatened by
my father if I failed to do as I was told. I wonder what life
would hold for me and how I would fit in to Christ Church?

My hope was there was not too much high church and the
accompanying, dreaded bells and smells – thinking about it
made me feel like a hypocrite. My parents were devout
Catholics but I had never found in religion what they had. For
me it felt like another way to control and coerce people in to
doing what was expected of them. Why were people
discouraged from actually living a life they would enjoy?
Committing sins was held over them like some gloomy cloud
they must fear for eternity. Is that what God really wanted for
the people? On the positive side, one could commit terrible
sins, confess, be forgiven, and then move on unblemished.
That would have its uses, I imagined.

As I got back into the car Andrews closed the door and then got in the drivers seat himself. I looked along my own seat and there sat my devoted teddy bear. He never argued with me and always made himself available for cuddles when I needed them. In that moment I realised how much store I put into the silly relationship we had. In some ways he was my only friend, believe me he knew all the secrets, all of them! I picked him up and gave him a hug, he looked at me with those familiar reassuring eyes. "I've never given you a name, have I? Don't worry, when we get to Oxford we shall find a name for you darling. Until then I shall just call you darling."

Andrews looked at me through his mirror. "We'll be off again then, sir," he said and added, "Do you need anything before we…"

"No, thank you, Andrews. I shall perhaps have another snooze but please wake me before we drive into Oxford as I want to take it all in."

"Yes, sir, of course, sir."

With that off we went again. The lushness of the Oxfordshire countryside impressed me and I enjoyed the fact the landscape undulated so dramatically. Seeing the locals in villages going about their day, and them standing to attention at the road side when such a grand car passed, made me smile. Who did they think I was? Did they always stand to attention to what they thought was passing gentry? Even the farm workers in the fields doffed their caps as we passed. How sad they felt they had to be so subservient and respectful. Did they do it out of habit, did they resent doing it. I often wondered.

These thoughts made me reflect on my own future from this point onwards. There were so many things I wanted to experience and I loved the arts and theatre and the new film technology. The possibilities seemed endless, exciting and full of as yet unknown opportunities. Literature was also a love of mine and I wanted to explore that to see if I could create something unique and wonderful to leave the world; to be like my favourite author, a modern day Edgar Allan Poe.

I loved the darkness and the glimmers of light his work stirred in me. But alas my heart sank when the reality of my pre destined duty once again enveloped me like some dark, sinister cloud. Gloom embraced me when I realised that my father would never let me explore these desires, instead I was to be groomed and manipulated to take over and become Lord of the Manor, Squire Clifton, the means of all existence to those working the lands and estates in Lytham and Scotland as well as my siblings and the wider family. I would be their means to an end. But, what of me? Did I not matter? What end would be in store for me!

I must have dozed off in my despair because the next thing I remember is Andrews waking me to say we were just entering the city of Oxford. It was mid afternoon and the sun was a golden orb with a few wispy clouds in a beautiful blue sky. The honey coloured stone of the buildings was burnished and warmed by the sun and had the look of an enchanted city that was confident of its place in the history of these islands. From this day forth I was to be part of it – at least for the time being.

We entered the city from the Woodstock Road and immediately the atmosphere on the streets was that of academia. Masters with their billowing black capes strode along as if desperate to get to wherever their destination was; their shiny brogues polished within an inch glistened and clattered as they pounded the pavements. Students mixed among them, some ambling and chatting lazily, others with more purpose and determination. Where, I wondered, were they all going and to meet whom? Friends, lovers, parents, the next lecture perhaps? Would they be on time or late?

As a backdrop to this hive of human activity were the ancient buildings. The Catholic Oratory of St Aloysius caught my eye as we proceed onto St Giles. A gaggle of nuns emerged into the sunlight herding a group of infant school children. Their black habits with striking white head bands made them seem somehow other worldly in this place and also stirred a feeling of guilt in me for being such a lapsed and bad Catholic. As I had that thought a rather stern looking priest approached them and started giving the nuns directions to some place. The car travelled on and I lost sight of them.

Proceeding down St Giles the towering façade of the Randolph Hotel came into view which sat on the corner of St Giles and Beaumont Street, opposite the Ashmolean Museum, that father proudly boasted of donating a rare fossil to, that I had heard so much about. I had thought of staying at the Randolph whilst at Oxford but my father forbade it and insisted I had rooms at Christ Church. The gothic splendour of the hotel attracted me and made me determined to lunch there frequently if at all possible. Standing on the corner was an odd and rather eccentric looking young man who seemed impossibly out of place. He had a rather battered looking satchel in one hand and clutched under his arm a rather small and scrawny looking teddy bear. I had the feeling I might meet him sometime. Then he was gone as the car turned into the Broad.

The journey through Oxford was mesmerising and I found myself looking forward to exploring this rather enchanting place. It may not be such a trial after all. The Sheldonian Theatre looked majestic in the sunshine and if the density of masters, dons and students could get any thicker then it did in this vicinity. It was almost like going back in time. That thought made me shudder with excitement.

As we turned I noticed a street sign that said Turl Street. This was a rather narrow street and the buildings seemed oddly claustrophobic so close were they together. As we passed I saw a dashingly handsome young man staring at me as the car slowly made its way. He had blond hair and rather delicious blue eyes and wore a tweed suit with great panache and a trilby hat tilted back off his face. Cigarette in one hand he looked cocky and self assured. I wondered why he stared so and as I started to feel uncomfortable he suddenly smiled and it was a smile that made any concern I had melt away to insignificance. I decided to set my expression as haughty and untouchable but I wanted to know more about him if I possibly could. That said, I thought as the car turned onto the High, I would probably never see him again.

Evelyn Waugh:

That was my first glimpse of him. I did not know his name but his odd perfection and profile captured my curiosity and I had to know more, see more, feel more. As I looked at him through the window of his car I felt a strange alignment as if we had met before even though I knew we hadn't. Not in this life anyway. I could see he was very tall by the way he sat slightly cramped in that elegant car. He seemed to me like a man who cared little for anything or anyone but himself. This is all nonsense of course because how can one feel that powerfully by seeing someone, no, glimpsing them for a few seconds, as they pass in a car? It was ludicrous. Maybe the drama of being a writer had spilled over into every day events and any sense of logic dissipated as a result. My God, I had to find out who he was and where he was going so I followed the car

Harry Clifton:

As the car pulled onto St Aldates and then into Christ Church the beauty of the buildings literally took my breath away. I had to pause a moment to gather my thoughts and whilst doing so suddenly felt very nervous about what lay ahead of me. This emotion surprised me as I rarely felt nervous about anything so wasn't sure what to do. Surprisingly it was Andrews who noticed this unusual reaction in me and said reassuringly, "Deep breaths, sir. You will be fine, it's probably the heat and all."

I looked at him and smiled a thank you as I had no words capable of escaping my throat in this moment. Instead, as Andrews got out of the car, I picked up my teddy bear and whispered to him, "Like a lamb to the slaughter I go…"

Holding the bear to my ear I heard him offer encouragement. "Do you really think I am brave," I said back to him, "that is so kind. You are my only true friend and confidant. The bear whispered to me again. "I know, I promised to give you a proper name after all these years and I shall darling." The Clock struck 3pm and then began to chime rather prettily I thought. I looked at my watch and it seemed the time was wrong.

Andrews opened my door and gave me a reassuring smile. He took off his chauffeur cap and clutched it under one arm. After I had emerged into the sunlight he began unloading my two large suitcases from the trunk of the Bentley. In the distance I could see a porter in a bowler hat and tail coat looking at us and waving. He then made his way towards us from the lodge.

"The weight of history and family expectations is upon me, Andrews."

"Yes, sir."

I watched him as he struggled with the heavy cases plus a small leather bag I had brought. He would be thankful I had the bulk of my things sent ahead in two large trunks so I had eased his burden.

"Is it not tiresome for you to be at my family's beck and call?"

"No,sir, not at all," he replied heavily of breath, "Not at all…"

Looking at him I found it hard to believe. His uniform was thick wool so he must be exhausted with the heat at the very least and never mind all the driving he'd done. He then looked at me and his face was mired in sweat. "You must be mad!" I said sincerely and with some incredulity too.

"I'm as sane as you, sir," he replied with some jollity, "now I should get this luggage to its destination…"

I watched as he managed to heave up the heavy cases and sling the bag strap over his shoulder. My teddy bear then whispered in my ear again.

"Oh, yes," I said to the teddy bear, "thank you darling for reminding me." I then turned to Andrews who had been joined by the very small, I had to peer down at him, bowler hatted porter, "Andrews, I need partridge eggs and some preserves as they were not ticked off my list. Please get mother to send you back with some."

"Very good, sir," he replied whilst standing there with luggage hanging off him precariously, "I will see to that."

"Are they even in season?," I said to my teddy bear, "Oh, mother will sort it out!"

The porter looked up at me with a puzzled expression. I cannot imagine why. Then said rather sternly "Follow me please, Master Clifton and your chauffeur…"

We did as asked.

Evelyn Waugh:

Having followed the car and observed it turn into Christ Church I stood and watched as he emerged from the car. There was something regal about him physically but I put that down to him being so tall - as I had suspected. He clutched a teddy bear closely and seemed oblivious to his poor chauffeur struggling with the heavy luggage. I watched as the college porter approached and led them away through the quad.

He must have rooms here then, so I know where to find him. My friend Bertie had rooms here too, so he can find out who he is and how I can meet him. I felt a wave of desire wash over me and leave that unfathomable tingling sensation across my skin that always followed. Here was someone special but I am not entirely sure why or for what reason. I decided to cut through to the Christ Church meadow as some of the accommodation overlooked that area and I could tell Bertie where his rooms were if I could catch another glimpse. My heart raced with expectation.

Harry Clifton:

As we walked through into the quad, the sun caught the south side and the accompanying splash of water from the fountain created a dream like atmosphere in the ancient walls of Christ Church. Apart from Andrews' slightly laboured breathing nothing but our footsteps disturbed the tranquillity.

"Excuse me," I said to the bowler hat ahead of me," could you clarify an anomaly for me?"

"Of course, sir."

"Why," I asked politely, "is the clock in the tower five minutes slow and," I added quickly, "why so many chimes?"

"We still work to Oxford Time at Christ Church, sir. It's five minutes and two seconds behind Greenwich Mean time."

"How peculiar," I replied, "not at all eccentric."

"When time was standardised," the porter replied with a little irritation, I felt, "in 1852 Christ Church preferred to remain on Oxford Time…"

The porter then, without a take your leave, turned and carried on. Andrews was breathing quite heavily by now and was no doubt glad to be on the move again. I took it all in, along with my teddy bear, and then realised he hadn't answered my other question.

"Why all the chimes?" I asked again.

The porter stopped and turned to look at me. Andrews also stopped abruptly and let out a loud sigh.

"101, sir, every hour."

"How absurdly wonderful."

We started walking again in a snake like procession across the quad.

"Henry Eighth," said the porter suddenly, "all to do with King Henry Eighth, sir. I'm surprised you haven't acquainted your self with the history before you arrived, sir."

I sensed that tone of irritation again, but this man was good at hiding what displeased him and rightly knew his place. So I thought.

"You see, Andrews," I threw over my shoulder, "we are amongst history! An accident of birth is what brought us here."

"Yes, sir…"

Hearing his labours with the luggage I said as we continued to follow the porter "How can you conform so easily? Had fate decreed otherwise you would be me and I would be heaving heavy luggage about." He gasped a reply of, "Yes, sir…" I replied swiftly with "Rebel, Andrews, why have you never rebelled against such injustice!?"

I heard a grunt and a groan from Andrews as he dealt valiantly with my luggage. To make him feel better about his position and show I appreciated him I turned and said to him quite sincerely, "Just as well we are as we are, master and servant, I can't imagine I could have heaved anything with success."

Realising I had stopped near the fountain at the centre of the quad, I looked up and was surprised to see a charming statue at its centre.

"This is the famous statue of Mercury," I asked the porter, who turned again wearily and slightly insolently, "isn't it?"

"Yes, sir."

My teddy bear gave the porter a dirty look at this point and then at me sympathetically. "You should learn to be more mercurial, Andrews. Conformity is so dreadfully dull." I then added, "You mustn't let my father bully you too!" The porter looked at me oddly so I added, "Don't you agree?"

"Your rooms, sir," he said as he turned to carry on, "are this way."

I was finding the porter's skilful insolence a little wearing but bit my lip lest I should cause a scene on my first day – well on arrival. That wouldn't do at all. But I made a mental note of this man's behaviour for future reference. Then to nobody in particular but the bear, "We are surrounded, darling, by lost causes aren't we?" As we trudged along following the silly little porter I suddenly felt aghast and thirsty all in the same moment. The events of the day were wearing thin and I was tired.

"I need champagne," I threw the demand over my shoulder to Andrews, "and I need it now!"

When I want something I want it and I was used to it being brought to me immediately. I didn't care from whence it came as long as it did. Having to wait was tedious and boring. These thoughts rattled in my head as we turned into a small doorway and I had to duck to prevent banging my head, this not a problem for the small porter or Andrews behind me. We then started to climb a stone staircase that twisted round alarmingly. It all looked positively medieval to me and I shuddered at what my rooms would be like. My teddy bear couldn't bear to look so he buried his head in my shoulder.

Suddenly my fears returned and I felt trapped and almost as if I was being imprisoned by Oxford and Christ Church. My desire to run and be free was never far away. I suspected those around me, especially the tutors and the dons, would view me with suspicion because I behaved differently and beyond what was considered normal. How I hated normal, how I hated the dreaded status quo.

With a heave of a large wooden door that swung inwards, my rooms were revealed to me, much to my relief, as the spiral staircase had left me feeling quite giddy by the time we got to the top. The rooms that were before me were full of light and surprisingly spacious as well. I feigned however an expression of under-whelmed disdain for the benefit of the little porter. He indicated to the mullioned leaded windows.

"They open," he declared as if a miracle, "quite easily." To which he demonstrated as if it was a wonder of the world.

"How very modern!" I replied with sarcasm.

At this exchange I noticed the two large trunks that had been delivered before our arrival and my mind wandered to the champagne that lay within. At this there was a sudden crashing at the door and the porter and myself swung round to see what the racket was. Andrews was there dripping with sweat having dropped the cases and bag he was carrying onto the floor. He looked as if he might have a seizure and he gripped the back of a chair whilst he got his breath back.

"The rooms will do," I said to Andrews, "they exceed my expectation actually."

"Very good, sir," he spluttered, still gasping to get his breath back, "I'm pleased to hear it."

The porter stood at the door with his bowler hat in his hand, Andrews still gasped to recover his lost breath and I crossed to the window that looked out over the gardens and the Christ Church meadow beyond.

You see, in spite of the irritated and rude remarks from the porter, I had done some homework and had studied a map of Christ Church and the centre of Oxford – it's why I knew the names of the streets more or less as we drove in. I didn't matriculate for nothing, although I suspected my father had made sure that I had decent rooms and had no doubt wafted a hefty contribution as a way of ensuring it. Being an old Etonian he was used to getting what he wanted and that had afforded some privileges for me, his son. Then it suddenly occurred to me and I turned to ask the porter.

"Do I have a valet?"

"Valet?" he said with a splutter. "No, sir, we do not provide a valet for you."

"Oh, dear," I said to my teddy bear, "Does this mean I must dress myself?"

"Shall I unpack, sir?" Andrews said, now with repleted breath.

"Yes, instantly," I said with desperation," I need that champagne."

The porter looked at us as if we were quite mad. He then put his bowler hat back on and walked to the door. As he left closing it he was heard to say "Good afternoon, sir." I replied rather loudly "There's nothing good about it!"

Andrews was already unpacking a trunk by this point and I walked to gaze from the window. As I stared out I was sure I could see that handsome man again standing looking up at the window. It sent a shiver through me. Had he followed me here and was trying to locate my rooms? I chastised myself for being foolish. How could I tell from this distance anyway and I am sure he wasn't the only good looking man in Oxford. It was just coincidence.

With these thoughts raging about my mind, I heard the pop of a cork and Andrews, bless him, then handed me a glass of champagne. How I needed that!

Evelyn Waugh:

It was him alright. I recognised him even from this distance and that profile was unmistakable. He suited being framed with a mullioned stone window opening. I was not surprised he gazed out over the gardens and meadow as it captured all of us in the end. Once under its spell it is hard to completely leave ever again – a little like Oxford itself – the tranquillity of it can be balm to a troubled soul. And he had a troubled soul I was sure. You don't know me yet, but you will. Soon. You are irresistible to me.

Harry Clifton:

Andrews had been busy unpacking as I sipped my champagne and stared from the window at the beauty of the landscape.

"Where would you like this, sir?" He said, slightly startling me out of my reverie. I turned and he was holding my Elephant's foot umbrella stand. So I indicated "By the door there," he placed it where indicated obediently, "It will remind me daily," I added, "never to be like my father and shoot innocent animals. Only an Elephant should ever own an Elephant's foot!"

With that I indicated with my empty glass I wanted more champagne. He picked up the bottle and replenished my glass and then he carried on with my unpacking in his marvellous efficient way.

Chapter Five

Bertie & The Hypocrites Club

Harry Clifton:

A few days later after settling into the routine, well as far as I did settle into any routine, I was up early and walking the eerily quiet streets of Oxford before the hustle and bustle of the academic day began. The traders of the Covered Market were unloading their wares from vans and even horse and carts and their activities made the surrounding streets even quieter. Soon the masses of Town and Gown would be going about their business and, as I had noticed, respectfully tolerating the other camp and vice versa. It is an anomaly from the permanent public and passing academic population of the city that never seemed to be fully resolved.

At least, as in days past, they no longer had street battles to determine who was dominant. They lived, at least, uneasily but together. One felt it immediately and being resident only a short time I sensed it.

There was bitter rivalry between the colleges and, so I heard, the dons could be ruthless in their determination to succeed to exalted positions within their respective circles. My tutor and lecturers at Christ Church, known by undergraduates reverentially as 'the house', had made a less than memorable impression on me from the outset. But then, as I had told my father and mother, I doubted the academic life here would suit me very much and it was highly improbable I would actually graduate.

Feeling somewhat weary and my head full of thoughts I could make no sense of (this was not that unusual for me) I decided to rest both my body and my brain by sitting at the base of the Martyrs Memorial next to the Randolph Hotel and gaze up that beautiful and wide thoroughfare of St Giles. Apart from an odd delivery van chugging along to the Banbury Road it was still fairly quiet. I could see through the windows of the Randolph and the waiters were busily preparing tables for breakfast, white linen table covers catching the sun as they flapped them open and then over the tables. The odd glint of silver as the cutlery was placed appropriately. I was thinking how smart the waiters looked in their starched white jackets when my mind turned to the poor Bishops this memorial was erected to remember.

Clutching my trusty teddy bear close I shuddered at the thought of the flames licking at their heels and them knowing that a certain, terrible death drew nearer and nearer as the flames intensified. Publicly burnt at the stake and all because they denounced Catholicism and declared themselves Protestants as a result of the reformation.

I wiped away a tear that had appeared from my eye and felt rather foolish. My father had often mocked me for my sensitivity, to him that made me weak which was the ultimate sin in his eyes.

His typical Victorian adventurer spirit and tough character was what one needed to survive this world. Or so he said, and maybe he was right. It confused me still if I thought of it too much. A voice then made me jump and dragged me from my thoughts.

"Are you alright?" He asked kindly, "Sorry if I surprised you. We met on your first day, I have rooms at Christ Church too."

"Oh, yes, hello…" I replied less than sincerely as I didn't remember him at all.

"Hello," he said holding out his hand, "I'm Bertie – Bertie Pemberton Billing."

I shook his hand. "Harry, Harry Clifton and this is my darling bear." I made my teddy bear wave at him and he smiled. He then sat next to me and we were silent for a few moments oddly comfortable considering we had literally just met.

"Why so glum?" he asked.

"I am consumed by the sins of our forebears and what they did in the name of religion."

"Gosh, that's bit heavy for this time of the morning," he breathed in deeply and then exhaled as if savouring the fresh smell of the new day, "Have you settled into your rooms and escaped the proctor's beady eye?"

"The Proctor is an ass," I said a bit dramatically as it made him chuckle, "he reprimanded me for drinking champagne in the gardens. I shall drink it where I like!"

"It's hell isn't it, I hate being told what to do."

"These Bishops were consumed by flames for daring to defy the Church of Rome and declare themselves Protestants."

"Well, I am consumed by hunger at this moment," he said with a definite twinkle in his eye, "do you fancy breakfast somewhere?"

"Does nothing disturb you?" I asked aghast at his indifference to the Bishops.

"God, no! I just try and concentrate getting through each day."

This made me laugh out loud and I loved his wit and personality. I fancied he was someone who also refused, like myself, to conform. I whispered loudly in my teddy bear's ear, "I think we are going to get along famously with Bertie."

"It never gets any easier though," he added dryly, "dealing with the day's events. Thank God for sex, eh?"

My teddy bear gave him a shocked look on the word "sex" and then buried his head in my shoulder. I did my best not to laugh but Bertie guffawed in a delightfully delicious way.

"I set out this morning on a mission to find a name for my teddy bear," I said as I stood up, "but I got distracted by the poor fate of the Bishops and then you!"

He stood to join me and looked at my bear and said to him, "Bugger the Bishops of 1555!" He then said to me "I'm not as unenlightened as you think, see...

He then guffawed that odd, infectious laugh again that developed into half snort and half grunt. I laughed with him.

He was gorgeous to behold and lifted my spirits immeasurably. "I like you, Bertie," I said sincerely, "would you like to help me find a name for my poor bear. I promised him I would."

"Certainly," he replied instantly, "we could walk along St. Giles and onto the Woodstock Road, there is a splendid café there." He smiled a beautiful smile at me and then unexpectedly he tweaked my teddy bear's nose and said "Come on then Mr. Bear, let's find you a name."

We linked arms and laughed as we crossed the road and started to walk along St Giles, It was coming to life now and more people started walking to and fro to get to their destinations and start the business of the day. I felt elated in Bertie's company.

"Lead the way," I said with drama, "I am yours to do with as you wish!"

"Best offer I've had in a while!"

As we proceeded along St. Giles, the gentle and beautiful rendition of church and college bells chiming the half hour gave way to a rowdy gang of what we called at Downside

"Rugger Buggers" who emerged very loudly onto the street from a side alley. They were fairly typical types, sporty like my father, with too much testosterone that made their brains work less efficiently. The cocky leader deliberately crashed into Bertie and then started taunting him. I admired the fact Bertie faced them down and did not let them get the upper hand. For me it was a shock as I had never encountered such close hostility before by a gang.

"Where are you off to boys," he said sneeringly as the others laughed, "Or is it girls?

The others gathered around us apart from one boy who hung back and looked a little embarrassed by the behaviour of his friends. Bertie seemed to know him, I thought.

"Hi Johnny," Bertie said directly to him, "not so friendly when you are with your rowing friends are you?"

"You know this nancy boy, Johnny?" Asked the ringleader as the others started teasing him and ruffling his hair. "Is there something you need to tell us Johnny?"

"His friend still has his teddy bear! Ahhh, what a pansy."

Bertie went for the kill "You know how I like a big muscle, don't you Johnny." He then winked at him. "Don't you?"

This deflected the attention to Johnny and they teased him mercilessly as he dragged them away, but not before he could give Bertie a sly conspiratorial wink. For good measure I shouted after them: "Grow up, chaps!" They so reminded me of my father and my young brother, who was destined to go the same way, I thought sadly. Bertie seemed completely undaunted.

"Just avoid the 'Hearties' if you encounter any…"

"They call you 'nancy boy' and 'pansy' just because you don't do sporty things or rowing?" I asked incredulous.

"Something like that," Bertie said matter of factly, adding, "but some of them like fucking each other - and me secretly."

This made me laugh delightedly and he soon joined in as if not realising his own wit and sense of comic timing. We carried on walking at a leisurely pace in silence and then sat for a few minutes watching the world go by. Bertie made me think about things.

"I hate people pinning labels to me," I said thoughtfully, "I like to think I am adventurous and open minded. I hate conformity."

"Even sex?" he looked me right in the eye as he said it.

"Especially that. Everyone is attractive and we should see each other as equal and try and shake off the shackles of what has been and explore what could be. Don't you think?"

We strolled on feeling like old friends. I glanced at his handsome profile and found it hard to believe we had just met a short time ago. It was like our souls had known each other before and had just picked up where they left off. The sound of the bells began to chime 10am and all across Oxford the sounds mingled and caressed to create a magical effect on one's ear.

"My father is a brute," I said sadly, "and doesn't approve of me and my bookworm tendencies. "What good is that?" he roars.

"Mine is dead," Bertie said bluntly, "but I didn't really know him at all. Brute or not, you are lucky to have one. I have no living family, just a trust administered through a solicitor in London."

"How ghastly for you," is all I could think of to say, "your honesty is disarming, Bertie." After a brief silence we carried on walking, to lift the mood and change the subject I said: "Now, let's find a name for my darling bear."

"Are you Catholic?"

"My family are." I replied rather taken aback. "They expect me to be, but I have too many sins!

"Since the slaughter of the last war," he said suddenly wistful, "and all the boys who died life has changed for our generation. I don't want to be constrained or dictated to anymore. I want to live, be free, sin as much as I damn well please!

We suddenly found ourselves surrounded by a cohort of women laughing and chatting and it made me feel unusually anxious for some reason.

"Oxford is positively pullulating! Let's go in here out of danger," I said feeling a rising panic. I suspect it was the sudden noise of all the chattering and laughing that set my nerves off. We found ourselves in the Catholic Oratory of St Aloysius. I pulled Bertie to a pew at the back of the church. The familiar smell of high altar and incense and candle wax pervaded, touching everything in its reach.

"What is that smell?" Bertie asked in a whisper.

"The end of innocence!" I said almost angrily. "You don't have to whisper either." It made me smile because people often resorted to whispering when they entered a Catholic church if they were unfamiliar with it. An instant subservience the priests would be proud of. "Were you ever religious?"

"Me? No, pure heathen," he said, "The fires of hell await me."

"My father," I said suddenly serious, "is a conundrum to me in some ways."

"Why?"

"I know he thinks I am too sensitive and doesn't approve and has spent years trying to toughen me up and make a man of me. That didn't work. He hates that I like books and calls me a silly bookworm and cannot see the point of it or the benefit of it for the responsibility I will have as his heir."

"I still feel I would rather have a father, even if he treated me like yours. It's better than having nothing."

"Yes," I replied taking a deep breath, "I'm not even sure why I am telling you this."

"I'm glad you are…"

"He has arranged for me to come here to Christ Church but I told him I will never get a degree as I am not hard working. Everyone thinks I am but I'm not. I don't care about it you see. All paid for by father, through his Estate Manager of course, like a business transaction. I also get £400 a year allowance, again managed by father's Estate Manager. Like I am some prized horse."

"I'd rather be a horse than an orphan."

"Dear Bertie," I looked at him with fresh eyes, "your desire is admirable and I understand. Better to have than have not."

"You are luckier than you realise. I get a cheque every quarter signed by someone I have never met. I have no idea if that money comes to me from love or resentment or forced obligation. It's soulless in a way."

"I told my father I don't want to inherit the estates in Lytham and Scotland when he dies. I don't think I am up to the job to be frank. I have no skill or desire and I hate anything to do with the land, shooting, hunting it all means nothing. I asked him to let my younger brother Michael inherit instead. He would do a better job, he has it in him, I can see that even at the age he is."

"What did he say?"

"He refused, said it would be impossible because of tax and death duties. I pleaded he ask his Estate Manager to look into it find a way to make it happen. But no, even they did not agree. I thought my father would have been glad to be rid of me. I just want to be free."

"I want to be loved," he said, "not just fucked."

As he said this, thankfully still in a half whisper, a nun got up and genuflected at Christ on the cross then scurried up the aisle and past us. We looked at each other and tried to contain our giggles.

"I like the name Giles," I said suddenly, "There is an irony to it." I looked at my teddy bear. "What do you think, darling?" The bear whispered in my ear. "That's settled then," I said holding him aloft.

"I feel flames licking at my ankles, Harry" Bertie said suddenly anxious and standing up, "Can we go?"

We quickly exited the church and found ourselves back on the Woodstock Road. The morning thus far had been a revelation to me – or rather finding Bertie had been a revelation. I had never met anyone remotely like him and probably never would again. This made me realise I had to cherish him and our new found friendship. Maybe I was finally starting to meet people that made sense to me and me to them. My kind of people. It sounded trite but it was true.

"Bertie," I said with real joy in my voice, "meet Giles. He suits his new name doesn't he?"

"Perfectly"

"I'm ravenous now."

"Darling," he said with that twinkle in his eye, "we must have breakfast first!"

I made Giles do a double take at the implication, this made Bertie snort his ridiculous laugh again to which I couldn't help but join in.

Evelyn Waugh:

As I turned onto the Turl from the High I marvelled at how much I still found Oxford charming and addictive.

I don't think I would ever tire of the city – thankfully it didn't tire of me either and my father was still holding out the hope I would get my degree. I suspected otherwise and decided my eccentric tutor had no intention of finally allowing me the prize. I couldn't blame him as I had been beastly and rather unpleasant to him whereas I should have bitten my tongue and at least tried to conform enough to get by – as had most of my contemporaries who had long gone. At times I felt like I was a lone survivor clinging to the wreckage of the stricken ship that was my university career.

Life has taught me that not everyone likes me at first sight – or closer inspection – but rebuffs still shock, however infrequent they may be. I actually think my character, general manners and charm are highly amusing and sought after. But I would, wouldn't I?

I was beginning to accept that my hated tutor at Hertford College has finally given up on me and finally sent me down without a degree. How do I know this? I have the letter in my pocket. To their credit, I mention this with gritted teeth; they have extended my time way beyond the normal that it takes to attain one's degree. But alas, as they pointed out, I had only completed eight terms instead of the required nine, so I had to accept the outcome and all because my mind had been elsewhere. It's harder to give up Oxford though, in that I fear I shall never succeed.

Seeing the red telephone box I mustered myself and thought it best if I call my dear old Pa. I needed to nurture my financial goose! I dialled the number and waited for him to pick up, then when he did I fed the machine coins as it pipped away and finally connected us.

"Pa? Is that you, it's Evelyn…"

"Hello dear boy."

"Did you and the board make any decision about my novel Decline and Fall?"

"Yes, good news, I persuaded them to publish it. We will see how it goes."

"That's splendid, Pa!" I retorted a little too enthusiastically I thought. "Can you deposit a hundred pounds into my account as an advance? I'm a little, well a lot actually, embarrassed financially."

"Good God, boy," he spluttered, "What do you think I am, made of money?

At this point I had to hold the telephone away from my ear so he could have a good old rant and tell me how ungrateful I was and how money didn't grow on trees. He would also, no doubt, ask if I had graduated yet and sorted things out with my tutor. I wouldn't burden him with that news just yet. After a few moments I said into the telephone:

"Thank you dearest Pa! I will speak soon and look forward to getting the proofs."

My father being a publisher meant I couldn't have been more lucky for a good start to my literary career. I then hung up rather quicker than politeness demanded. I didn't worry as I knew he would pay the money into my account. He always did. As I had this thought I noticed one of the dons from my college coming towards me. It was obvious he had spotted me as he glared with a barely masked fury etched across his face. I guessed he had heard the news of my ultimate shame. He stopped right in front of me as I emerged from the telephone box, I could see a nerve twitching on the side of his cheek.

"Damn you, Evelyn," he blurted out with spittle, "you're a scholar. Sent down? You should be ashamed wasting your talent and your life!"

With that he marched off grunting and muttering to himself which, to be honest, I thought very funny. St Aldates is an odd street as it is both old, old fashioned and some of the houses, now with occasional shop fronts, reminiscent of Tudor buildings. As I made my way to the Hypocrites Club located in rooms above one of these houses, with a bicycle shop on the ground floor, I wondered if Bertie had invited the intriguing newcomer to the club. Clifton his name was. I looked around and then went into the door that had stairs leading up to the Hypocrites.

The bare wooden stairs were steep and narrow with a perpetual coating of dust from people's shoes. They were also slightly rickety and lopsided because of the age of the house – in many ways that perfectly described the members of the club as, let's say, we were all free thinkers and non conformists who refused to 'fit in' to society and its expectations.

The club was founded originally in 1921 by John Knatchbull Lloyd, then kept going and frequented by myself and my lover Alistair Graham when we met after coming up to Oxford. We gave a voice to 'the love that dare not speak its name' and also had the audacity to go into the streets and 'frighten the horses', as Wilde and Mrs. Patrick Cambell once famously remarked, and warned against respectively. So thus we refused to care and make hypocrites of ourselves and others like us.

Many of us were actually sexually fluid and enjoyed all types of sexual partners. We did of course want to shock, but taking the lease on the floors above this bicycle shop to create a private members club gave us a space to be who we were and damn convention. Rather delightfully and wickedly it was opposite Christ Church too. The motto, rather tongue in cheek, from the Greek ode by Pindar that translated into English as: 'Water is Best' We all thus became Hypocrites as we drank alcohol heavily – at least I did. Others had various pleasures of addiction, but my life long love of alcohol and sex started here. We always enjoy looking for new members.

This was the stomping ground for most of my time at Oxford, and as a result I wasted a good deal of time, but it kept me sane. My spirit and nature abhors authority of any kind apart from my own. It also provided me with the most inspiration for my novel ideas and the characters therein.

Sadly the university became aware of its less than shining reputation and were determined to close it down – we resisted for a long time.

Harry Clifton:

I awoke to the chimes of Tom Tower striking 9am, immediately followed by the eccentric 101 strikes. The oddness of it still made me smile but I freely admit it was starting to wear thin now it had become a constant every day occurrence.

Through the open window of my rooms I could hear the bustle of the day and indistinct chatter of those passing by on their way to respective lectures. Next to me still sleeping lay the handsome profile of dear, sweet Bertie. His modesty barely covered but his naked beauty plain to see.

His breathing was even and he seemed to be deeply asleep. I had started the habit of counting the damn chimes of the clock almost without realising. I admonished myself and declared it to be a slippery slope!

"You're muttering," Bertie said suddenly taking me by surprise, "I was having a lovely sleep…"

"I'm counting the chimes." I replied rather obviously.
"Don't bother counting," he said closing his eyes again, "there are 101 every time."

"I know, but it is bizarre!"

"When Henry VIII died," Bertie said suddenly serious, "there were 100 students at Christ Church and they added the first student to join after his death to the number. So 101 chimes it was and has remained so ever since."

"Not only does this place have its own time," I said rather baffled by it all, "it has this odd ritual to commemorate a long dead mad monarch."

Bertie laughed as he flung the sheet off himself and me leaving us naked to the world. "And," he added with that twinkle in his eye, "Tom Tower that houses the clock actually looks like a giant phalus!"

"You are incorrigible but absolutely right," I said laughing with him, "quite a big one too!"

"We should get up," he said wearily and somewhat resigned without making any effort to move, "we have lectures today."

"How tedious," I said yawning, "I shan't be going as I'm too tired and they are insufferingly boring."

"They will throw you out."

"No they won't. My father pulls the strings and pays them handsomely for me to be here."

He turned to look at me. "It must be comforting to know," he said teasingly, "that you are cushioned from the harsher realities of life."

"I know. Nobody could accuse me of being a hypocrite."

Suddenly Bertie sat bolt upright and looked at me suspiciously. He then lit a cigarette for us both and handed me one. He smoked with panache and I sputtered and coughed with mine. After a couple of attempts I stubbed it out and lay back down.

"Actually," he said looking at me, "you would make a fabulous hypocrite."

"Thank you very much."

"I'm serious," he said stubbing his cigarette out and laying back next to me, "I have been meaning to ask you to become a member. You would love it."

"A member of what?"

"The Hypocrites Club! Well, to be absolutely correct, it's a drinking club now. I took over the lease when the original club was closed down by the university. But we still call it that but unofficially. It's still deliciously decadent."

"But I'm not..."

"Darling Harry," he said laughing, "that's the whole point. We do things and enjoy life and each other without being hypocrites. You see?"

"I think so," I said still not entirely convinced, "and it sounds intriguing."

"There is someone who would like to meet you, but I can't and won't say who. You will have to come along tonight and find out."

"We'll see," I said warily, "I'm not accustomed to secret admirers."

"Oh, you will be," he chuckled and then sat up looking down at me, "so you must promise to come. You will won't you?"

I grabbed him and pulled him back down into the bed and pulled the sheet over us. "Only if you are a very good boy..."

Chapter Six

2023 - Lytham Hall

Undertaking research into Harry Clifton's life nearly one hundred years later I quickly realise that he was a man born in the wrong time. Had he been at the same point in his life today, he would have fitted into the world and been very contemporary. Unfortunately for him he wasn't, and he was so out of kilter with the world dominated by his unforgiving father, that he emotionally imploded to the point I'm not convinced he knew who he really was, once all the dynasty expectations and demands were stripped away. Underneath it all I feel he felt quite inadequate, due to his father's aggressive tactics, some would say bullying, and also ill-equipped intellectually to deal with his birth right as heir. His temperament was, I think artistic, dreamy and other worldly.

Hi father had become more and more intolerant, some say due to his declining health, "of the damn bookworm" that he could not believe was his son, so different was he from his own character. He declared "he wanted to make him [Harry] tough and a worthy successor" to the estates for the security of the family dynasty. In the book The Clifton Chronicle it gives us an insight into the hostile father son relationship in 1925:

"Harry genuinely wanted to work and become a scholar or journalist, but, when with his father during holidays [from school], life was sometimes unbearable. There were short periods when Talbot [his father] was more charming and interesting than any man Harry had ever met; but then there were long periods of gloom, suspicion, anger and bullying. He insisted on billiards every night and Harry was severely rebuked for missing an easy shot, yet woe betide if Talbot got beaten by anyone."

This is interesting in that one suspects that Harry, who unsurprisingly hated billiards, had seen his father rage if anyone had the temerity to beat him at the game, that Harry made a conscious decision not to try to avoid his father's wrath. Whatever he did, it seemed, he couldn't avoid conflict, or win.

Harry was then, it is recorded, "delighted" that in the end he went to Oxford as it gave him, aged 19, his first experience of real freedom. He also thrilled at, "the store of wisdom and knowledge one could dive into." The agent for the Clifton estates that arranged his allowance of £400 per year [not a small sum in 1926] – paid quarterly – was William Whinnerah who became Harry's point of contact for all things financial rather than his father directly. This I am sure Harry found a blessing rather than a curse!

William cautioned Harry about getting into debt and stressed the importance of living within his means whilst at Oxford. He wrote encouragingly: "I hope your expenditure may keep well within your allowance if for nothing more than the extremely comfortable sensation it will afford you, but in any event do not, I beg of you, ever make application to any outside agency for monetary assistance."

Sadly, as much as he did try, within four months Harry found himself hopelessly overdrawn at the bank and had to write to William asking for a loan from his next quarter's allowance. He managed to charm William into assisting him "just this time" by refusing the estate manager's offer to ask his father to get him a car. Harry wrote to William to say:

"I answered 1.) That I could not afford it [on his allowance] and 2.) That I did not want it. Both of which are quite true and I do hope he says nothing to father altho' (sic) he has already mentioned it to mother."

William replied: "Thank you very much for your letter which if I may be permitted to say so, is an excellent one and to the point."

Harry was also struggling with thoughts of the future and what would happen if anything happened to his father and he inherited and had the weight of the Clifton estates thrust upon him:

"The other day father replied to a question of mine – that it would be better if Micky [his younger brother Michael] were to be heir – that it would be unfair to the other children.

But surely the death duties which father said would be heavier in that case, could be arranged, could they not? This is what I would like to know and also since this involves the coming of age, to try and avoid it. I realise that you are already making arrangements in which I do not personally wish to concur. I write to you instead of speaking to father as you are such a good counsellor and I have tried mother but she always makes specious arguments against my views. If only I could get father to agree with my plans everything would go simply. But although this is no sudden resolve (over a year old in this form) when I suggested the metamorphosis of Michael and myself he just said that I was speaking, without thinking. The first thing that came into my mind; not understanding that I had been thinking without speaking for a long time. I am afraid he would think I was being ridiculous and might be very angry and therefore I am asking your advice as I would prefer not to idle away time till (sic) I was twenty-one pretending I was a perfect Clifton."

There is something very mature but heartbreaking about this letter as Harry clearly feels he is just not cut out to be his father's heir. Aside from the constant battles and feelings of inadequacy his father engendered in him, Harry it seems is looking for a way out as he feels it would be better for the family. It is truly telling that he had more confidence discussing this with William rather than anyone else in his life. I also admire the fact that in spite of his parents obvious belligerence towards him, and knowing it would aggravate his father's wrath; he tried in his own way to secure the future for the Clifton family by trying to get them to see his brother would be a better heir. Remarkable really in many ways. The letter went on to say:

"I do not know how much independence I will have after I am twenty-one as my idea is that if I have enough money after that I will give up sport [which he hated], cease being a gentleman (at which I am very bad) and become a student. I am trying to draw you to the main argument that if father would accede to my wish and put Michael in my place, postponing the coming of age festivities for another nine or ten years [when Michael would be 21] I could begin my career as a student right away. At least, could I? Would father agree? Or do you think he would consider it very selfish and prevent my ever becoming a student? I am neither learned, talented or a genius. But I am no sportsman and never will be one and if allowed to work now I may be able to fill some position, perhaps even make a little money later"

This letter does make sad reading because it shows us the turmoil he is experiencing and his feelings of inadequacy towards his abilities and his non existent grasp of life's realities too. He really has no idea how the system he was born into works and his efforts are in vain. He concludes with his thoughts on Oxford:

"I realised when I went to Oxford how hard men do work and realise I know nothing compared to others. And the worst of it is that my sisters, who have never worked – I had almost said my whole family – think that I (an inveterate idler, hardly able to get into Oxford, hardly able to stay there) work hard.

"It is a queer and unpleasant situation. I see almost no prospect of getting a degree and yet my family think I work hard. In many places the atmosphere, the conversation is worth a book a day to the young man who is at the same time diligent in himself. Here [meaning himself] there are no books in the atmosphere and no diligence in the undergraduate. And yet the irony is I am considered to work hard. I wonder what your advice will be? I tremble that you will wish me to do the (for me) twenty-one-ster farce. I hope you may think my projects reasonable.

Good bye, your affect.
Harry.

P.S. Forgive my troubling you – take it as a tribute to your wisdom. May the preparations for December year [his 21st Birthday] and the attendant difficulties …both vanish and melt…I pray and hope."

William wrote to Harry to reassure him and to say that perhaps he had taken his father's bluster too much to heart, explaining his father was of a different generation and that his "pursuing the usual method of gingering up, successful in ninety-nine percent of boys" had not actually worked in this case. He also told Harry his father had not factored in his "extreme sensitiveness" reminding Harry that his father had been quite ill for the past two years. He implored him to consider also that if he did abdicate in favour of his brother he might live to regret it. William went on to say:

"Your extreme sensitiveness and modesty are liable to become a burden unless you watch them but you can never be anything but a gentleman, whether you elect to wear the purple or prefer to earn your living quite independently of your great birthright. By virtue of your birth alone you are a personage of importance without taking into account your own charming personality, and what might be quite a proper choice for one of your age in an ordinary position in life, is not always permissible to the eldest son of an old County family – Noblesse Oblige."

William Whinnerah the Estate Manager was a positive influence on Harry as well as having his best interests at heart. He managed to defuse many of the highly charged situations that arose between father and son and, one suspects, mother and son too. He was also an expert where the finances were concerned and did his best to tutor Harry to have fiscal responsibility where his allowance was concerned.

Walking into Lytham Hall today one is surprised that such a grand Georgian House can feel so homely. But it does. The grander rooms and formal dining room on the ground floor are all beautifully proportioned and presented to the visitor like they are still lived in. Praise must go to the trust and the managers of the Hall for initiating such an excellent recreation. One feels that the family may return any moment to the empty rooms.

The Clifton family portraits are also rather splendid and the chronology starts with the Tudors and ends with the 20th century Cliftons. Many of these portraits were stored away and rediscovered by the trust that now operates the estate. Thankfully they were not lost.

In the main entrance hall that leads to the grand staircase – and it is one very grand staircase - there are two huge portraits that dominate. One is of John Talbot Clifton, Harry's father, known as Talbot. He was a typical Victorian adventurer and a handsome, strong featured virile looking man who was also very tall for his time. The other of Harry's mother Violet Clifton, who seems witheringly tall herself and has an imperiousness that could have come from one of her decedents, a certain Ellen Gwynne, known as Nell, who bore the famous basket of oranges at the Theatre Royal, Drury Lane, who was King Charles II's mistress, and for whom she bore an illegitimate child. So Violet could claim to have royal blood in her lineage. For eternity they are now destined to look down rather disapprovingly, as if wondering who all these strangers are in their home.

On the grand piano are silver framed black and white images of Harry and their other children and family members in informal poses that make you feel like you are intruding on some private possessions whilst the owners are absent.
It can't help but make one feel a little sad that instead of the family thriving, and more current pictures adorning the main house, the last of them are preserved in aspic for posterity as if time has stood still.

The formal dining room has a long elegant table that is presented as if a grand dinner party is about to commence, one can imagine the butler and footman polishing the glasses and silver one more time to make sure everything is perfect and ready for their master and mistress. More family portraits from centuries past gaze down at this theatre and wonder where the family are now.

As the sun bursts through the windows and lights the room there is visible dust in the air that will slowly settle on the unused china and glass ware until a preservation volunteer comes along to gently clean everything again. A dinner party laid out that no family or guests will ever experience, nobody will ever sit at the table. No Housekeeper, butler, footmen, maids, cooks, chauffeur, gardeners, or gamekeepers making it all possible. Like a ship without a crew. I can't help but think of Harry and his father arguing and fighting over some trifle and Violet attempting to calm the situation.

Their energy seems to still permeate the house and echoes of them are never far away as if at any moment they will all come striding through the door and take you by surprise.

As you pass through there are discreet guide volunteers who will, if you ask them, impart their knowledge on the rooms, the history and the family and other relevant facts about the Cliftons. There are no ropes and barriers, as one finds in National Trust houses, just discreet requests that you don't sit on the antique furniture or touch any of the treasures that dress the house so beautifully. This alone adds a reality to the experience and creates the atmosphere of a real home for visitors.

One thing that troubled me about the guide volunteers is that they describe Harry as "an awful man" or "that terrible Harry" and it strikes me as odd and a part of me refuses to believe that he was all "bad" or as "selfish" as he is made out. It all seems a little one dimensional to me in terms of a character analysis of Harry. This for me is highlighted by the way the other family members and his mother and father are considered and talked about with respect and affection. For this reason I became more and more intrigued by Harry and wanted to find out what really happened and why he behaved as he did.

This thought occupies me as I enter the grand staircase. It is a double cantilevered stairway that splits into two flights after the initial wide stairs lead to the first landing. As you climb this initial wide staircase a portrait of Violet Clifton looks at you quizzically and her eyes seem to follow you. The height of the ceiling and the intricately decorated plaster ceilings and mouldings were certainly created to impress. To show there was wealth here with the Clifton family. It is rather awesome really and you feel slightly humbled being there.

I can understand why Evelyn Waugh was impressed when he first came here and on his subsequent visits, in a letter from the 1930s to Lady Asquith he wrote:

"A very beautiful house by Kent or someone like him with first-class Italian plaster work. A lap of luxury flowing with champagne and elaborate cookery (sic)…Cliftons are all tearing mad. Mrs [Violet] Clifton more sombre and full of soul."

Similarly the brother of the Tsar of Russia, but to him, compared to the Winter Palace and the Kremlin perhaps it was all very ordinary. There will have been many other guests who would have climbed these stairs, perhaps on route to Violet Clifton's private sitting room for an appointment, who would have felt nervous and rather insignificant. Potential staff on their way to be interviewed - or estate managers and local dignitaries, to discuss the charity events and social functions, that Violet would attend. All life went on here.

As you enter the private areas of the house on the first floor there is a cosiness that is rather unexpected after the grandness of the ground floor and the staircase. In the bedroom once occupied by Talbot and Violet Clifton one gets a sense of how tall they were. The bed, which is still in place, was made for them. It dominates the bedroom. The bathroom and dressing rooms lead off and are decorated and conserved to an excellent standard to create a moment in time.

Violet's sitting room is adjacent and still has her red plush furniture and splendid double aspect windows looking out over the parkland. Another bathroom and a small bedroom are also off this room.

Harry's room is along the hallway that also leads to other bedrooms and a small intimate dining room on the first floor. There you will also find the other more practical staircase that services the house and obviously made it easier for the staff and family for everyday coming and going. This staircase leads you to the second floor that also has a number of rooms and bedrooms. Unusually for this kind of Georgian Hall the staff did not sleep in these rooms – they were reserved for guests – the staff had rooms in the quarters housed in a separate building attached to the main house via the kitchens and service area.

One of the rooms on the second floor is decorated using the original paneling from the former Tudor house that was on the site but demolished to make way for this much grander house. It has a feeling that is slightly oppressive and the ceilings are lower in this part of the house. Next to this is a room dedicated to the history of the Benedictine Monastery that occupied the site prior to that. This made me think of Harry being sent to Downside School run by Benedictine Monks, where he was so unhappy with the sports regime. It must have been terrible to endure if you are not a sporty type and more artistic. I felt for him.

During my research I discovered that, like Harry, his father was far from perfect when it came to money and responsibility. Talbot caused much angst for the previous

Estate Manager when he was 20 years of age! He was taken to task for spending money he didn't have, running up gambling debts and even causing a scandal by taking Lillie Langtry, the famous socialite and mistress of the Prince of Wales, as his lover. She was many years his senior at the time. A letter from Lily Langtry to Talbot dated circa 1890 gives a flavour of her ardour for him but it seems to be less than reciprocal:

"My darling Talbot

I was so sorry to say goodbye and to feel that we had wasted the last three days quarrelling. Why won't you let me come with you. Will you be glad to see me if I come out to America? I feel that I must see you again soon. I was so pitiful to see the poor coach left behind – I wept all the way back and feel so blue – Do be a good boy and don't drink too many brandies and sodas, you will kill yourself if you do – and write to me from Queenstown to say you care for me, my own darling, and telegraph the address that will find you in America…God bless you, my darling boy.

Love you – L
18 Pont Street
S.W"

One of Talbot's sisters, suspicious that Langtry was more interested in the Clifton money, wrote to him as a warning: "there is a report in London that Mrs. [Lillie] Langtry, finding her acting not a success, is pretending illness, has thrown up her engagement, and is going to follow you out to America to induce you to marry her."

It would seem the affair fizzled out on both sides before any such disaster could take place. Talbot had been a worry financially for his excesses for some years. The Estate manager, Mr. Fair, wrote after Talbot had run up a £200 gambling debt – a considerable amount of money – and Fair must have felt duped when he discovered the real reason for the money:

"It did not occur to me that Talbot had drawn on me to pay a gambling debt…The Manchester and County Bank has a branch and sub manager in Lytham and I felt that to dishonour the Bill [cheque/draft] would bring disgrace and dishonour upon Talbot – I was assuming that he had received value of some kind for it [£200] If however it was to pay a mere gambling debt I must admit I have made a mistake."

This was all at the time Talbot was about to inherit when his grandfather passed away. His grandmother Lady Cecily Clifton, who had brought him up from being a small boy when his father died, was in despair at his behaviour.

This all makes one wonder if Talbot's fears for his own son, and the reason he was so hard on Harry, was because he feared he may have inherited his own traits of irresponsibility. I wonder if Harry knew all this about his father's past at this time. Surely it is something he will have discovered as he got older that perhaps fed into his own resentment. Could this explain Harry's actions once he came of age and inherited the Estates?

By 1927, whilst Harry was at Christ Church, Oxford, time was starting to run out for Talbot Clifton. Harry carried on regardless in his own eccentric way. By 30th January 1928

Harry had seen his parents as they passed through to London on their way to Dakar for one of their adventures. Harry noted: "We all kissed one another goodbye last Wednesday, which was a surprise."

More shock and surprises were on the horizon, they just hadn't come into view yet. Ones that would change their lives forever.

John Talbot's mistress the actress Lillie Langtry – she became infamous in Victorian society after her affair with the Prince of Wales (later King Edward VII). Born in Jersey she was known as The Jersey Lillie.

Chapter Seven

Hedonism

Harry Clifton:

After a particularly lazy day spent mostly in or on my bed in my rooms at Christ Church, I decided to take up Bertie's offer and grace the Hypocrites Club with my presence. I had nothing to lose and could always leave if it didn't suit me. I did have quite an aversion to enforced jollity that one encounters at parties – be they at Oxford or anywhere else for that matter. But, I wondered, perhaps this 'drinking club' might be sufficiently entertaining to not bore me too much – and he did make it sound intriguing.

I pondered this as I bathed and then dressed in my white tie for a formal college dinner that I had to attend prior to going on anywhere else. I wondered if Bertie would be at the dinner or if he would abscond and suffer the wrath of the Proctor and his tutor. I had been admonished my self again for drinking champagne in the gardens and the quad. It was insufferably tedious – or rather they were. What harm did it do?

As I dressed and then made my way down for dinner I imagined my boredom at the speeches yet to be made by the stuffy academics and tutors. They would all be sitting hawk like on the top table, glaring at us all to find some fault with our dress or manner. It really was like being back at school in some ways. I disliked giving speeches and abhorred other people giving them, especially as they were so dry and uninteresting and mostly self congratulatory. It was like walking back in time entering the dining hall with its great vaulted ceiling and stained glass windows. Like some high priest or cardinal of the church, had devised a way to overwhelm the senses of poor mortals that almost made your knees buckle in an involuntary way. Thankfully I had had a couple of glasses of champagne in my rooms to numb the effect it had on me. I was of a mind to genuflect but for all the wrong reasons. This made me smile as it pleased me that only I knew what thoughts were in my head.

As anticipated the speeches were dreadfully dull and the food, although adequate, was more so. Typical stodgy fayre that sat like lead shot in your stomach for hours afterwards. Thank goodness the champagne I had secretly drunk dulled the pain of the indigestion. At my earliest opportunity I fled and collected another bottle of champagne from my rooms.

The evening was lovely for the time of year, the trees bare and lifeless against the moonlight with no promise of spring that was as yet, alas, so far away. I sat looking at Christ Church

Meadow and revelling in the beauty of it at any time of day or night. It had a peace to it that was balm to my soul. I must have looked slightly incongruous to the odd passer by in my white tie, tails and supping champagne direct from the bottle. I imagined my mother's horror if she could see me and it made me laugh out loud to myself. Love, or the concept of it, genuinely puzzled me. Usually people who said they loved me were the ones who treated me badly or raised their voice at me, or got annoyed with me, or pointed out my faults; or wanted something from me – usually a loan! I was not sure I was capable of any kind of love.

The bicycle shop on St Aldates, above which was the Hypocrites Club, was just through the Christ Church gates and across the road – not far – but it seemed a million miles away at this moment. I hesitated because it was the unexpected, I wasn't sure what that would be and, made worse, by Bertie telling me that some mysterious person he refused to name wanted to meet me made me all the more apprehensive. Who would want to meet me? I had already experimented with things at Oxford I would never have dreamed of in Lytham or Islay. Could there be more secrets inside me? Did I have the courage to face them head on and deal with the consequences? Oh, dear, life can be jolly hard and one never knows what to do for the best. "What is the best," I thought and then decided to get on with it because I needed distracting; I did not like spending long periods of time in my own head. That was a frightening place to be.

Evelyn Waugh:

The club was busy and full of the usual crowd. Looking around there was all life here still and the lesbians who loved to dress in tails like men and slick their hair back, whilst their more feminine counterparts draped off their arms in conventional flowing dresses - more Joan Crawford than Bette Davies - who were both, to my eye, rather masculine anyway. But what did I know. The jazz music played on the piano with a heady beat and the smoke lingered thickly in the rooms whilst the barman did his best to supply drinks on demand. The hastily adapted floor and table lamps added to the atmosphere, by being covered in multi coloured silk headscarves that muted the light and cast glorious shades of colour across people complexions. Boys in drag dressed to perfection flounced and purred and flirted with hearty boys who liked nothing better than other boys. Other boys with pretty faces who wore barely anything at all and snared whatever handsome man they could, dragging them willingly to the back rooms where they could fuck.

Looking across the room I could see Bertie wearing nothing but high heels and a feather boa around his neck. His body was perfection and the light glimmered on his smooth skin; he liked to shave all his body hair off. He was sipping from a glass of champagne and I could imagine all those repressed souls out there in the world gasping or clutching their pearls in shock at what went on here. They were the hypocrites in my mind because they didn't have the guts to be who they wanted to be; do what they wanted to do; fuck who they wanted to fuck. This made me laugh out loud and even over the music Bertie heard me. He looked across at me and winked whilst pouting a kiss. Those lips of his had caressed parts of me that nobody else had. I felt my erection and remembered what he had done to it.

Alistair came towards me with two glasses of gin. I blame this place for nurturing my love of alcohol, I doubt I could live without it now, but then I doubted I would want to.

These beautiful people all had one thing in common. They had the guts, at least here, to be themselves. I toasted them and sipped my gin. Alistair and I had been lovers since we met when we first came up to Oxford, our relationship continued and was useful when I needed someone who was feeling fuckable – and vice-versa. But our lust had waned, or at least it had for me, and we remained friends.

"A little under-dressed aren't you?" He said looking at me a, little distastefully, I thought. "So many new faces…"He looked about with an expression of someone who had seen it all before – and he had. He was referring to the fact that on my arrival Bertie had dragged me upstairs and undressed me apart from my underwear. I still had my shoes, sock suspenders and socks on and he also put my bow tie back on even though my chest was bare. He then put bright blue eye shadow on my lids and some red lipstick on my lips. He also grabbed my cock and licked his lips but I said no. Tonight I wanted something new. Something fresh. Something daring.

Alistair looked at me and seemed bored. "Do we have to stay here?" He said over the music slightly shouting. "Nothing I haven't seen or had before old boy."

"I'll catch you later," I said dismissing him, adding "You go, I'll see you tomorrow."

Then I saw Harry enter the club and he looked a vision in his white tie. I watched as Bertie went over to him and flirted deliciously with him. Alistair could see my attention was on someone else and sounded petulant and annoyed, which turns me off completely.

"Are you not coming," he said rather put out, "You can be such an ass."

"Don't be such a bore, darling," I snap at him, "you know how much I hate that."

"I'm not in the mood for an argument," he said huffily, "Fuck you!"

"And I'm not in the mood for your whining. Just leave, I'll see you tomorrow."

I watched as Alistair flounced off glaring at people as he went. The bodies around me embrace and kiss and writhe with sexual energy. I can smell the sweat of expectation and sex in the air. The smoke seemed thicker and the music louder and there in the distance was this gorgeous man who stood head and shoulders taller than most. I cross the room and feel the naked bodies on my skin as I pass. Hands clasp at me and touch me intimately but I am oblivious. I have eyes only for him. I then find myself standing next to them.

"Evelyn wants to meet you," I heard Bertie say to Harry as I approached. "You are a lucky boy."

"A girl?" Harry said, puzzled.

Bertie laughed at this and grabbed me and pushed me in front of him. "Evelyn Waugh meet Henry Talbot de vere Clifton."

I was speechless and just kept staring at him.

"I prefer Harry," he said, adding with a smile "Why Evelyn, isn't that a girl's name?"

"My parents fault," I said raising my voice so he could hear me, "they wanted a girl." His eyes locked on me and mine on his. "Besides, I'm not fussy, I can be whatever you want me to be." I was sure he blushed but couldn't be sure.

Bertie laughed and then kissed us both on the cheek. I stared at Harry and then grabbed him and started to dance to the heavy throb of the jazz music. He didn't resist or object, he danced with me and we drank champagne from his bottle. I was entranced and he was mesmerised with what was going on around us.

As we danced to the hypnotic beat of the jazz the bodies around us writhed and screamed their pleasures and the sexual energy carried us all away to some other place that only hedonism and liberation allows. This gave me an out of body experience and I seemed to watch from above as the naked bodies writhed and copulated below and Harry and I danced at the centre of this frenzy of lust.

Bertie and a naked girl also danced either side of us. The girl rubbed herself against us and around us like some rampant snake slithering and sliding her hands over us feeling my erection. Harry seems to be oblivious to everything and trance like allows himself to be caressed and handled, the firmness of his body enticing and exciting. His lips were kissed and licked. There was no hypocrisy here as they removed his clothing.

Harry Clifton:

I awoke to the dawn chorus with a pounding headache. I stumbled from my bed and realised I was naked, but carried on to close the windows and mute the din the birds were making at first light. I staggered back to the bed and sat down. I realised immediately that I had drunk too much champagne last night and that perhaps I had done things I could not remember. My head felt like it was full of bubbles and my mouth was dry as dust. I knew I shouldn't have had that champagne before I had gone to that club. The club? I remember smoke and music and lots of naked people and dancing. I was dancing with Evelyn and that girl but mostly Evelyn. I had never danced with a man before; I had never danced with a nearly naked man and a naked girl before either! Oh, dear, what had I done?

The clock in Tom Tower struck six and I had to endure the hours and the 101 chimes. I buried my head under my pillow in frustration and desperation. The people I had met whilst at Oxford and the way they lived was worthy of a fantasy. I never knew such people existed and it gave me hope for the future and the world. I seemed to fit in with these eccentrics so completely. It was utter bliss for my soul. Comparing my parents and my family with these people made them seen dry and alien to me – as if they truly belonged to the last century. I collapsed back into bed and pull the sheet over me.

Over the course of the next few months I spent a lot of time with Evelyn. We went out of Oxford to Boars Hill and had a picnic of all things, and seeing the city from that perspective made the reality of Matthew Arnold's famous "dreaming spires" come alive. Somehow being lazy there and eating sandwiches, boiled eggs and sipping champagne made all well with the world.

"I'm going to be a famous novelist," he said triumphantly, "the entire world will know of me." He looked and smiled and raised his glass to me.

The sun caught it and reflected in his eyes and he seemed to radiate all the confidence in the world. He laughed delightedly as he accidentally sipped his champagne and it dripped down him because he missed his mouth. Even that didn't fluster him or dim his confidence. I was in awe.

"Are you listening to me, Harry?" He asked as he changed his position and sat cross legged, "My inspiration comes from all those old fuddy-duddies and eccentrics in the colleges down there. They take themselves so very seriously, but you see I see the humour and tragedy in their lives."

"Isn't that being a little unkind?" I asked with seriousness. "After all they must have had hopes and dreams and maybe being a fuddy-duddy Don at Oxford was it?"

"I hadn't considered that," Evelyn said with a twinkle in his eye, "maybe I should consider people's dreams and desires more before I parody them in my novels. You're a good egg, Harry."

"Now you are making fun of me, Evelyn!" I said haughtily but for fun. "You are a bit of a fuddy-duddy yourself if truth be known. Not in a priggish way, just the way you always seem to see the odd in people and not the full roundedness of them."

"I'm a very good judge of people generally," he said a little deflated, "usually if I think them fuckable, then they have appeal."

"You are incorrigible, do you know that?" I sighed with resignation. "Of course you do. I love your mind and the way it thinks. It leaves the rest standing."

We gazed into the distance and enjoyed the view in silence whilst entertaining our own private thoughts. I had no idea what went on in his head, which is perhaps why I liked him so much. I wondered why, with his obvious intellect and curiosity for human nature and all its foibles, he liked me. To me I seemed terribly dull – and sure I would be to know but he seemed to see something in me.

"Do you think people find me fuckable?" I asked him without realising I was going to say it. My frankness even shocked me.

"Always, darling boy! Always…"

"That's heartening to know," I said slightly reassured, "I struggle with the concept of 'love' though. Do you?"

"I think," he said as his mind pondered the question, "most ordinary Joe Bloggs believe that to say they love each other, and convince them selves it's true, means it's okay to fuck. It makes sex acceptable."

"Acceptable?"

He turned to look at me and put his glass down. I turned to get the champagne bottle from the ice bucket – it still made me smile that he brought a bucket with ice for a picnic – and replenished our glasses as he spoke.

"Sex has been oppressed, at least talking about it and accepting that everybody, mostly, does it." He laughed and picked up his glass. "Take my dear parents for example, even though they have children they would be shocked – shocked to the core – to think anyone imagined they ever had sex."

I shuddered at the thought of my own parents. "Yes, I see what you mean, I can't, or don't want to imagine my parents…"

"You see," he said laughing, "we have all been conditioned by society to block it out. But behind the respectable façade they are all at it. If they weren't none of us would exist my dear boy."

He sipped his champagne and bit into another cucumber sandwich thoughtfully. I watched his profile and tried to describe in my mind what made his so different and so appealing. On the surface he was a nice looking man but not overly handsome. He just had something indefinable that drew me to him.

"My father had an affair with Lillie Langtry," I blurted out, "Edward VII's mistress no less. She was ardent for him I understand. He must have been good at sex."

Evelyn almost choked on his sandwich. When he had recovered himself he looked at me and guffawed. "Now that's a claim to sex fame if ever I heard it. How do you know?"

"There are letters hidden away, my aunt told me, and she has them still. They thought Lily Langtry was trying to trick father into marrying her because of his money. He doesn't know that I know."

Evelyn got onto his knees and walked with them across the picnic blanket. He sat next to me and put his arm around me. It felt like the most natural thing to do.

"You are an inspiration to me, Harry, do you know that." He smiled at me even though I felt embarrassed by his words. "As a writer I see your uniqueness and one day I may use your inspiration for one of my books or my writing. That makes you special."

"Thank you," I replied with a smile, "I think you will make a marvellous author one day if you keep at it. It's a shame you flunked your degree though and got sent down."

"Fuck 'em, Harry! They will be sorry," he said with what I thought was a tinge of regret, "the world will remember my name when they are all forgotten. I will always be associated with Oxford in spite of my tutor's spite towards me."

"I like the fact that adversity makes you more determined. Most people would be defeated and give up."

"Never!" After a moment he added, taking me by surprise, "Do you have any dreams?"

"I've always wanted to be anything but who I am." He turned to look at me with a shocked expression on his face. "Aside from that I wanted to be a creative writer or journalist, the new film industry has captivated me too. I love Edgar Allan Poe stories and think some would make excellent films."

"Then you must do it, of course. Sod this habit we Catholics have of being secretive, although to be honest I struggle with it and have resisted converting as yet, my sins overwhelm me sometimes, but we must burst out and show the world what we have to offer. My first novel 'Decline and Fall' is all about parody really, and the hypocrisy and eccentricity of our ruling elite."

"I cannot wait to read it – will it be published soon?"

"My father is working on it – hopefully I will get the proofs through soon."

"How exciting for you."

Evelyn suddenly jumped up and wound up the picnic gramophone he had brought along, as it played the scratchy record he started to dance about like a maniac whilst singing along to a song I didn't recognize – Love Is The Sweetest Thing by Al Bowly. When he lost the lyrics he just hummed and "ahhed" along, oblivious to how out of tune he was. Sometimes I wondered what on earth made him tick, how that brain worked, what he was going to think up next.

The effort was too exhausting because he was too unpredictable to fathom beyond what was before you. I could understand why some people found him unbearable to be around for long. I liked his differences and his suspicion of his faith. That all resonated with me – somewhere secretly inside of me – which was, I thought as I laughed out loud, exactly what a Catholic would do!

"Where," he said suddenly, jolting me from my reverie, "is that annoying bloody teddy bear you carry everywhere. It's very odd you know, but he would be handy to dance with right now."

"I left him in my rooms, he hates picnics." Saying this out loud made me realise the absurdity of it, so to change the subject I added "Besides, he has a name now."

Evelyn twirled and danced like a drug induced dervish, all the while laughing and smiling like a maniac. I wondered at his lack of inhibitions and his devil-may-care attitude. I imagined he even enjoyed public speaking! I shuddered at the thought.

"Come on old boy, let yourself go!" He shouted joyfully. "What did you call him?"

"Who?" I asked momentarily confused and having lost the thread of the conversation amidst all the racket. The gramophone had started to wind down so the music became rather drunk.

"The teddy bear!" He shouted laughing.

"Oh, yes, I was out with Bertie and I called him Giles after St Giles. We had called into St Aloysius Church on the Woodstock Road and it just came to me."

"Good God, Giles!? What a damn awful name, 'Giles' sounds like some boring accountant who ends up living on Boars Hill."

I though about this as he whooped and twirled and laughed at my ridiculous choice of name. I felt rather offended at that moment and wished I was limber enough to leap up and trip him up. "I rather like it, at least he has a name now," I said defensively, "At least it's not a girls name, Evelyn!"

"That was a bit below the belt, Harry." He said with mock indignation, then added blithely "Besides I would have called him Aloysius, yes, Aloysius, after the church, that would suit him better. A good Catholic name too!"

Now that he said it I realised how nice it sounded and thought perhaps he was right. "It sounds a tad pretentious, don't you think? Aloysius?"

"Nonsense! It sounds just right, and, I shall call him Aloysius even if you don't."

As he said this he collapsed in a heap next to me on the rug and laid back looking up at the sky. He pulled me down to join him. His breathing was heavy and he was sweating after all the exertions of his dancing. His profile was beguiling as ever and I found it hard not to stare.

"Can I kiss you?" He asked suddenly and without a hint of embarrassment that took me by surprise. As I had decided to be a less brittle rather than an overtly bright young thing, I said yes with a confidence I didn't actually feel. He pushed himself up on his elbow and looked at me smiling. After a moment he leant in and kissed me rather spectacularly on the lips. His full lips were moist and warm and inviting, mine felt dry and chapped but I let it happen. It was an experience like no other. It certainly didn't feel wrong.

Then we just lay there looking at the sky and content just to be in that moment. Eventually he said kindly: "You must be who you want to be, Harry. Let the world see the real you, you must promise me that. Will you, promise me?"

"Yes," I said feeling rather other worldly, "Yes, I will, and I promise."

"Good," he said, wearily.

We then feel asleep and were oblivious to reality.

The Hypocrites beckoned and we climbed the rickety, dusty stairs and passed the discreet doormen. We had drunk too much champagne and that made our ascent more difficult and hilarious to us – those who have experienced this whilst drunk will understand. It's like trying to climb a moving staircase. We were laughing so hard when Bertie appeared, wearing his usual next to nothing, and seeing our state joined in with the laughter but helped to haul us into the club.

We drank more, which under the circumstances was probably not a wise decision, but the atmosphere and the music carried us away. A beautiful dark girl was dancing on a chair to the strains of Gershwin, a saxophone player in full drag on another, the crowd in this small cramped space spread over two rooms were writhing and dancing in various forms of undress. I marvelled, as all life was here.

As she sang we started to dance round her, Evelyn and I encouraging others to join in, and as we danced we started to strip away our clothing to liberate our bodies and allow ourselves to become as one with the others. This really was the stuff of fantasy and I realised that I no longer felt awkward or reticent being nearly naked among strangers. Evelyn cared nothing and would happily dance as he was born and to hell with it. I began to feel dizzy and slightly sick but no doubt the copious amounts of champagne were playing hell with my insides and added to that I couldn't remember the last time I had eaten. I carried on dancing in spite of this and nobody noticed.

Bertie had rescued our clothes and placed them on a chair for safety. He then passed round a lit cigarette, or more accurately hashish, and we took long heaving puffs and I naturally found myself coughing uncontrollably because it wasn't something I usually engaged with. It made no difference to the effect and before I knew it Bertie, Evelyn and I were dancing as one so close were our bodies. It was spiritual in a way, like I could walk through walls or on water, anything was possible. Until I started to feel terribly sick.

Looking around I could see all these people writhing and fornicating and suddenly the smoke and the smell overwhelmed me and my nausea increased and I started to sweat and feel that I would faint at any moment. My heart was beating erratically and then thudded hard as if trying to escape from my chest, my vision blurred and I could just make out Evelyn who was talking to me and slapping my face. I couldn't understand what he was saying but I could feel his breath on my cheeks – but his face refused to remain in focus. He came towards me and I thought he was going to kiss me again but instead he must have grabbed me and put me over his shoulder to stop me collapsing and to get me in the fresh air. The sudden movement made my head seem to spin off the planet and all whirred before me making me wretch and my nausea rise again, my heart hammering in my naked chest.

My heart reminded me of the Edgar Allan Poe story that was one of my favourites – "The Tell Tale Heart."

I suddenly panicked thinking my heart was going to stop and oblivion beckoned but instead I felt a slap and the cold splash of water over my face. Then Evelyn and Bertie were calling my name. I opened my eyes and they were there and I could focus on them, as I did, I lurched forward and vomited violently on the pavement with a great splooshing sound. I immediately felt better.

Evelyn grabbed me and stood me up, my legs like jelly and I wobbled precariously which made me laugh out loud. I felt like a helpless child. Bertie helped him get my arm round his neck and Evelyn them held it firmly whilst supporting my weight.

"I need to get him home," Evelyn said to Bertie as he kissed him on the cheek, "Once he's had some fresh air he will come to."

"Take him into the Christ Church gardens, the proctors won't catch you if you're quiet." Bertie said conspiratorially, then added "Use the side gate."

"Good night, darling Bertie!" I slurred and realised it was hard forming words. "I feel drugged…"

"It was the hashish on top of the champers," Evelyn said amused, "you'll be right as rain…"

I watched bleary eyed again as Evelyn gave Bertie another kiss on the cheek and then walked me away. Bertie waved and then vanished back up the rickety stairs to the club.

Evelyn managed to get us into the garden via the side gate without anyone noticing. We must have been there a while as when I was lucid again he was sitting there deep in thought. He had made a good effort at dressing me but my shirt was still undone and I felt and looked, no doubt, as did he, like a couple of dishevelled tramps. I grabbed his hand and he turned to look at me.

"Can we go to bed now, "I asked, "I need to go to bed and lay down. I'm better now, I think…"

He put his fingers to his lips and smiled. "Shhhh," he whispered, "someone will hear."

I attempted to stand but was still unsteady which made me giggle and in turn he giggled at me giggling.

There is nothing so infectious as someone trying to be quiet and serious and the other person giggling. It's impossible to resist and our sides were aching with the effort.

"Come on dear boy," Evelyn said standing me up, "let's get you to your rooms."

"And to bed?" I replied in a stage whisper half of Oxford could have heard. "You must get me to bed…"

"Not for the want of trying dear boy, not for the want of…"

Before he could finish a voice cried out in the dark, "Who goes there?" Quick as a flash Evelyn hurled me and himself into the nearest bush and then clasped his hand over my mouth as the whole thing made me want to laugh louder. After a moment a pair of legs scurried past.

"He's gone to lock the gate!" Evelyn said, "that means I can't get out. Shhhh, here he comes."

Still with his hand clamped over my mouth the legs scurried back and after a few moments we heard a door close. Evelyn released his hand from my mouth. As he did I kissed him. He looked at me and smiled.

We then heard a voice whisper. "It's okay now you can come out." We looked at each other puzzled and then realised it was the dark girl who had been dancing naked at the Hypocrites. We emerged from the bush looking more dishevelled, if that was possible, with bits of the said bush stuck to us and in our hair. It made us all giggle again.

"Come on, this way," she said barely audible, "I have rooms on the next floor to Harry," she said quietly, adding, "my uncle is the proctor…"

With that she led the way and Evelyn dragged me along with him keeping me upright and quiet. I suddenly had an urge to sing, barely had a sound escaped me when Evelyn clapped his hand over my mouth again.

Once we got back to my rooms, Aloysius was there staring at us disapprovingly as we all staggered in still giggling. I realised I could call him nothing but that now that Evelyn had said it. I remember Evelyn taking off my clothes and sitting me on the bed and he then started to remove his own. The girl was still there cuddling Aloysius, to whom she had taken an instant liking.

The next thing I remember is waking up to the dawn chorus and realising that Evelyn and I were naked and in bed with just a flimsy sheet covering us. I tried to remember what had happened but my mind was a blank. I went to move and regretted it.

"Ouch," I said clutching my head, which made Evelyn wake with a start, "Champagne gives me a frightful head! Full of angry bubbles…"

He looked daggers at me for waking him and then the sound of the birds made him wince. "Bloody birds," he exclaimed holding his hands on his ears, "should be illegal to make that din at this time of the day…"

"It's the bubbles," said a voice from beneath the sheets. Suddenly she emerged, the girl from the night before, and smiled at us clutching her own head. "Oh, hello again," at that instant the clock chimed 7am, "I must go!" She said with urgency and leaped out of the bed leaving Evelyn and I sheetless and giggling again in spite of our hangovers. We then watched as she nakedly hopped about pulling on bits of clothing until she was decent enough to leave for her own rooms.

"You boys are such fun," she said hopping, "I enjoyed getting acquainted with your…" here she paused perhaps for dramatic effect and then with a glint in her eye and a sly wink added, "considerable attributes!" Evelyn and I spontaneously grabbed the sheet to cover the said attributes. She grabbed her shoes, gave Aloysius a kiss, and then stood by the door and opened it a crack to make sure the coast was clear. "We must do this again sometime," she said sounding serious, "Toodle-pip, chaps!" As she slipped out the door she whispered, "Don't tell the proctor!"

Then she was gone. We laughed and pulled the sheet over our heads. I snuggled up to Evelyn, and him to me, and I couldn't for the life of me remember a bloody thing. More's the pity!

The next thing I remember is Evelyn's voice calling me more and more insistently.

"Harry, Harry!" he called. "Harry, wake up please…"

I opened my eyes and could see the sky and for a moment I was totally confused and didn't know where I was or what had happened. I then felt splashes of rain on my face which I wiped away.

"Harry," cried Evelyn, "Come on and give me a hand, it's raining and everything is getting wet. Grab the picnic blanket will you?"

I sat up and watched as he bundled the picnic basket and other things into the car. The rain had become heavy and we were getting soaked.

"Harry!" he shouted, "Quick!"

Leaping up I grabbed the picnic blanket and made a dash for the car. Once safely inside we sat getting our breath and orientating ourselves. The rain hammered and drummed hypnotically on the roof of the car. Our wet clothes making us feel uncomfortable. I looked across at Evelyn and felt really sad that it had all been a dream, one he knew nothing off.

"What's the matter?" He asked seriously. "Are you ill?"

"No, no," I replied forlornly, "Just realised that something I thought important, wasn't really, it never happened."

With that he started up the car and drove us back into Oxford. We didn't talk much, my mind was on other things, he was concentrating on steering in the rain, I revelled in my thoughts of a land that might-have-been!

Chapter Eight

Death & Duties

Harry Clifton:

It was a day that I shall never forget. It started out absolutely normal and, in an Oxford way, quite unremarkable. The birds sang and the sun shone on this late March day. I had invited some friends for drinks to my rooms in the afternoon. Strangely, that morning, I had tripped over my Elephant's foot umbrella stand that I loathed for what it represented, but had to remind me of what not to be and do.

"Bertie has done a remarkable job with the club, I'm amazed it was as easy as taking on the lease and opening as a drinks club," Evelyn said enthusiastically to Alistair, "he is a genius really."

"It wasn't that hard, Evelyn, "replied Bertie laughing, "we still had all the customers as they had nowhere else to go, poor dears."

Alistair was slightly bemused by this and exclaimed "Even those of us who have left," he then looked at Evelyn, "and those who were sent down, still come back to the club?" Rather sad lot really, aren't we?"

"Of course, Alistair," said Evelyn, "I can't imagine why you would be surprised, of all people, happily taking advantage of its charms and male members, and you still come yourself don't you?"

"I think it's rather remarkable," I said, "that its mystique remains and it keeps going at all. I have never been anywhere like it with or without my clothes on!"

They all looked at me and laughed and then Bertie went round filling up everyone's champagne glasses. As he did there was a firm knocking at my door and we all froze for a moment.

"Yes?" I called out as I mimed to everyone to hide their champagne glasses and the bottle lest it be the proctor, "I'm just coming."

I crossed and opened the door to see the little porter with the bowler hat. As he stepped inside he removed his hat and handed me a telegram. The others looked on expectantly. I read it and then crossed and sat of the edge of the bed.

"What is it," asked Evelyn, "are you alright?"

"Here," said Bertie, indifferent to what the porter might think, "have some champagne…"

I took the glass from his hand but didn't drink it. I just stared ahead whilst a million thoughts rattled machine-gun-like through my brain. The porter shifted uncomfortably from foot to foot, so I sensed that he might already know the contents of the telegram.

"Will there be any reply, sir," he asked sheepishly, then after a moment, unsure what to do because of the silence, "Will that be all?"

"Yes, that's all, "I said, quickly adding "and no reply. Thank you."

The porter put his bowler hat back on and left, quickly closing the door behind himself.

"Harry," said Evelyn, "what is it?"

"I've inherited it…"

Evelyn crossed to me and took the telegram from my hand and read it. Once it had sunk in he looked at me aghast. "His father's dead." He looked at the others to make sure they understood, and then added "In Tenerife, the Canary islands…"

"Oh, darling, how sad," said Bertie, "how unfortunate."

"So sorry," interjected Alistair sounding uncomfortable, "that's a blow."

"He was on his way," I said a little dazed, "with my mother to Timbuktoo."

"That is a real place?" said Bertie, making Evelyn and Alistair laugh uncomfortably. "Well I didn't know it was real" added a rather indignant Bertie. They all regained themselves and become suddenly quiet. I looked up at them all.

"I have inherited it all! I am the master now. I'm free. Free!

Evelyn lifted his glass "I propose a toast. To the memory of Talbot Clifton may he rest in peace and long live the new Squire Clifton, Harry." They all chanted "to Harry" and sipped their drinks.

"I'm really free," I said still rather unbelieving of the news, "I can't take it in."

"Well," said Evelyn, "not quite so free - you will no doubt have the dreaded death duties to contend with now."

In that moment I had no idea what he was talking about but with the fullness of time the reality of death duties would become clear to me. For now, I had to deal with my father's death and step up to the plate I supposed.

The next couple of days were a blur and, apart from a letter from my mother, it all felt a little unreal and I couldn't apply myself to anything so great was the shock. In that letter from my mother telling me of the final couple of days. I read it over and over and wished I could have been at hand for her.

"Darling Harry,

There followed two nights and a day of calm when no one but the doctor came into the room. I trusted that your father might die thus in peace. Love was visible to us in the cabled hopes of friends and the towns-people, and in gifts of flowers from people in Tenerife; the room still full of Lilies and love.

Your father was terrible with pain and sweat. Between your father and me lay a threefold silence, and a reserve; the reserve of our particular natures, and the reserve of our breed and the reserve of our race. Neither of us dared, by words, to add an edge of sharpness to the steel of our suffering.

I felt I was being dragged over stones and through briars, God knows what your father felt. Watching him, I thought of a slow felling of a forest tree. The doctor said to me: 'With that will and that superb body there is, I think, no other sickness from which I could not have saved him.'

At six o'clock on the last morning your father said to me: 'I know that I am dying,' and I answered him: 'Yes, you are dying. There is nothing that can save you, because you have another illness [lung cancer] that you do not know you have.'

So I saw my beloved, your father, gasp away his life which too was my life. I only whispered to him, at the end, 'godspeed' on his last journey. Suddenly he sat stark up and looked at a far corner of the room. All the blue of his eyes was restored, and the brightness of them. Without terror, without pleasure, he looked fixedly as at some strange and unexpected thing. A few moment later, still sitting up, he died."

I managed to make arrangements to have his body shipped home on a cargo steamer. I will take this last journey home with him. We will make our way to Lytham. Once in England, then my wish is that he be buried on Islay. He loved that place like no other.

With love
Mother"

I was numb but for the wrong reasons. Tears refused to come and I felt oddly unemotional. This talk of 'love' seemed anathema to me.

"I will travel by any ship," mother declared, "whereon the coffin can be put where I am allowed to be near it, and where, too, it will be blessed by the winds and the sea…"

Mother was lucky to get any ship to agree to transport a dead man as it was unheard of. Most would be buried at sea with no argument; the reason my mother failed to attempt to bring father home alive but ill lest that happened en route. However the Norwegian owned San Jose was a little fruit cargo ship and agreed to take mother and father's coffin.

"His last journey," she told me on arriving in London, "befitted the explorer. The coffin was lashed to the taffrail on the boat-deck; sun and moon, wind and spray upon it, and English flag over it. The Spanish firemen, passing the coffin on the way to their stoking, murmured a few words of prayer for Talbot's soul, and, taking the watches on the bridge deck, a young Spanish apprentice prayed."

She intended having father's body embalmed to ensure it could endure the final adventure and eventual internment on Islay. Even strangers could pray for this man that was my father but I could not – not even in death.

My tutors were informed and I was given permission to leave for my father's funeral. It seemed absurd that my mother had decided on a public display rather than something more dignified and discreet. Thus I went to Lytham to meet my brother and sisters who travelled down from Islay for the first stage of father's final journey. Staff were instructed to prepare the house for our imminent arrival. Mother would travel up to Lytham by train with my father's remains.

We eventually gathered at Lytham Hall with father's coffin, thankfully closed, placed on velvet covered trestles in the Gold Room, with copious vases of lilies and assorted candles and incense. His presence even in death guaranteed a muted and hushed nervous reverence in his children. My sisters would weep quietly and Daffodil especially so as she wanted her father to bellow and rage as he had in life. Michael was lost and wandered hopelessly about the place with the dogs who themselves sniffed about as if looking for him.

Mother was serene and quiet mostly but her eyes told of a mind far, far away in some other place of memory where father lived and was vibrant again. It was stifling and almost unbearable. The clutching of rosary beads and muttered prayers gave the house the feel of a convent. Even the staff were sombre and some even wept! I did not weep, could not weep, for a father I suspected didn't even like me very much.

As a result I found myself confining my person to my room and reading Poe. The irony of this didn't escape me and his prose of hauntings and the mysterious occult were not lost on me, and in a way felt comfortingly inappropriate at this time. Had mother known she would have been horrified. Father, I doubt, would have understood this world where my mind frequently wandered to find a solace of sorts from the bullying and anger he wrought upon my childhood soul.

> *"Lo! Death has reared himself a throne*
> *In a strange city lying alone*
> *Far down within the dim West,*
> *Where the good and the bad and the worst and the best*
> *Have gone to their eternal rest.*
> *There shrines and palaces and towers*
> *(Time-eaten towers that tremble not!)*
> *Resemble nothing that is ours.*
> *Around, by lifting winds forgot,*
> *Resignedly beneath the sky*
> *The melancholy waters lie..."*
>
> *[E.A. Poe]*

My solitary escapes allowed me to reflect on the freedom I had flourished under at Oxford. It could be said that some of the happiest times in my life were spent there, but I knew it must now end. The thing that nobody in the family spoke of was that I was now master; it was as if they didn't want to believe it, and if they refused to acknowledge this truth, it would go away from gnawing at their minds. It gnawed at mine too leaving me shivering with cold sweats but it was a truth I could no longer try and deny, and I had to face that destiny head on – no more thoughts or possibility of handing Michael the responsibility. It was now mine until my own death to do with as I saw fit. Nobody ever again, I thought, will ever have to endure and suffer what I have. I will make sure of that.

Evelyn Waugh:

I saw Harry off from Oxford and couldn't help wonder if he was going to cope with all the responsibility that had now been thrust upon his young shoulders. He was a sweet man and we had created a bond that is unusual for me as I prefer to treat people I meet as transient and for life's pleasures.

My own father was pressing me to get some kind of work because, I imagined, although he never actually said it in a brutal way to me, he had tired of supporting me financially. So he had arranged for me to have an interview at the Daily Express who were looking for journalists and writers for news and feature editorials. After having a disastrous spell as a school master in Wales, that lasted just a few weeks, I accepted that hanging about Oxford after being sent down was probably not the wisest thing for me to do. So off to London I go to try and earn a crust!

My novel 'Decline and Fall' was underway from the publishing perspective and I had so many ideas for more. They will have their day eventually I'm sure.

Harry promised to let me know when he gets back to Oxford. I will look forward to seeing him again and hearing all his news and what he plans for the future.

Harry Clifton:

I was mesmerised by the sight of the tall, black ostrich plumes fluttering hypnotically in the very gentle breeze. They seemed hopelessly exotic at this sombre time. It then struck me that some poor Ostrich had to lose these feathers, did they lose their life also in the process, to allow these adornments to sit atop the beautiful black horses heads? Why, I thought, do animals have to suffer so horribly at the hands of people. Like my father who had so joyously hunted and killed, it baffled me.

My mind then turned to the meeting I had had with the Estate Manager, William, yesterday. He made it depressingly clear to me that although I had inherited nominally on my father's death, it would not be legal until my 21st Birthday some months hence on the 16th December. That is when I would reach my legal 'majority'. The estate was now subject to punitive death duties. This rather pernicious form of taxation had been introduced with a review of the tax system in 1914.

It meant that the trustees had to make an agreement with H.M. Treasury to pay off these taxes, some as high as 40% of value, and I was informed that this would take at least five if not six years to complete. The money would come from the income the estate had from land leases, rents, shooting rights, farming and agricultural profits from Lytham Hall estates and also the Islay estates in Scotland.

"Does this mean I can have an increase in my allowance," I asked William rather shaken at this news, "at least a small one?"

"Alas, sir," said a sombre William, "that will not be possible immediately," adding rather pompously, "although you did recently received an increase from £400 per year to £500." He said this kindly but, I thought, irritatingly.

"Am I not," I asked with some sarcasm, "the possessor of some eight thousand acres of prime farmland in Lancashire, sixteen thousand acres of shooting and stalking in Scotland and my estate receiving ground rents from the towns of Lytham, Ansdell and St Annes-on-the-Sea. It is hard to now be the owner of all this and receive a mere £2,000 a year for spending money."

"I am sorry, sir," he said, obviously not though going off the look on his face, "but until we settle the financial obligations regarding death duties with the Treasury…"

"Yes, yes," I said rather annoyed, "it's daylight robbery and like stealing from the dead."

"I understand, sir, but technically you and the estate are liable for this tax."

"So, if I refuse to pay they will send me to prison will they," I spat out rather petulantly, "Let them try."

"Probably not, sir," he said annoyingly calm, "They would just take possession of enough of the estate property to pay the debt."

It then occurred to me that my mother had thus far spent a fortune on bringing father's body home, having it embalmed and preserved, then parading it to Islay via Lytham whilst creating a spectacle for all to see.

"My mother has of course managed to get the money from the estate to pay for the funeral and all that has entailed since father died in Tenerife?"

"The cost has been agreed and covered, sir."

"I bet it has," I said angrily, "Meanwhile in the midst of all the weeping extravagance I, as master, cannot benefit fully before the taxman has his share."

"Of course, sir, we all offer you and the family our sincere condolences at this sad…"

"Sad for who?" I spat out. "I want to see all the accounts for Lytham and Islay estates as soon as everything is finalised. Savings and cost cuttings will have to be made immediately."

"Yes, sir," he said very calmly, "I will be joining the estate workers in paying our respects at your father's funeral tomorrow."

"I hope I will now be shown the same lofty respect everyone seems to have had for my father."

This was my parting shot before I left rather abruptly. If only the damn man would have shown some emotion and spirit. Once I had calmed down I accepted that I had no idea that death duties would be involved, I just thought it was all mine to do with as I pleased. How wrong I was.

Looking from the drawing room window at the black plumed horses drawing the hearse I suddenly had an awful, hollow feeling in my stomach. I felt like an imposter as all around me was sobbing, wailing, punctuated by my mother's annoying stoicism.

Why was she so embarrassed to show the world the emotions she felt. Her demeanour seemed to make her taller and the black mourning clothes, along with a rather dramatic swathe of black netting covering her face, made her seem aloof and untouchable – beyond the emotional reach of me or her youngest child Michael.

Outside the hearse waited as the horses bobbed their black plumed heads irreverently, the grooms and undertakers in their black tailcoats and tall silk top hats standing to attention waiting for the coffin and the family to emerge. The other carriages plumed and draped with black velvet. They all stood motionless apart from the light breeze which ruffled pieces of clothing; like eerie waxworks that would suddenly burst into life and stop your heart with fright. In that moment I wished I was anywhere but here. Still no tears came, no feelings of terrible loss or anguish. I began to question whether I had the normal human emotions. The cost of this also irritated me.

My mother suddenly stood and said imperiously to us, her children, as if we were all infants, "Come now children, we must escort your father on his journey." Suddenly the sound of a piper playing whined and then started a lament. The sound was like a herd of cats screeching to me, I hated bagpipes.

To the lament the sad procession of family emerged from the family door at Lytham Hall following father's flag draped coffin. The pall bearers gently carried the coffin which, I thought absurdly, why so gentle he can't feel anything. Off on the green a clutch of estate workers had gathered all suitably dressed and holding hats and caps in their hands, with most looking at the grass. William the estate Manager was there and he looked right at me and nodded his head.

The bearers slid father's coffin into the hearse as two grooms steadied the horses. A spray of pungent smelling Lilies was placed atop the coffin followed by lots of bowing and nodding of heads. My brother and sisters were in the second carriage, and my mother and I were in the first. An undertaker opened the door for us, and taking off my top hat I followed mother and we sat side by side. As the door clicked shut I heard her let out a sigh of relief. I hadn't realised it was such an ordeal for her, but I wish I felt the same. Guilt swamped me again. Will I never be rid of feeling inadequate?

The piper took his position at the head of the hearse, I could just see the horses shifting and a little spooked by the sound of the pipes whining out the lament. The grooms mounted the hearse and then we started on our way to the Catholic Church for the thanksgiving service before we all boarded a train that would take us to Scotland. Driving through the parkland the estate staff were out in force to pay their respects. I fiddled with my top hat perched on my knees feeling like a trapped bird – a raven.

"Don't fidget, Harry," mother said haughtily, "It looks unseemly to the mourners."

"Was this spectacle really necessary," I said putting my hands at my side, "It's ridiculous."

"You father had a standing in the community, of course it is necessary." She turned and looked at me coldly through her veil. I turned to look out the window wanting this to be over. "How," she added, "could you even say such a thing – and on a day like today too."

"It's obscene," I said through gritted teeth, "You should have let them bury him in Tenerife where he died."

"That is a wicked thing to say. The train will take us to Scotland, then the ferry to Islay, and he will be interred there. It's what he wanted. It is where he was happiest."

"Ludicrous waste of money," I said and felt her stiffen next to me, "At least I can't disappoint him anymore. That, if nothing else, will make me happy. Nobody cared, especially not him, if I was ever happy." The bitterness I said this with surprised me and I suspected it had been deeply buried within me for a long time.

"No matter what you might think, your father loved all you children," she said with what I thought was a suppressed sob, "and wanted nothing but the best for you." She suddenly placed her hand on mine and I froze, mother never expressed herself with overt physical gestures to comfort us. "You didn't make it easy for him."

"He's the past now," I said rather coldly, "I am in charge now."

"Yes," she replied pulling her hand away and folding it into her lap, "that's what worries me."

"I hate Islay, the house there, and everything it stands for."

"Yes," she said knowingly, "did William discuss the death duties with you? If you are wise you will allow him to guide you."

To me this circus was pointless because I found it impossible to forgive my father for the way he had been with me all my life. Mother was no fool, she knew that the death duties would curb any impulses I might have to spend excessively in my new position. That is why she seemed so smug and serene and her tone expressed that even if she didn't say the actual words to me.

As I watched the estate workers standing so well turned out and respectfully to catch a glimpse of their old master's funeral procession, the whine of the bag pipes droning on, I wondered if they would feel the same reverence for me when my time came? As we passed through the huge ornamental entrance gates for Lytham Hall, the cortège moved out into Lytham itself. The piper remained by the gates as we passed and his lament faded into the distance. "Thank God," I muttered to myself.

In that moment I decided the first order I would give the staff on my return would be to chop up and burn the billiard table my father loved to humiliate me with so much. I would watch it burn with joy! This thought made me smile for the first time that day.

"Once upon a midnight dreary,
While I pondered, weak and weary,
Over many a quaint curious volume of forgotten lore,
While I nodded, nearly napping, suddenly there came a tapping,
As of someone gently rapping, rapping at my chamber door.
'Tis some visitor,' I muttered, 'tapping at my chamber door –
Only this, and nothing more.

Ah, distinctly I remember it was in the bleak December,
And each separate dying ember wrought its ghost upon the floor.
Eagerly I wished the morrow; - vainly I had sought to borrow
From my books surcease of sorrow – sorrow for the lost Lenore –
For the rare and radiant maiden whom the angels named Lenore –
Nameless here for evermore.

Deep into the darkness peering, long I stood there wondering, fearing,
Doubting, dreaming dreams no mortal ever dared to dream before;
But the silence was unbroken, and the darkness gave no token
And the only word there spoken was the whispered word, Lenore!"

[E.A. Poe]

Islay

Kildalton Castle near Port Ellen on the Hebridean island of Islay had been my father's happy place. This, mother insisted, is why he must be interred there to rest for eternity amidst the wildness and the serenity. His memories of Lytham Hall as a boy were not happy ones and in that we had something in common. The estate on Islay he had purchased in 1922 when he had to abandon our estate in Ireland when it became independent from the British – as did so many of his aristocratic and landowning contemporaries I hated Kildalton, Islay and everything it stands for. It is bleak and joyless when the weather from the Atlantic batters it for several months of the year. As I derived no pleasure from hunting, shooting and fishing I was happy to avoid it whenever possible and now that I am master I can please myself.

The journey to Islay with my father's body was torturous and seemed, to me at least, but not my mother, a pointless and sentimental journey. Nothing brings back the dead no matter what you do for them. Watching my mother sitting in the guard's van with father's coffin all serenity and still the doting wife; I wondered if she thought that he would somehow miraculously arise again to life once back at Kildalton. The thought made me shudder. Somehow though I felt that she had that hope and that was what ensured she retained her composure.

Once on the ferry to Port Ellen, made rocky and uncomfortable by inclement weather and rough sea, we watched as she spoke gently to father's coffin oblivious to us children. As the drizzling rain soaked our clothing, I did my best to reassure Michael who still sobbed and couldn't understand what death really meant. Daffodil was subdued, an unusual state of mind for her, and clung to my hand as she watched mother from afar in her composed grief. My two older sisters muttered over their respective rosary beads and did little to comfort anyone of us but themselves. It made me realise that grief, this new emotion, or was it an experience, manifested itself in very different ways in people. The British way was to be stoic mostly, repress those feelings and present a calm and mannered façade to the world; much as mother and father had wanted me to do with my person in light of my destiny. "Be more normal," they had said, "hide your eccentricities," they demanded. I was, in this moment, glad I had done neither.

As the ferry approached Port Ellen in the drizzle and low cloud gloom, I could see a clutch of estate staff waiting at the dock all dressed somberly and suitably grief stricken. The piper started up and the whine of the bag pipes once again assaulted my ears with 'Flowers of the Forest.' This made Michael and Daffodil cry but I wondered if it was the sentiment of it or the terrible din. I looked around and felt detached and griefless in the drama in which I had to play my part. I would be glad when it was over.

Once docked my father's coffin was again gently carried and put onto a carriage with great reverence. My mother followed the piper looking tall, refined and elegant in her distress followed by me and my siblings who were all moving sombrely in their wake.

The drizzle continued and soaked us through almost immediately but on we marched and rode in carts to Kildalton where no doubt, I thought, a roaring fire would be blazing in the fireplaces and hot milk drinks, whisky and supper awaited.

On that journey I wished more than once that I could feel something, but grief eluded me. Beady eyes watched me as they knew I was the new master. "What will he do?" I imagined they thought as I passed, "Will he change things?" Their positions I am sure were also at the forefront of their minds and I couldn't blame them. They had no need to think of things like the death duties, but those tax impositions would surely affect them eventually. It would not bother me greatly if I never returned to this island once this was over. Being master had not changed the way I thought of this place, and my father's ghost watching everything I did held no appeal and I imagined him reading Poe's 'To One in Paradise' as he haunted his beloved Islay – this poem, at mother's request, after mentioning it to her, I had agreed to read at the graveside the following day:

"Thou wast all that to me, love,
For which my soul did pine –
A green isle in the sea, love,
A fountain and a shrine,
All wreathed with fairy fruits and flowers,
And all the flowers were mine.

Ah, dream too bright to last!
Ah, starry Hope! That didst arise
But to be overcast!
A voice from out of the Future cries,
'On! on! – but o'er the Past

(Dim guld) my spirit hovering lies
Mute, motionless, aghast!

For, alas! alas! with me
The light of Life is o'er!
No more – no more – no more –
(Such language holds the solemn sea
To the sands upon the shore)
Shall bloom the thunder blasted-blasted tree,
Or the stricken eagle soar!

And all my days are trances,
And all my nightly dreams
Are where the dark eye glances,
And where thy footstep gleams –
In what ethereal dances,
By what eternal streams."

[E.A. Poe]

As father's coffin was lowered into the ground I could feel my heart thumping in my chest. Was this heart his also? Would the sound of my heartbeat forever remind me that he who was dead was still alive in some way in me? I shuddered and watched as the clods of earth were shovelled on top to fill the gaping hole. Mother's sobs, for now her composure was broken, stirred the silence and others sobbed too. As the earth covered him the sound of my heart beat diminished and I felt like I was once again in control of myself.

Mother said that on returning to Kildalton she had been caught off guard at the sight of "the birds he had fed, coming to the door for crumbs – they undid me. He was dead – but they, brief singers, still nested in the home trees."

This, I thought later, became a good metaphor for what was to come, but my overwhelming memory of that day was once the estate staff and undertakers had gone and mother and I stood alone at the grave. She wept and wailed uncontrollably and I had no words or actions that could offer her solace. It was then I realised the power of a love that can be possible between two people. It was a kind of love I knew nothing about and never felt I had been shown by another living being; even them. They were lucky to have found that in each other. Some never find any kind of love, let alone that kind. In that moment I envied them and I wished I could have embraced her and allowed her to weep on my shoulder. But, it was not my shoulder she craved.

The drizzle drizzled and we stood saturated with the weight of life and emotional consequences. Things would never be the same. Had I been Poe's 'Raven,' I would have flapped my wings and flown away, never to return.

Chapter Nine

2023 - An Errant Heir

It is hard to believe that just one hundred years later the legacy of the Cliftons' has almost vanished, thanks in large part to the recklessness of Harry and the way he happily squandered his family estates for personal pleasure. One wonders if there was not perhaps an element of spite in his actions, seemingly hell bent on destroying the dynasty so nobody would ever have to go through what he had been subjected to by his father. Looking at the remnants of the estate today, and especially its only surviving treasure, Lytham Hall, one can't help wondering how he could so blithely destroy what had taken so many centuries to assemble.

His desperate desire to pass on the responsibility to his younger brother Michael fell on deaf ears and made his father rage at him for spouting, in his view, such ill-informed nonsense; and aside from everything it would have impacted severely on the death duties owed by the estate if this had happened, so maybe the common sense and fiscal elements escaped Harry. But why did nobody bother to explain this to him and at least treat him like an adult and educate him on the matter instead of again berating him. It is hard to fathom looking at it today, but at the time it was a fairly normal procedure. You accepted your lot and be damned!

Surely his desperate plea to the Estate Manager, William, when his father failed to take him seriously on relinquishing to Michael, would have been an ideal opportunity to try and educate Harry and reassure him. To be fair to William he did attempt to do this within the social limitations of the time. At the end of the day it wasn't his job to be a social worker to Harry; that duty was his parents who, to be fair, were too wrapped up in their own world to want to molly-coddle their son and heir. Their affection for their children, if any, seems to have been stilted at the very least and at worse a little detached. In that time people did not consider their feelings as any excuse to shirk or shy away from duty. Everything was about duty and one's place in the world and where you stood on the social spectrum. Nobody much cared about personal feelings of any sort.

Before returning to Oxford, Harry took a trip to Spain and got conned into a business deal that he thought would be his salvation and earn him plenty of money until the death duties had been paid. Agraz was a fruit syrup derived from oranges and grapes – or lemons – which was used like a cordial. Harry was convinced he could establish the brand in the British Isles. A consignment was sent to Lytham Hall from Spain where it was stored for future sale. William the Estate Manager agreed to send him £126, and Harry wrote back:

"I have now £84 in the Midland Bank and £20 in my pocket to carry on. So if you would allow me £100 on my horse, I could start business straight away out of income and I could sell my samples anyway, so I am not risking much for a wonderful drink and perhaps a splendid business."

The horse in question Harry had purchased after his father's death and, within year he had, still at Oxford, become the owner of "an Alvis saloon car which he then sells and buys anew Chrysler, and has a racehorse – and an overdraft of £854." [a huge amount of money in 1929] William the Estate Manager is horrified at this largesse and writes to Harry pleading with him to be sensible and to stop spending money he doesn't have. Harry writes back in agreement and suggests that, "I ought to start doing some work other than literature." This is odd as he does not have any kind of literary career that would earn him money, it is more of a career ambition. Sadly one he would never really fulfill.

Harry had also managed to upset his mother by letting out Kildalton on Islay to American shooting parties so she had to move herself and the children back to Lytham Hall and take up residence there once again. This all in an effort to economise and save money for the estate. In spite of this Violet was pleased with Harry after a conversation she had with his Oxford tutor who told her:

"He would never pass exams, nor learn very much, [but] he was full of literary promise and may add something to English letters."

One can't help feeling that this was something of a back-handed compliment of sorts and that everyone, including Violet, was trying still to see the good in Harry and that he was at least trying to make something of life.

By the time he returned from Spain to go back to Oxford he had purchased shares in another racehorse. In spite of how things looked and his play of being sensible there was a shock when William discovered he was again overdrawn at the bank to the sum of £750, in addition to the £1,250 he owed the trustees for requested advances to get him out of a financial mess.

Worse was to come. He sent William a telegram saying: "In terrible debt like last year." It transpired that he owed bookmakers over £600 for gambling debts. He also stated that:

"My plans for the future are to live, probably in London, and learn music. I am, as you can imagine, thoroughly repentant, but the same thing happened last year, so perhaps that is not much good."

William sent Harry a rather terse and forthright reply: "You appear to have betted persistently over an extended period and that your gains should show such an infinitesimal proportion of your losses may convince you of what everyone else was previously aware, that betting is a Mug's game – spelt with a capital MUG."

William arranged for these betting debts to be paid [as Harry no doubt banked on] but also made him agree that the bookmakers be informed, as part of the payment deal, that they should no longer take any bets or do business with Harry.

Oxford also lost its appeal and Harry left, and was thus sent down without a degree. This is something he would have in common with Evelyn Waugh who was also sent down.

The days of the Hypocrites Club and 'the drinking club' as it became known was also ending. Interestingly the original Hypocrites that Evelyn joined, was to all intents and purposes shut down in 1925 after a nun was found trying to get into Balliol after curfew – said nun turned out to be a male student in drag – so the licence was revoked.

The club's lease was then taken over and it reopened and was known as "the drinking club" frequented still by many of the Hypocrites original members – even Evelyn Waugh visited to club on his return visits to Oxford up until 1928 – but it was never seen as debauched as the original, not publicly anyway. It finally closed for good, on the insistence of the university – in 1929.

Harry travelled abroad visiting several countries, starting in France, then on to Egypt and Colombo and finally settling for several months in Saigon. He seems to have decided he would be a travel writer, he perhaps got the idea from Evelyn Waugh who did similar journalism trips, but in spite of writing articles and sending them to William at the Estate Office with instructions to send them out to editors for potential publication; sadly there were no takers and they languished unread.

This was, it seems, a story that never ended in terms of Harry's excess with money and William's constant battle to

keep him on a level playing field. All was in vain and the bigger disaster for the family and the dynasty was already on the track that would lead to its ruin.

He found a passion for India and was tricked and conned mercilessly into business deals that came to nothing. He seemed unconcerned by it all and came to imagine he was a successful businessman. This was of course complete self delusion and a constant headache to William who was constantly sorting out the financial mess he created.

As I sat on the bench looking over Lytham Hall's grand façade and the gardens beyond, it seemed incomprehensible that just 100 years before this estate was still thriving and providing so much employment for the local area – not to mention all the farms and land that were producers of crops and animal produce. How could one man manage to erase hundreds of years of family toil?

The sun shining illuminated the Georgian splendour of it all and a melancholy seemed to permeate the very atmosphere of the place. People walking by seemed to take all this for granted and were more focused on their children or dogs. Some, with interest in the history, either entered or emerged from the hall tours as others made their way for a coffee, lunch or even afternoon tea in the café. It was all a world away from what had gone before.

Had the family continued what would be happening to the estate today, I wondered? Would they still own Kildalton on Islay? Would Lytham Hall be open to the public or have remained a private house?

Thankfully this would carry on and even though the land surrounding it is tiny compared to what the Cliftons did own, it had survived and now its future looked promising and assured.

In my mind I still imagined these people from the past as they continued as characters in a story of my creation that gave them life again. It was neither pure fact nor pure fiction, it was somewhere in-between, but they were once again alive and well in my head. Besides, is it so fanciful to imagine, considering Harry's eccentricities, and the fact he had rooms at Christ Church, where, in 'Brideshead Revisited' Sebastian Flyte had rooms, that a connection is probable? Flyte has been attributed to a few of those Waugh met at Oxford, so it's not beyond comprehension that the character is bits of each of them. If nothing else, it fired my imagination in wanting to tell this story.

Chapter Ten

Evelyn Waugh
The End of The Roaring 20s

Evelyn Waugh:

Harry never really settled after his father's death, even though he couldn't wait to get back to Oxord and his friends, it made him restless and his new sense of freedom meant that the first thing he jettisoned at the earliest opportunity was his studies at Christ Church. He never felt academically suited to it anyway and had been here more on the orders of his father but that no longer mattered.

As for me 'Decline and Fall' had finally been published by my father's publishing house Chapman & Hall, London, and had been a greater success than even hoped for. I was now, to some at least, even more than an enfant terrible, usually scorned at with lots of shaking heads and comments using the word disgusting. But if people constantly bury their heads in the sand of life and refuse to see what happens around them, they can hardly blame me for using all life as inspiration for my characters. I would assure them with a smile that I had much worse in the planning – even they could be used as my muse. This invariably shut them up and I would offer a rather terse and forced smile and perhaps an unforgivable expletive too. Their faces I would never forget. Manners? Mostly, they had none anyway.

The final straw was the complete closure of the drinking club, formerly known as the Hypocrites Club. The Dean of Balliol, himself rather questionable when it came to the subject of morals, had put the university under intense pressure to close 'the drinking club' altogether. As the university authorities were rather against undergraduates indulging in copious alcohol they didn't take much persuading.

As it happened I was in Oxford and had decided to call at the club to see Bertie and also, if he was there, catch up with Harry. As I approached and turned on to St. Aldates I knew immediately something was afoot by the police and vans outside the club entrance. I also saw the Dean with a police sergeant pointing to the club entrance door and then scurrying into a doorway to watch. To avoid being seen I did the same and observed from the shadows. There was little doubt in my mind this was a raid and would have terrible consequences for anyone found in the club at this time of night.

The sergeant in charge called for his men to take out their truncheons, in that moment I knew this was not going to be pleasant, the sight of this had made me start to sweat; it was pure luck that I was not inside the club and my heart went out to those that were. There was no way I could warn them; that made my position worse. My heart beat wildly in my chest as I heard the shrill sound of the police whistles and then the hammering down of the door and the sound of boots thundering up the rickety stairs.

The gathered police rushed into the building leaving one or two to watch over the police vans that stood ready, rear doors agape. Soon I could hear shouting and screaming and I knew without seeing anything that there was violence and brutality. I felt sick and wanted to retch but I dared not lest I be heard and alert those police out side to my presence.

Eventually they started to drag the poor boys and girls out onto the street and bundle them into the police vans. They made for a sad sight in their drag and other attire, the lesbians and transvestites being humiliated, the musicians and pianist haughty with fear, some silent in their shock and others sobbing with distress. I found it hard to believe that this kind of horror can happen in a civilised society.

Suddenly from the corner of my eye, with a background of shouting and abuse as bodies were unceremoniously bundled and hurled into the vans; shrieks of pain along with defiant words of resistance which I admired under the circumstances, I saw the Dean of Balliol speak to the sergeant and then walk away hurriedly. The betrayer deserting the scene of his creation, the coward I thought, scurrying away like a rat. As it happened he came my way and as he passed he suddenly froze and turned to look at me with fear on his face. I stared at him emotionless and said nothing. He fled after a few seconds without saying a word.

My thoughts then turned to Bertie and Harry. I hadn't seen either of them being dragged out of the club so was praying that perhaps they had by some miracle not been there.

Once the vans had driven off and all was fairly quiet, I walked along the street and could see no more police but the door to the club was in pieces so accessible.

I entered and ran up the stairs, the main club rooms on the first floor were a mess, all the furniture toppled and broken glass on the floor. The bar was a mess of broken bottles and all the bottles behind had been smashed up deliberately. The smell of spirits was overwhelming. The door to the upper floor had also been smashed open and hung off its hinges. I crossed and heard voices so quietly went up the stairs. The sight that caught my eyes was like something out of a horror story.

Bertie's body was swinging slowly by a rope. He had hung himself rather than be caught and arrested for homosexual activity. His life would be ruined; it being illegal to have sex with another man or love him. He would have feared this meant prison and he would have never been able to bear that. Two policemen were trying to cut him down. He was naked apart from a feather boa and his outrageous eye make up made the scene more hateful and hideous. I gasped and the two policemen turned startled at being disturbed, but I ran.

We all knew the risks and in the end it's why we conformed; even though every part of us screamed at the injustice. I would have my revenge on the Dean of Balliol for closing this and the Hypocrites down. He was the hypocrite!

I made my way to Balliol and by climbing over a garden wall I managed to get in. Sneaking past the porter's lodge I made my way to the centre of the main quad, most of the rooms faced this as did the academics' quarters. I stood there a moment savouring my triumph at getting in undetected. I opened my arms and took a deep breath and then at the top of my lungs I shouted:

"The Dean of Balliol sleeps with men," waiting a few seconds until windows started to open at the noise, I repeated, "I said, the Dean of Balliol sleeps with men."

I twirled round and round as more lights went on and windows opened and then I saw him at a window. The smug look gone from his face. Then I shouted again:

"The Dean of Balliol has sex with men. He's a hypocrite!"

I laughed with pleasure and heard the students cheering and laughing. The porter came out of his lodge and started to chase me from the quad. I could easily out run him and managed to scramble back over the wall and into the lane and then I ran as fast as I could to Christ Church. I had to tell Harry that Bertie was dead.

As I made my way there I could see images of us all in my mind having fun and enjoying happier times. Bertie was such a beautiful soul and he didn't deserve to die like this. Something had to change. His smiling face looked at me in my mind's eye and I promised him his death would not be in vain. But I knew I was a coward in life and I feared being discovered the same as he did. I recited a poem as I thought of him laying dead never to smile or laugh again.

"And autumn will lay a still,
Cold finger on your beauty, and
Dim your liquid eyes and suck the
Juices of your lips. This living
Dream you are shall see eclipse
And I'll not mourn you in my
Waking state, wide-eyed and
Frozen of heart."

[A.L. Rowse]

I stayed with Harry that night in his rooms and we cried for Bertie's loss together. It made us both determined to live fully and change the world.

****

A couple of weeks later Harry and I stood at the graveside watching Bertie's coffin being lowered into a deep grave. Apart from us there was just the undertaker and a handful of people who knew him. As he had committed suicide several vicars had refused to attend and officiate at a service or the grave. So, the service was abandoned and he was buried in the paupers' section of Rose Hill council cemetery on the fringes of Oxford – set on the side of a hill it was a bleak and wind swept place that offered little comfort to those visiting the dead that lay here for eternity. The tips of the Oxford spires could be seen in the distance through the trees but they offered no consolation here. For such a bright, vivacious and extraordinary man it was an unfitting end and tribute for his short life.

Harry sobbed and threw a single rose down onto the coffin. I watched as the others did the same, but for me it was a gesture full of sentimental tones that left me cold and angry. He should still be alive and looking forward to the rest of his life.

"How could they allow this to happen?" I said with a sad heart, "What harm did he ever do to anyone."

"What courage he had," Harry said, "More courage than any of those who chose to persecute him through fear."

"They couldn't even allow him respect here, to see him off with dignity." I said angrily. "He deserved better, we must never forget him and the world must change."

"He would be pleased we are here to see him off," I said, "he knew we loved him as an equal."

"I thought you would have brought Aloysius," I said it before I realised I had even thought it, "He loved that bear."

"I did," Harry said looking down at the coffin, "I couldn't let him go alone, he would have been lonely, so they are together for eternity now."

I looked down at the coffin as the grave diggers started to shovel great clods of earth into the grave. The first few shovels made a sickening thud, thud, thud, as they hit the coffin. I couldn't believe that Harry had done that for Bertie, I knew what that bear meant to him. I put my arm around his shoulder and, looking about noticed the others had gone, so we walked slowly to the cemetery gates leaving behind forever a dear friend whom we would miss for the rest of our lives.

Chapter Eleven

Putting On The Ritz
& The White Goddess

Harry Clifton:

I hadn't seen Evelyn for at least a couple of years and in that time I had spent a lot of time traveling, discovered the allure of Monte Carlo, especially the casinos, India, the Far East and also continually fighting with the estate Manager over money. The vile death duties were still not completely paid but on the bright side I had been to Hollywood and could see money to be made in the new film industry. I had made new friends and advisors who remained faithfully by my side.

Sitting in the ballroom of The Ritz Hotel a new singing sensation called Al Bowly was crooning accompanied by the Ray Noble Orchestra. As he sang the lyric "Remember me /

Just keep me in your memory / I'll never forget the day we met / For the sake of auld lang syne." I couldn't help but think of dear Bertie, which made me feel quite emotional and teary; that was an emotion I never usually had to deal with thankfully. Bowly's voice was like a yard of rich velvet, so I could understand why people loved him. The couples dancing on the floor were, however, more entranced with their partners than his dulcet tones which seemed a bit rude.

I saw Evelyn as he entered and asked the waiter where I was. He pointed in my direction and when Evelyn saw me he smiled and made his way over. I stood to greet him and we embraced. We sat and I poured him some champagne from my bottle.

"Darling Harry," he said gleefully, "How are you? I've missed you."

"You look well, as always." I said as I hugged him affectionately. I gestured him to take a seat.

"What luck to find you in London, and in such grand surroundings," he said looking around, "I've never been in the Ritz Ballroom before."

"Yes, I have a permanent suite here now for when I am in town," I said rather grandly, "It makes life so much easier."

"Living your best life then?" he said with some irony that was not lost on me.

"Yes, I also have a suite at Claridges."

"Why?" he asked, bemused now.

"Well," I said seriously, "if I go for a walk down Park lane and get tired I have somewhere to go."

I could see by the shocked expression on Evelyn's face that he wasn't sure if I was being serious or pulling his leg. Al Bowly continued his song and I noticed more of the audience had stopped to pay attention. We listened until he finished singing and then applauded with everyone else. The orchestra then carried on with dance music and couples laughed and twirled and flirted with each other as they glided past us oblivious of anything but the dance floor and each other.

"I wanted to ask you a favour," I said looking directly at Evelyn again, "It will be a chore but we can make it fun."

"It sounds intriguing."

"I need to travel up to Lytham Hall and wondered if you would come with me?" I said, adding, "My family are unbearable and you being with me would help to make it fun."

"I'd be delighted," he replied in a flash, smiling, "What an adventure."

"That's settled then," I said quietly relieved he had agreed, "I need more champagne…"

He picked up the bottle and began to refill our glasses. "…and we need it now!"

The ballroom at the Ritz was, like everything else in this hotel, gilded to within an inch of its life; sometimes a little too much. The sight of the couples dancing exaggerated their own fake façades and one tried to imagine what they looked like stripped of their finery and jewels – paste or real as it was hard to tell the difference. The odd old duchess sat with some money hungry gigolo and there were also single men in white tie and tails, but probably no underwear, working the room like wolves on the prowl for prey – preferably rich prey. It was all rather seedy.

"This zoo," I said conspiratorially to Evelyn, "must be a gift for your character studies. Pity that most are so vile and rather dull when you actually talk to them."

"That is why it is better to keep them at a distance," he said watching a particularly handsome young man leaning against a gilded pillar, "they don't disappoint then."

"Your first novel 'Decline and Fall' turned some heads," I said laughing, "I loved the title. It still makes me laugh."

"Darling," he said not taking his eyes of the young man, "they practically swivelled right round in some cases, some even fell off!"

"Everything has to be hidden away to conform and create the illusion of respectability, life, it's so terribly false!"

"Just like the diamonds that old duchess is wearing," he said turning to look at me, "I heard she had to sell the real ones to survive but she won't admit it to anyone. She even keeps them in her bank vault and they go along with it. Anything can be bought."

I noticed the young man had moved closer and was keeping his eye on Evelyn. So very obvious what his game was, but those around seemed oblivious, so wrapped up in their own fantasy relationships and worlds.

"Yes," I said to Evelyn pointedly, "even attractive young men?" I indicated with my eyes the ever closer young hustler who seemed intent on catching our attention.

He looked at me and laughed. "No, that's for another time. Tonight I'm all yours – for dinner at least!"

"How is your new novel?"

"Just published after much argument over the title, they gave in and let me use Vile Bodies!"

"Sounds perfect," I said as I stood up, "My mother will loathe it!"

Evelyn stood and laughed. "That young reprobate playwright, what's he called, you know he wrote The Vortex?"

"Noel Coward?"

"That's the chap. I agree with him when he said 'It's discouraging to think how many people are shocked by honesty and how few by deceit.' You only have to look round this ballroom to see that…"

"I think we would get on famously with him," I said to Evelyn as we walked across the ballroom, and the young man smiled at me which disarmed me somewhat, "I booked a table in the main restaurant for dinner."

"Excuse me, sir," said this handsome boy suddenly, catching us up, "Mr. Clifton, sir, my friend wishes to make your acquaintance, Brian Hurst is his name, sir, he asked me to give you this if I saw you tonight." He handed me a letter, so I took it.

"What is your name?" I asked him more sternly than I intended, "Can he not ask me himself?"

"My name is John, Mr Clifton," I am Brian's personal assistant and he is making a film at Gainsborough Studios tonight but asked me to come here in the hope I could pass this on to you, sir." He smiled delightfully at Evelyn and then me. "Thank you gentlemen, I am sorry to have disturbed you."

With that he was gone. Evelyn looked at me and I at him as if not quite being able to believe what had just occurred and also how wrong we had been in surmising the young man was on the game – as they say!

"What a shame," Evelyn said, "I'd started to feel rather fuckable tonight and now my hopes are dashed again."

"Never mind," I said laughing, "perhaps you need to find a spirit guide. That might help."

I looked at Evelyn's face and knew that I had shocked him by that last statement. It was more delicious because he was trying to work out what on earth I had meant by that. I loved that we had so much in common and that our respective eccentricities, and catholic guilt, made us interesting company for each other. I always thought that Evelyn suspected that my independence would be my downfall but in that, up to now, I had proved him wrong. I am not sure he would approve of me dabbling in the occult though, which might be a bridge too far even for him. We shall see.

The dining room at the Ritz never failed to impress me and I used it several times a week. The views across Green Park were splendid and my favourite table that, miraculously, was always available for me, made the best of it. The gentle chink of china and the clink of crystal glasses always created an atmosphere of hushed elegance. The waiters in their smart white tie and tail coats and the sommeliers in their maroon and ruby red silk jackets always a pleasure to observe and be served by.

As we walked through the main promenade to the restaurant I had opened the note and read it. Evelyn watched and then couldn't help himself. "Well," he said impatiently, "what does it say?"

"Mr. Hurst is a film producer and director and is looking for backing for a new project." I answered honestly, "Oh," I exclaimed, "he wants to adapt a Poe story for the screen. That's right up my street." I put the note in my pocket.

"Just make sure, Evelyn said seriously, "that he doesn't take advantage financially."

"Dear Evelyn, you are such a cynic, what am I to do with you."

The Maitre D' of the restaurant glided swiftly to us on seeing us enter. "Good evening, gentlemen. Your usual table is ready Mr. Clifton." He gestured to us and we followed.

"Evelyn, I simply cannot wait for you to meet my new friend," I said excitedly and savoured the confused look on his face, "I dine with her every Tuesday evening here at the Ritz."

Once we arrived at the table the Maitre D' pulled out a chair and said, "Good evening, Madam." He waited a moment and then pushed the chair in slightly as she sat. He then offered myself and Evelyn a chair.

Once the Maitre D' had left I turned to look at Evelyn and said: "Now, you mustn't be shy, Evelyn. I would like to introduce you to my spirit guide – the White Goddess – and she is utterly charming." I looked at her, "Don't worry dear, he will be fine in a moment or two." I then looked back at Evelyn and waited for him to respond.

"Good evening, my dear," Evelyn said to her, "Harry has told me absolutely nothing about you!"

"Good evening, madam, gentleman," the sommelier said as he reached the table, Evelyn watched in awe as he smiled at the White Goddess, "Champagne, sir, he said to me."

"Yes, please my good man. For all of us, please."

I watched Evelyn as the Sommelier filled our three glasses with champagne. The Maitre D' then arrived with menus, which I waived away. "The White Goddess and I will have our usual fish, thank you. Mr. Waugh may wish to choose differently.

Evelyn took the menu and started to read it. He seemed to relax and I was so pleased he was meeting my White Goddess in person. She was very happy also and her smile lit the room for me. She was very beautiful and very knowledgeable about so many things. I can't imagine how I managed without her guidance. Evelyn handed back the menu and ordered.

I then raised a toast and we three raised and our glasses and I recited some of Poe's poem 'Song' thus:

> *"And in thy eye a kindling light*
> *(Whatever it might be)*
> *Was all on earth my aching sight*
> *Of loveliness could see.*
>
> *That blush, perhaps was maiden shame –*
> *As such it may well pass –*
> *Though its glow has raised a fiercer flame*
> *In the breast of him alas!"*

The three of us then clinked our glasses for the toast and I smiled at Evelyn and the White Goddess, content to be with my friends.

Evelyn Waugh:

For me it was a first and, to be honest, once I accepted the total madness of the situation I did begin to enjoy and actually believe that Harry and the Maitre D' and the sommelier and staff could actually see the White Goddess. Did this make me as mad as them?

It awed me that the hotel staff went along with this and served food and addressed the White Goddess as they would any other guest. Harry chatted with her happily and responded with nods and laughs to her replies. At one point he laughed at something she said and after a pause looked at me puzzled, so I laughed as well and we all carried on. For the hotel, I am guessing it was about the money. What did they care if they served an expensive meal to a woman, sorry, a goddess, they couldn't see?

"Harry," I said suddenly remembering, "I meant to ask, do you miss Aloysius?" I then looked at the White Goddess right in the eye and added, "He must have told you about his teddy bear?"

At that Harry laughed delightedly and clasped his hands. "I forgot to say, dear Evelyn. Aloysius came through during a séance and told me, through my White Goddess, that he and Bertie are happy on the other side." He smiled and then leaned in to whisper to us both as he placed his hand on her imaginary hand as he looked at me. "He's a bit jealous of my goddess."

"That's a shame," I replied, thankfully gulping back some more champagne, "I was so looking forward to talking about him."

Quick as a flash Harry replied "Come up to my suite for cocktails! We can have some fun."

"Will you be joining us," I asked in the direction of the goddess, the champagne making this feel more absurd, "for cocktails, too?"

"Don't be silly," Harry replied, "she has a separate suite and gets tired after dinner, don't you darling?"

At that Harry got up and pulled out her chair. He then went through the motions of kissing her on both cheeks. I just stood and smiled in her direction.

"It has been a pleasure," I said, "to meet you." I stood feeling rather foolish.

I noticed other diners looking over at us rather oddly but being British they didn't say anything but just smiled and nodded politely.

"Good night, dearest darling," Harry said, "sleep well."

He gave her a little wave and watched her go. The waiters all gave her a little bow as she passed. I decided at that point I had had too much champagne but needed more!

"She gives me great financial advice and guides my investment choices and helps me deal with William the estate manager when he argues with me over money. I had the chance to purchase over a thousand Scottish tweed men's suits and had a buyer in the Middle East, but he argued with me over the practicalities of such a business opportunity, but I got my way. Sadly they didn't take off over there, I can't imagine why really as they were such good quality. But, talking pictures is the next big thing, and I am writing poetry and taking piano and singing lessons."

I picked up the bottle of champagne from the ice bucket and stood. Harry got up and we thanked the Maitre D' and left the restaurant on the way to Harry's suite through the main hotel to the lifts.

"Do you pay for the White Goddess to have a permanent suite here as well," I asked but knowing the answer, "I'm just curious…" I added when he looked at me oddly.

"Of course," he replied with complete seriousness, "where would she sleep otherwise?"

I shook my head and laughed. It was utter madness but madness that was beyond comprehension in some ways – is that lunacy? How would anyone outside of this think it was ever believable that a grown man like Harry could sell tweed suits to a country that had forty degree heat? I gave up thinking about it because it made my head hurt. Flinging my arm across his shoulder, with the champagne in the other hand, I laughed a laugh of the insane. Insanely!

Chapter Twelve

Lytham Madness – 1930s

Violet Clifton:

The weather had been thoroughly appalling in Lytham but not as bad as it could be on Islay, so there were some blessings in this life. As I had this thought Lomax, our butler, came in the drawing room with logs for the fire. It was a chilly day. All this accompanied by some awful din on the new wireless contraption.

"Lomax," I said rather abruptly, so made him jump a little, "has everything been prepared in the guest room?"

"Yes, ma'am."

With that I ran my finger over various surfaces to check for dust, making sure the maid had done her job. I thought about the chauffeur…

"Lomax, can you ask Andrews to stop making that awful noise with the motor carriage…"

"The horn, ma'am?"

"Horn indeed," I said, "It's very undignified and vulgar. Don't you think?"

""Yes, ma'am," he replied dryly, "But it does prevent him running over the ground staff."

"Tell them," I snapped, "to be more agile then."

I was sure that behind that polite, professional façade of his that Lomax was sometimes laughing at me. Why I couldn't imagine. The din on the wireless got to me, so I crossed to the table.

"That frightful din," I said frowning fiercely, "why the Savoy hotel allows it is beyond me."

"The Savoy Orpheans, ma'am," he said, dryly again, "with Al Bowly."

"Orpheans?"

"The orchestra's name, ma'am."

"What a ludicrous name!" I retorted with a sarcastic laugh, "The world and its tastes have gone to hell in a handcarriage."

"Handcart, ma'am."

"Don't be impertinent, Lomax. You know exactly what I mean."

"Yes, ma'am."

I crossed the room rather loftily, that not being hard as I was insufferably tall, and sat by the side of the fire. Lomax crossed to me and handed me my book I'd been looking for.

"There it is," I said with irritation, having spent an age looking for it earlier, "You must stop hiding things, Lomax. Where was it?"

"On your writing bureau, ma'am."

"Oh," I said rather embarrassed, like I had been caught out telling a lie, so I changed the subject, "What is the name of the guest – and friend of my errant son?"

I sat there flicking through my proof copy of 'The Book of Talbot', my homage to my darling husband. I still missed him every day and wished he were here to shout at everyone and cause his general havoc. Oh to hear his footsteps approaching again and not know what to expect on his arrival – good mood or bad mood – or fury. The house seemed so quiet and morgue-like without him. I had hoped his ghost would haunt us but thus far no sign.

"Did you hear, ma'am," said Lomax looking at me oddly, "Waugh, ma'am."

Having lost track, I looked at him irritated and snapped rather too hastily "Do shut up! We don't want another one of those, do we?"

Lomax looked perfectly usual and unruffled by my hot-headedness, and I was thankful he was used to me and the daily drama he had to endure with my family.

"Evelyn Waugh, ma'am. That is the name of master Harry's friend."

"Oh, is it?" Silly name but she might be a prospective wife so we must keep such thoughts to ourselves.

With that I crossed to the window and looked out on the parkland. The drive was winding ahead and as yet nothing indicated anyone arriving. I felt nervous but wasn't sure why. Living back in Lytham had taken some getting used to but at least we didn't have to endure the Atlantic winds in all their unleashed fury in this part of the world.

"Lomax," I said turning to look at him seriously, "I want to say something important."

"Yes, ma'am?"

"My son's name," I said as seriously as my temperament would allow, "is Henry not Harry, so please, now he's master, don't keep indulging him. He has too many unfortunate traits as it is without us pandering to his whims."

"Tea, ma'am?"

He said this in a way that let me know he understood without having to utter a word. Butlers like Lomax were so hard to find. He was first-class indeed.

"Desperately so," I said, "desperately so…"

"Yes, ma'am."

"Let me know as soon as they arrive."

"Yes…"

I cut in before he had finished. "Lomax! How many times must I tell you not to over use 'ma'am' – it becomes tedious."

"Yes, ma'am."

As Lomax left my daughter daffodil came in full of vim and vigour! Too much so for my liking and she had a lugubrious look that I recognised of myself at that age. Nearly sixteen is a tedious age and time for a girl, she's neither here nor there, or anywhere inbetween.

"What is all the fuss about, mater?"

I watched a she collapsed like a rag doll on the sofa, so inelegantly too, which I disapproved of. "You are too headstrong," I said sternly, to which she smirked. Smirked! "Just like your father." She laughed and I added crossly "Oh, do sit up straight and make yourself respectable."

"Before long, you'll be having me carted off to a nunnery to join Hermione and Avia I suppose."

I despaired of this child sometimes and her fearless application of insolence worried me. It was a slippery slope to outright rebellion. "Your sisters," I said rather crossly, "are at a retreat – they are not nuns!" I crossed to look from the window again in the hope it would calm me. "This sense of the dramatic is a very unattractive trait, Daffodil."

"Oh, good!" One should always have something unattractive to offer the world. Perfection can be terribly tedious."

With this she laughed hilariously as if she was watching some musical comedy. I looked at her and wondered what her father would say if he could see her – what he would think of his son and heir who, having been sent down from Oxford without a degree, now seemed determined to gallivant across the world rather than face his responsibilities. Looking at Daffodil sitting all crumpled and ungainly annoyed me suddenly. "An untidy girl however is of no use to anyone – even herself. Look at you, tidy yourself up." My tone must have made her realise she was near the end of my patience as she harrumphed loudly and tidied herself up, straitening her dress.

"Is the King coming," she asked sarcastically, "or the Queen?"

"Don't be insolent. You may be sixteen but you are not too old for a good old fashioned slap. Do try and behave like a lady."

She looked daggers at me as only a girl her age can; I sighed and sat by the fire feeling exhausted by the day already.

"I can be charm itself," she said rather defiantly, "I'm just misunderstood."

"One day," I answered brightly, "I just may surprise you and welcome royalty to the hall – don't forget that…"

Daffodil cut in and finished my sentence haughtily, or an attempt to mimic my voice, I wasn't sure which, but I hated it, because it made me aware that I probably drone on about the same stories too frequently for comfort. "…we entertained the Tsar of Russia's brother for a shoot! Or at least father did. I miss him beasting around in a temper."

This last bit she said with a sudden melancholy to her voice that made me aware of how much she missed her father. There was also sadness in her eyes when she spoke of him that pulled at my heart strings.

"Quite," I said smiling at her kindly, "I'm not sure your father would have approved of your turn of phrase either. 'Beasting' indeed! He loved you very much."

She suddenly got up and walked briskly to the window and looked out. She was suddenly impatient and I suspected getting bored with the conversation. "We can't live on past stories with defunct Russian royalty forever…"

"Your father and I were very proud of that association."

She let out a rather silly, over the top, sigh and then turned to look at me. "Yes, we know!" She turned to look from the window again.

"As a mother," I said pointedly, after a moment's pause, "I would have hoped my youngest daughter at least would be a comfort in my widowhood, but alas no."

She turned and looked at me rather aghast I thought. She tutted this time and crossed to the sofa and flopped herself down – she was incapable of doing this elegantly and I shook my head in despair.

"Comfort?" She said looking at me bewildered, "Mater, I'm not a blanket."

"Is it not bad enough," I said a little too defensively, "that your brother squanders every opportunity as heir to your father's estate. We have had to leave Islay to come here and live as he refuses to pay the upkeep of anything properly. What, I say, will become of us? He'll have us eating gruel next!"

"Harry is a petulant, spoilt ass!"

"Daffodil!" I exclaimed, slightly horrified at her remark, "I will not tolerate such crass language – especially when we are expecting guests – sometimes I wonder if you are my child at all."

"Why do you always defend him," she said in a tone I had not heard her use before, "he will probably marry some awful shrew of a woman and he will continue to make us live on a pittance. And still you would stand by him."

"It is my duty," I countered feeling rather defensive, "Something you need to learn the value of or you will regret it later in life – as an adult – which you are not. He is my eldest son, your brother, and master of the family now. We must do everything we can to support him and if that means making economies until the death duties are paid then so be it."

I collapsed back in the chair feeling less like a mother and more like some Shakespearian tragedienne. I felt sick and tired of this constant worry over the finances and what the future held for us all. Daffodil must have sensed my inner despair as she crossed and sat on the arm of my chair and looked at me kindly.

"Mater," she said without a trace of waspishness, "he takes you for a fool – he cares little for us or the estates. He's more interested in those racehorses he's stabled here and his trips to Monte Carlo and goodness knows where. Stop being so subservient to him – he's not father."

I grabbed her hand and kissed it. She was a one off and I couldn't imagine having this kind of relationship with my other children. She was, in some ways, strong and forthright like her father had been. I missed that. I missed him.

"Like it or not Daffodil," I said with a sigh, "he is the eldest and we have no choice but to respect that fact – it's how things work – as much as we may disagree. It is a matter of great sadness for me to know, in my heart, that Michael, as he gets older, would be more befitted and efficient in his management of the estates."

Daffodil laughed and then squeezed my hand reassuringly. "Considering you can say that knowing that Michael is currently thirteen years old, and still at boarding school, speaks volumes of your opinion of Harry's abilities. Just try, mater, and see Harry for what he really is, that's all I ask…"

"You, young lady," I said rather more brightly, "ask too many questions, are wise beyond your years at times, and need to keep those opinions to yourself. And his name is Henry!

She jumped up all breezy again and looked out the window. "You are on a losing wicket with that, mater, he only answers to Harry, so best get used to it. Everyone else has."

I crossed and stood next to her looking at the empty parkland and drive. "Where are they Daffodil," I said rather forlornly, "they should be here by now."

Evelyn Waugh:

Having travelled up to Lytham by train we were relieved to see Harry's chauffeur, Andrews, waiting for us at the station with the Bentley. A few hours on the train had been uncomfortable, despite our first-class seats, and the food described as 'lunch' was abominable to say the least – luke warm, undercooked stew and dumplings and week old, dry plaice. Thankfully the wine selection was not too hideous, and they did have some champagne, so that alleviated our angst somewhat. Unfortunately by the time we reached Lytham Station Harry was, well not to put too fine a point on it, very tight. He managed to hide it with panache, but was tight just the same and, I say honestly, I was not far behind him. His mood had changed the nearer we came to Lytham, he seemed to dread his inevitable arrival.

Once in the car it was not too far to Lytham Hall and the very grand, imposing, entrance gates soon loomed ahead, then we passed through, onto the drive that would eventually lead to Lytham Hall. The grounds seemed ridiculously lush and green but Harry suggested there must have been plenty of rain to make it so. The mature trees lining this outer drive were impressive and had obviously been sentinels for several generations. Looking at Harry he seemed more and more agitated the nearer our impending arrival, that said the drive seemed to go on forever.

"Beautiful parkland," I said cheerily, "very impressive…"

"Is it?" He replied with no emotion in his voice at all, and then added coldly, "To me it's hideous." With that he took out a hip flask of whisky and swigged some back.

"Take it easy on the booze," I said, "if I were you…"

"Well," he snapped back, "you are not me are you!" He took another swig and then offered it to me. I shook my head. I had a feeling it was going to be a difficult couple of days.

"Steady on, Harry," I said irritated, "I'm not the enemy."

He seemed to gasp a petulant gasp (if such a thing exists?) and then shouted out to the chauffeur dramatically, "Andrews! Stop the car."

We had just passed some smaller inner gates and Andrews slowed down and stopped the Bentley. He came to a halt just on the curve of the drive that gave us a view of Lytham Hall itself. Harry got out of the car and I followed, I was taken aback at the beauty of what was obviously a fine Georgian Manor in perfect proportions. From this distance it was impressive enough to give me a shiver of appreciation.

Harry stared at the house and then looked away as if he couldn't bear it. I continued to admire it and couldn't wait to investigate and explore it further. He suddenly turned to look at me, his complexion was very pale and he looked as if he might be sick. But I guessed it had nothing to do with the alcohol he had consumed.

"This," he said sadly, "is where my family live"

"I'm looking forward to…"

He turned and cut me off and blurted out: "You'll hate them and this place. They put great store in tradition and all that."

"Nothing wrong with tradition, Harry," I said to try and lighten the moment, "After all, I've come to realize, albeit reluctantly, we all have to conform and toe the line in the end."

He looked at me as if I had slapped his face. "Do we?"

We just stood staring at Lytham Hall as if rooted to the spot. It struck me as terribly sad that Harry felt as if he was a stranger and had no place here. I began to see him in a different light and had also noticed how drink was beginning to affect him. Looking at the hall again, I thought to myself, were his family really the monsters he made them out to be?

"Come on," he said suddenly, "let's get this over with. Shame our Nanny is dead, she would have been worth meeting – but I can still show you the nursery." He looked at me and smiled and a chill ran through me. It was as if his personality had changed and he was that other Harry. As he got back in the car he said: "I'll be glad to get away, I'm off to Hollywood next week to see how it all works in this film making business."

That was the first I knew he was going to America and Hollywood. That was so typical of Harry. It must be the Catholic in him I thought, laughing to myself. We have to have our secrets and our sins - especially our sins!

Violet Clifton:

Daffodil was preening herself in the mirror; fussing her hair and pinching her cheeks to get some colour into them. I had noticed she seemed paler than usual of late and wondered if the move back to Lytham had affected her more than she let on to me. Perhaps she was pining for that estate manager Gerald, who she had had a crush on and embarrassed him and the family. She had no filter emotionally, I thought as I paced back and forth and then to the window again - I stopped and peered to make sure I was seeing what I thought I was. "How very odd," I said, and this immediately got Daffodil's attention, "Andrews has stopped the car on the turn of the drive."

184

At this Daffodil rushed to join me at the window. "What on earth are they doing?
Maybe they changed their mind about coming in? "She said this with some sarcasm and added, "You know how whimsical Harry can be…"

"Oh, dear," I said with a sigh, dreading the worst, "I hope Henr…Harry is alright?"

"There you are doing it again! He's a grown man, mater. Stop treating him like a child and then perhaps he'd stop acting like one."

"That ship," I said rather forlornly, surprising even myself, "has long sailed, sadly."

Daffodil harrumphed about and then came back to stand beside me at the window. I suddenly felt very melancholy and couldn't explain why. Maybe everything was just getting too much for me. Try as I might to keep this family intact I felt at times the seams were determined to pull apart. As she peered into the distance to where the car had stopped she suddenly gasped with a tone of delight.

"Harry's with another man!" She clapped her hands a little too gleefully, "Evelyn isn't coming then, whoever she was. Hurrah!" To my shock she then did a little twirl of delight completely unselfconscious. It unnerved me as to what kind of a woman she would become eventually.

"Don't be so rude," I said crossly; which she ignored and began preening in the mirror again, "We must do our best to be polite to whoever it is Harry has brought as a guest."

""Do you think," she said excitedly gazing at herself, "my lips would look more luscious with some red lipstick?"

I looked at her aghast and not a little bemused "Certainly not! I forbid it," I said crossly wondering where she got these ideas. "Luscious, indeed!?"

She harrumphed again and flopped into the armchair with a dramatic sigh of despair. "My hopes of being remotely glamorous dashed again," she said, then added, "Am I always to be a drudge like you?"

I was shocked at her insolence to the point I found myself about to laugh with amusement which, of course, I suppressed immediately so as to not encourage her. "If your father were here," I finally remonstrated sternly, "he would give you a good spanking my girl."

"But he's not, he's dead!"

I was about to lose patience with her when there was a sharp knock at the drawing room door and then Lomax entered.

"What is it, Lomax?"

"Master Harr…Master Henry has arrived ma'am with Mr. Evelyn Waugh."

"Lomax," I said cutting Daffodil off, "It seems we must call the master Harry."

"Yes, ma'am."

Daffodil had now burst into fits of giggles and seemed beside herself and her own excitement, "Gosh, mater, it's a man with a girl's name! What a hoot!"

"The master asked me to inform you they will settle in their rooms and will join you imminently, ma'am."

"Charming," I said a little despondent as I had hoped my errant son would rush to greet me first and introduce his friend, "That will be all, Lomax, thank you."

"Yes, ma'am."

Lomax left and Daffodil continued with her delight at Harry's friend being a man. I really did worry for her moral compass as it seemed slightly unseemly to be so enamoured with a man she had yet to meet. I shook my head and sat on the sofa.

"Come on, mater," she gasped, "it's like an adventure and nothing much exciting happens around here does it."

She looked at me gleefully and I couldn't help but laugh. In that moment she really did remind me of her late father's gusto for life and adventure.

Evelyn Waugh:

The view from my first floor room was very pleasing. I was impressed by the hall and the entrance staircase especially had some exquisite Italianate plaster work. Harry had followed me in from his room nearby along the landing. There was only a shared bathroom but needs must and these Georgian halls rarely had adequate plumbing wherever they were. Those who built them could afford free standing baths and copious staff to run up and down stairs with buckets of hot water and later down with waste water. Those were definitely not the days!

Harry had joined me and slumped into the armchair and took yet another swig from his hip flask. I bit my lip, determined not to cause any more friction in that regard.

"I can't bear it," he said sullenly, "I can feel my father's presence in this place still – he has his beady eye on me."

"Isn't that the premise for Poe's 'The Tell Tale Heart?'" I asked as I turned to smile at him, "didn't the murderer become paranoid about an old man's eye?"

"Yes, and the sound of the victims heart beat haunts him and sends him mad, until he confesses the body is chopped up under the floorboards."

Just as he said that, I started to move to the bed when the floorboards beneath my feet creaked eerily on cue. This made us feel horrified and shocked and then amused all within the space of a heartbeat. "We all have issues with our parents, Harry," I said brightly to try and lift the gloom, "Most of us just get on with life and hang the past."

"That's alright for you to say – at least your parents supported your artistic temperament and didn't try to crush it."

"We either sink or swim to survive our own misery," I smiled and then thoughtfully said, "I have some news…"

I was unable to elaborate as at that moment there was a knock at the door and Lomax the Butler entered with my case. I smiled at him.

"Sorry to disturb you gentlemen," he said delightfully, "shall I put this on the bed?"

"Yes, thank you," I said with a smile, "that would be perfect."

"Shall I unpack for you, sir?"

Harry suddenly jumped up in a rage and crossed to the door and flung it open. He glared at Lomax "For God's sake, Lomax," he spat out viciously, "we were having a private conversation!" There followed a stunned silence where I tried to look reassuringly at Lomax. Harry suddenly started to tremble but not with rage – the effects of the champagne and whisky taking hold I thought.

"Of course, sir," Lomax said in a purely professional tone that impressed me terribly, I assumed this behaviour of Harry's was nothing new, "I apologise. Your mother asked me to tell you she is expecting you and Mr. Waugh in the drawing room when you are ready."

Without further ado Lomax exited gracefully and Harry slammed the door after him. He then took another swig of his flask. I looked at him suddenly annoyed and embarrassed by his behaviour.

"That was vile, Harry," I said angrily, "A man is judged by how he treats his staff."

With that retort from me he slumped in the chair again and his mood changed to one of self pity. If there is one thing I cannot bear in anyone it is self pity!

"I am a disgrace," he said sullenly, "aren't I?" He looked at me but my patience was wearing thin, then he added, "It's this place; it's why I asked you to come with me. There are too many ghosts…too many…"

I looked at him and shook my head in disgust, determined not to indulge this nonsense.

I then crossed and stood right in front of him and looked down at him still slumped in the chair.

"Right!" I said, more of an order than a request, "come on, stand up!"

He slowly stood until he was looking me right in the eye. I then slapped his face hard. The shock and expression on his face almost undid me but I held firm in my annoyance with him. He held his cheek and tears sprung to his eyes and he just gawped at me unable to believe what I had just done. Suddenly we both burst out laughing at the ridiculousness of it and with complete spontaneity hugged each other.

"Come on now dear boy," I said heartily, "let's make the most of it and at least have fun. It's only 24 hours, how bad can it be?"

Harry smiled more like his usual self. "You see," he said, "you are the tonic I need. It's why I asked you along." He then added almost casually, "What is the news you wanted to tell me?"

I had forgotten amongst the drama I was going to tell him something sensitive, but decided to pass it by for now. "Never mind that now," I said with a shudder, "let's go and meet this dragon of a mother I've heard about."

This made him laugh and the sparkle returned to his eyes. "She really does breathe fire! You'll see when she has singed the edges of your considerable ego."

"As long as it's just my ego, darling," I said regally, "let's go."

"Never fear," he said holding the door open for me, "we shall go into battle arm in arm and face her down."

With that I followed him along the landing and waited whilst he collected his jacket from his room. I looked again at the grand staircase and found myself just as impressed with the second sight. The view of it would never tire, I decided.

Harry was a complex and a damaged man. I couldn't help but be moved by him and his inner turmoil. The shadow of his father loomed large over him and haunted the corners of his mind. I was concerned about his drinking, but could understand why he used it to numb inconvenient truths and memories. Catholics had guilt inbred in their genes and require no training to wear a self-inflicted hair shirt. I should know!

We made our way down the grand stairs as if we were at some state occasion. It made you walk taller and stand straighter so imposing was its countenance. As we got to the bottom and entered the main entrance hall there was an imposing portrait of his father John Talbot Clifton, the Victorian adventurer and scandalous lover of Lillie Langtry. It has to be said he was an imposing, handsome and very attractive specimen of manhood. I could well imagine why women swooned when under his gaze. It made me more curious to meet Harry's mother to see what had finally attracted that man to want to marry.

Being a creative and a writer my mind began to explore the possibility that Harry's story, and that of his family, needed to be told; immortalised somehow. The inspiration for his inclusion in such a story would no doubt come to me in time – it was too powerful a tragedy already not to – and his mother couldn't be all that bad, could she?

We crossed to the drawing room doors and Harry looked at me slightly ashen faced. I winked at him reassuringly, he then took a deep breath and then he opened the doors with a flourish and we marched in – literally – which must have looked rather comical. Violet stood as we entered and his sister Daffodil, sat pertly on the edge of her seat on the sofa.

"There you are," his mother Violet said rather sternly, as if we were an age late for a fixed appointment, "Are you quite settled and comfortable in your room Mr. Waugh?"

I crossed to her determined to keep things light and pleasant. Taking her hand, I shook it elegantly. "Please," I said smiling, "call me Evelyn, delighted to meet you both."

At this formal exchange Daffodil giggled charmingly and Harry gave me one of his askance looks and then crossed to the drinks cabinet. This latter move I felt perhaps a little unwise considering his consumption thus far today and the effect of alcohol on his rapid mood swings. That said, I felt I was in it for the long run so decided to go with whatever occurred.

"Is the sun over the yardarm yet," Harry announced to a disapproving look from his mother and more giggles from Daffodil, "Well it is somewhere in the world. Anyone fancy a tipple?

I stood looking out over the parkland and had to admit the landscape was tremendous, every aspect seemed to catch it afresh and as beguiling as the last. The drawing room itself was rather cosy, for a large formal room, and the frozen disapproving stares from long-dead ancestors in huge family portraits gave a feeling of someone always having their eye on you. I understood what Harry meant now that I was amongst the Cliftons.

"I have to say, Evelyn," said Violet matter of factly, "I thought you were a girl. My hopes were raised that Harry may be bringing home a prospective bride."

Daffodil burst out with her adorable giggles and interjected: "Well I for one am relieved that is not the case!"

I smiled at her as I found myself quite taken with her odd and outspoken eccentricities.

"Nobody asked for your opinion, Daffodil," said Harry sternly, "what happened to speak when you are spoken to young lady?"

At that Daffodil got up and threw Harry a dirty look that almost made me laugh out loud but I managed to check myself in time. She came and stood next to me still looking into the room.

"I think," she said pointedly, "it's divine you have a girl's name, Mr. Waugh."

"Please call me Evelyn," I replied with a bow and a wink of reassurance, "Everyone else does," then whispered to her, "amongst other things!" This tickled her humour and let her know I was on her side.

"His parents wanted a girl," Harry said, "he spent the first two years of his life dressed as one before they finally accepted the inevitable."

I watched as Violet almost broke her pearls, so tight did she clutch them at this news.

"How trying for you...." she said averting her eyes, "Parents can be difficult at times."

"I'm used to it," I said a tad too brightly, "but at least it marks me out."

"It can be tiresome being different, Evelyn," she said relishing saying my name, "my parents called me Easter Daffodil because I was born on Easter Monday. At least Daffodil is the least of the worst options!"

"Daffodil," exclaimed Violet with a hurt tone, "We love you and it was your father's idea. He thought it amusing at the time."

"Yes, at the time," declared Daffodil, "cute as a baby but no so much now I am older. Imagine if I live to be an old woman called Daffodil?"

Harry swigs his rather large drink alone as the rest of us had declined anything.

"Cheers everyone!" he announced loudly, "Evelyn's book has caused quite a stir, hasn't it?"

He looked at me glaring slightly so I assumed this was his way of attempting to engage me in changing the subject - for what reason I had no idea. Violet was meanwhile glaring at Harry disapprovingly.

"It's a little early, you know how I hate you drinking too much," she looked at me and then back at Harry, "I could smell it on you both when you walked in."

This made me feel like a naughty school boy caught doing something inappropriate. I blushed slightly and this of course made Daffodil giggle again. Looking at them all it occurred to me that had I not already created a character similar to her in Vile Bodies, Violet Clifton could have been an inspiration for Lady Throbbing! She may come in useful for some character in a later book though, I told myself.

My first impression on meeting them, at least these two members of the family, was that the Cliftons were all tearing mad. From what I had been told the late father had been considerably more torn than the rest. Violet seemed to keep him alive in her mind, imagining he was elsewhere on one of his swashbuckling adventures – forever in Timbuktu perhaps? That I thought would make a good book title. Having spotted her proof copy on the desk entitled The Book of Talbot, I assumed she had written some tome in honour of her great love. For love him she did still even in death. No doubt she would force that on me later.

The one with any resilience against this utter madness was the oddly named, but terribly charming, Daffodil. Whatever it was, she had it in spades! Harry on the other hand was floundering about and seemed devoid of any anchor or influence to curtail his extravagances and erratic emotions.

Just being in this room with such emotionally repressed humans was akin to a stormy channel crossing and left me feeling exhausted. I began to feel rather vile myself for such uncharitable thoughts towards my hosts.

I suddenly became aware that all three were staring at me oddly as if waiting for a response to something. It was then I realised I had drifted off into my own thoughts. Daffodil came to my rescue by repeating the question.

"Are you writing anything else now 'Decline and Fall' is a success? Are we research of sorts?" She looked at me expectantly.

"I have been working on another book…still drafting."

"Half the aristocracy," Harry said, his words slightly slurred, "of England think the characters are based on them in 'Decline and Fall'…"

"You seem," said Daffodil seriously, "a bit intellectual to be my brother's friend…"

"It is a dreary sounding title," said Violet, "is it very depressing?"

"Not at all," I said honestly, "in fact I hope just the opposite. Never judge a book by its cover – or title – I say. I did a few weeks teacher training at a terrible school in Wales, it's based on that mostly."

"What are you calling the new book," Daffodil asked eagerly, "something delicious I hope."

"Vile Bodies!"

At this Daffodil giggled, Violet took a sharp intake of breath and clutched her pearls again and Harry got up to replenish his drink.

"This new book interest me more by the minute," Daffodil said teasingly, "is it very shocking? The title suggests it might be."

"Daffodil," said Violet tersely to admonish her, "asking so many questions is impolite." She then looked at me directly and smiled as she said: "Of course I shall never read any of your books. I tend to avoid cheap novels."

Violet said this to me with such honesty and with no obvious malice at all as if it was a matter of fact. This made me laugh out loud.

"Well maybe you should read them, mater," said Daffodil, "it might broaden your view of the world."

Violet shook her head aghast at this. "My view is quite broad enough, thank you!"

"Well," said Daffodil looking at me conspiratorially, "I think you have anything but a vile body, Evelyn. Have you ever been in love?"

Harry took his glass and crossed to the window. "That's enough, Daffodil!"

"Well," she said defiantly, "I hope you research us and discover why we are all as mad as March hares."

"Don't be absurd," Violet said annoyed, "remember your manners."

"Mother is writing a book, Evelyn," said Harry naughtily, "about my father's heroic life. She has called it the Book of Talbot."

"How very interesting," I said with as much sincerity and interest as I could muster, "What a touching tribute."

"Yes," said Violet nonchalantly, "it is being published by Harcourt, Brace and Company, New York, who are, as you will know, very selective and distinguished publishers."

She said this in a way that supposed I was published by some street urchin in awful London by comparison. This I let go as, I had to admit, Violet said things that came directly from a long past generation. One where everything was done as tradition demanded and nobody deviated from that structure. I suddenly felt very claustrophobic.

"I don't suppose, mater," said Daffodil haughtily mocking her mother, "that Evelyn will ever read your tribute book to father but it will be a burden I carry with grace."

Daffodil winked at me and I delighted in her wickedness and humour. Violet looked wounded and Harry just swigged back another drink.

"Sometimes, Daffodil," Violet exclaimed, "I could cheerfully slap your face. Have respect for the memory of your father."

"Will anyone in this family," Daffodil shot back, "ever respect me and my feelings?"

Violet literally looked as if she had been shot, the look on her face was priceless, I could see the thoughts in her mind. How could anyone care about or respect a girl's feelings in the scheme of things.

"Don't," Violet said violently, "be absurd!"

There ensued an awkward silence that in reality lasted a few seconds but felt like three months. The atmosphere seemed chillier and chillier.

"So you see, Evelyn," Harry said quite calmly, "we are worse than even I could have prepared you for."

Harry crossed to refresh his glass and managed to knock over a bottle that went crashing to the floor making a terrible racket. Physically he was showing signs of being drunk.

"Maybe," I said lightly, "I should get you upstairs, Harry."

"He is tired after travelling," Violet said blinding herself to the obvious drunkenness in her son, "Dinner is at 8pm and we usually meet for an aperitif at 7.30pm."

Violet gestures to Daffodil that they leave. She sighs heavily but complies. As they make their way I smile at them.

"Thank you for making me so welcome."

"Hope to see you later, Evelyn." Daffodil said following her mother. Then they were gone. I felt like I had been hit by a whirlwind and suddenly felt rather tired myself. Harry had slumped into a chair and was in the process of nodding off, no doubt exacerbated by the drink.

I crossed to him and pulled him up, putting his arm round my neck and shoulder. "Come on old boy," I said kindly, "let's get you upstairs…"

"I told you so," he muttered, "I told you so…cold as a sliver of ice isn't she."

I knew he was referring to his mother. It suddenly occurred to me that not a moment of affection or genuine love seemed to pass between mother and son.

That fact made my heart ache and I began to understand why Harry was so detached and alone. An awful sadness enveloped me and was almost unbearable. Imagine, I thought, how he must feel?"

All this went through my mind as I hauled him up those bloody stairs to his room. He was like a dead weight hanging off my shoulder and his legs barely able to support him. I was hoping that some of the staff or the butler would appear but there was nobody to be seen. I had a feeling that where Harry was concerned this was not unusual.

Harry flopped onto his bed and I lifted his legs up and made sure he was comfortable before removing his shoes and loosening his tie. He was less than coherent but managed to grab my hand clumsily and attempted to pull me onto the bed – I resisted and he gave up and just looked at me for what seemed an age.

"I told you so," he murmured, "don't leave…stay a while and talk to me…"

It was almost pathetic really. I watched as he suddenly succumbed to sleep having resisted it for too long now. Looking at him in repose like that he had the look of a small boy and it made me realise I experienced real concern and affection for this man beyond what my patience would normally endure. I covered him with a rug and left him to sleep.

Wanting to clear my head after all the drama, I decided to go for a walk in the parkland. It was a pleasant day but still a little chilly with the wind but that suited me as it blew away the cobwebs in my mind and freshened up my senses somewhat. I felt rather tired myself and realised how high maintenance it was dealing with people who seemed to fall short of normal emotional intelligence. It struck me that perhaps I noticed these things more, especially the deficiencies in people, because I saw them from a writer's perspective. Whatever, it made me glad to be me and to do what I did best.

As I reached the lake – more of a large pond really – approached through a rather delightful tree lined avenue, it began to drizzle slightly with rain. I pulled the collar of my coat up and lit a cigarette. In the midst of all Harry's trials and tribulations I was wrestling with my own emotional turmoil, in some ways it made me feel uneasy, but also made me feel relieved that I had reached some sort of definitive decision about my life ahead. I had decided to conform and convert fully to the Catholic faith and also entertain the idea of marriage again, and children. In this moment I thought of Bertie and what a hypocrite he would think me, Harry too probably, as they were two of the most unconforming friends I had ever had. I was becoming the kind of person they despised. I would forsake, of course, my homosexuality. That would mean living a lie. I didn't have the courage not to.

I must have been out a long time with my thoughts. As I returned through the rose garden from the mound I could see Lomax and the staff preparing the table for dinner and the light was beginning to go – going off what I could see, and been promised, only the finest food and champagne was permitted in this family. That remained to be seen. It had become grey and overcast and I shivered as I made my way into the hall and ran up the stairs and to my room. I rested briefly and then used the bathroom and dressed myself and wondered what state Harry would be in and if he was still asleep.

Once ready I made my way to his room and quietly let myself in. I needn't have bothered. Harry was sitting on the edge of the bed and half dressed. I'm not sure he had bothered to bathe before doing this but decided not to comment – he seemed a little uncoordinated still but his will was steely as ever.

"I must dress for dinner," he said irritated, "these fucking shirt studs!"

Having never heard him use that particular language before I guessed he had been fumbling with the said shirt studs for some time. He then got up and walked to the drinks table and my heart sank.

"It might be for the best," I said trying to calm him down, "if you don't come down for dinner, I will tell them you are unwell, shall I?"

Harry has picked up the whisky decanter and is looking at its emptiness rather puzzled.

"Fuck," he exclaimed, then shouted, "Lomax!"

I had to think quickly as I didn't want to get Lomax into trouble and be the cause of more unnecessary drama.

"Don't blame him," I said with an air of authority I didn't feel, "I emptied the decanter."

He stopped and looked at me and I could see he was trying to process what I had just said. He had that look, like his mother earlier, on hearing something they didn't want to, that he had been shot.

"Why?" He said rather puzzled, childlike even, then repeated it "Why?"

"Because," I said with utter determination of purpose, "I hate seeing you like this. You are a terrible, awful, drunk and, to be frank, a bore with it! For the first time since we met I have found myself disliking you intensely. There, I said it."

He stared at me shocked and it made me wonder in that instant if anyone had ever delivered such a diatribe at Harry. Then, unbelievably, he just burst into floods of tears. He dropped the decanter on the floor and flopped into the chair sobbing again.

I crossed to him and picked up the decanter and placed it back on the table. His pathetic demeanour moved me, where as with anyone else I would have berated them for being silly and told them to grow up. Maybe therein lay the problem and why he managed to spark such unexpected caring reactions from others at his behaviour.

"Dear Harry," I said as I lifted him up and put his arm round my shoulder again, "so childlike." I walked him to the bed, "Come on darling boy you need to sleep this off."

"Don't desert me," he sobbed, "don't…"

"Never." I said smiling to myself, as I had no choice in this instant.

I got him on the bed again and déjà vu prevailed. I laughed out loud and took his waistcoat off and the one shoe (the wrong foot though) he had managed to get on in his determination to dress for dinner.

Once he was comfortable I realised that he was again asleep. I wished he still had Aloysius to put in his arms, so instead covered him with a rug. There was then a knock at the door.

"Come in," I said more brightly than I felt, "come in."

Lomax entered looking concerned. "One of the maids said she heard the master fall, sir."

"It was me, Lomax, I dropped the decanter." I crossed to the drinks table and picked it up and handed it to him. "Can you take it away, please."

"Of course, sir."

"Can you let Lady Clifton know that Harry will not be joining us for dinner. He is unwell and I have put him to bed. Nothing to worry about, just a slight cold."

"I will tell her directly," he said with no hint of his thoughts on the matter, "Can I get you anything, sir?"

"No, no thank you, Lomax."

Suddenly there was a loud noise coming from somewhere in the house. It sounded like a boy screeching and bashing furniture with something. Lomax looked at me and could see my bewilderment.

"Sorry, sir, that is master Michael. He returned early from school for the holidays and has just discovered his mechanical toy car."

"Oh, I said, bemused that another Clifton was upon us, "how lovely for him. How old is he?"

"Thirteen, sir."

With that he was gone and I rushed to my own room to get myself together before having to face Violet for dinner and defending my cheap novels again. The racket carried on from the thus far unseen Michael. He needed a good clip round the ear by the sounds of it!

Once I had composed myself and tidied myself, I opened my door and made my way to the staircase gallery. There, I beheld, a thirteen year old boy who was at least, it seemed, seven foot high, the likes of which I have never seen before. He zoomed past me in his ridiculous toy car and never gave me a second glance. A maid came rushing after him and nearly collided with me, offering a hurried "Sorry, sir" as she sped past. As I descended the stairs, I heard the boy screeching about the unfairness of having to go to bed.

By the time I reached the dining room all was quiet again and Violet gave no indication anything untoward had occurred and never mentioned Michael to me. It wasn't until I entered the dining room that I discovered, rather bizarrely, that there were separate tables, as you would find in a restaurant or hotel. The look on my face must have said it all as I had entered rather flustered at being late. Daffodil giggled again, but this time it was not so amusing. I rather hoped she had other charms and character traits to share with us for entertainment if nothing else.

"We started without you," Violet said quite brightly, "please excuse the table arrangements we find it serves us better than being clumped on one large table; especially when we are all in residence."

"Yes, of course," I said, sitting at a two table laid for one, "apologies for being late."

"Time was marching on," she said, "so we started without you. Hope you don't mind."

Lomax offered me some wine, I acquiesced without really looking what it was, or tasting it, as I was past caring really, I then realised it was champagne.

"Harry is a little under the weather I'm afraid," adding after they looked at me blankly, "nothing serious, just a cold."

"Is he drunk again?" Daffodil asked matter-of-factly, adding, "I expect he is."

"Daffodil," said Violet sternly, with an accompanying withering gaze, "That is quite enough."

"He will be fine in the morning," I said as Violet turned to smile at me, "must have been all the travelling. I have to say I am quite tired myself."

"This is such a bore for you," said Daffodil cheekily, "dear Evelyn."

I suddenly found myself ridiculously amused by their ridiculous behaviour. It was like something from a PG Woodhouse novel but not as funny. I found myself finding this constant carping and sniping at each other tedious; my limit was, I realised, fast approaching, how dare they treat me in this unjust and inhospitable way. To make matters worse they seemed oblivious to it. I checked myself and dragged myself away from these thoughts as they would lead to no good.

"The lamb is very good, Evelyn," said Violet, "it's from our own home farm."

"From Harry's home farm. He owns the lot you see," Daffodil said pointedly to me, "we just accept whatever crumbs he throws our way."

"I'm sure Harry means well," I said for the lack of knowing what else to say, "and I'm sure he will always take care of his family."

"No, he doesn't," Daffodil replied, "it's why we are moving back here as he refuses to the proper upkeep of the Kildalton on Islay."

"Daffodil, that's enough!" Violet said with barely contained anger. "It is not good manners to discuss family business with guests."

Lomax brought my meal at this point so a silence ensued. Everything was cooked to perfection including the seasonal vegetables. I was glad to focus on eating for a while and decided separate tables were, after all, a splendid idea and should be more common at country houses. Violet and Daffodil ate their meals and Lomax cleared the plates away. She then turned her attention back to me.

"I hear you are converted," she said, to my surprise as I had not discussed this with anyone since arriving, "Does the Catholic faith suit you? You are busy, what with writing as well. I hadn't realised you had been married."

"One disastrous marriage," I said, "however mistaken and brief, was I thought, enough for me." I was trying to work out how she knew this as it was something I never talked about.

"Divorced and Catholic," she said, with obvious some relish at my discomfort, "not something you stumble upon very often."

"I divorced before I converted. My first marriage was a mistake, we were too young and foolish. We both realised immediately! Common sense prevailed."

"That's terrible news," Daffodil said playfully, "I had such hopes for you and me." She winked at me which made me laugh. Violet looked daggers at her.

"You must forgive my silly daughter's ludicrous childish presumptions and fancies," Violet hissed like a snake, "She has these silly fantasies that are far removed from life and reality."

"One day, Daffodil," I said, rather oddly insulted by Violet's words, "you will realise you have had a lucky escape! I am a dreadful catch and would be wholly unsuitable as pretty much anything." I laughed a hearty laugh to make my point. If you can't beat them, join them was my motto now.

"I imagine you are right," Daffodil replied naughtily, "besides, you would run like the clappers from being entangled in this family."

Lomax brought in a cheese platter and then topped up the champagne glasses, and also Daffodil's water, then quietly left.

"I am intrigued," I said to Violet, "how you knew of my conversion and divorce?"

"Sorry, how rude," she said insincerely, "I spoke to a friend at the Spectator who knows your father. It's a small world isn't it?"

I drank back my champagne and stood up quickly which surprised them. "I'm so sorry," I said feigning a yawn, "It's been an awfully long day and I am so tired, so if you will excuse me I shall say good night to you both." I was intrigued as to why they looked at me askance but I was too tired to care. I hadn't been rude, just honest.

In spite of tiredness I left the dining room and took the stairs two at a time, so desperate was I to get to my room and get these people out of my head. It felt like they were draining the life from me. I collapsed on my bed and must have fallen asleep almost immediately. When I awoke I could see, from my position on the bed, the moon from my window. I could also hear voices in the distance – raised voices – in fact the voices of Harry and Violet arguing.

"We need to discuss Kildalton," Violet said despairingly, "the house is in need of repair and the grounds…"

"It can rot for all I care," Harry's voice bellowed, "I will never agree to spend a penny on the Islay house. I hated it when father was alive and I still do!"

There was silence and then a final "Never mention it again!" from Harry followed by a slamming door. I then thought I heard sobs.

I suddenly felt like a stranger. Harry seemed hell bent on a path of destruction to exact a pointless revenge on his dead father. He could see no irony in his actions. I decided I no longer had the energy or the inclinations to help him. I had my own demons gnawing at my door to contend with. So I had betrayed youthful ideals by conforming to society's expectations and pressures. Me, a practicing Catholic? What a hypocrite I am. I had loved the brief life I led where I could be who I truly am, the one I was now turning my back on for good.

Harry was going to Hollywood so it might be years before I even saw him again – if I ever did. The way I felt in this moment in time it seemed possible that I never would. I undressed and as I did I saw Harry wandering the grounds in the moonlight like a lost soul. I no longer had the energy or the inclination to run after him. I got into bed and slept instantly.

The birdsong woke me and, as I hadn't closed the drapes, the sun was filling the room with its warm glow. As I sat up in bed and swung my legs out I noticed an envelope that had been pushed under the door. Once I had adjusted my eyes to the sunlight and gathered myself I stood up and crossed the room to pick it up. I sat back on the bed to read it – it was from Harry.

"Darling,

I am so sorry I brought you here. I could bear it no longer after the way I treated you, and couldn't face you, so will already be on my way back to London and the Ritz to prepare for my Hollywood sojourn. My mother will not succeed in destroying our friendship (as is her wish) but I need some time before we meet again to get used to the fact you belong now to the other side (Catholics!). Thank you for caring and trying.

Much Love

Harry"

This turn of events surprised me very little. It was typical of Harry to focus on his own needs and leaving me here in Lytham as he fled back to London left me feeling rather relieved if I was honest. In that moment I decided to have my fill of breakfast and scarper myself as quickly as possible. The house seemed impossibly quiet as I made my way across the landing and down the first stairs – as I turned to descend the final flight I spotted Daffodil at the foot obviously waiting for me.

"He's gone," she said, as if this were news to me, "left before anyone was up…"

"I know," I said smiling, "he left me a note."

She looked at me impossibly attentively for a couple of seconds, as if I were a subject under a magnifying glass. "Were you lovers?" She asked matter-of-factly.

"None of your business, darling girl. You can be very impertinent!" With this I laughed to mask my slight embarrassment at being grilled by a teenager.

"I like to think you were lovers, at least that would have shown he had some taste." She said this with a seriousness that defied her years. "I shall always think of you as my lost opportunity. It's hateful to think of you marrying some day – and to a woman who doesn't understand you."

"That will be a tragedy all of my own making."

"Maybe," she said teasingly, "we'll meet in the next life and be a similar age." She saw me looking over her shoulder towards the dining room. "Don't worry, you won't have to face mother, she has gone to repent and confess her sins at church."

I looked at the portraits of Daffodils mother and father staring down with, I thought, more of a scowl than yesterday when I had first seen them. I nodded to them, "They have much to answer for." I looked at her intelligent eyes, "you'll be alright though, tough as old boots!" She laughed delightfully and we started to walk to the dining room. "A more glamorous analogy would have been nice, but yes, you are quite right. I am nobody's fool." She turned to look at me suddenly serious, "We must remain friends, too."

"Yes," I said sincerely, "we must."

With that I headed into the dining room but instead of joining me she kissed my cheek and scampered away. "Sorry, I have to look after Michael…" she said as she went. I shook my head and made my way to my single table to have breakfast alone – and what a hearty one it was too. Lomax was as always brilliantly poised and efficient, as were the glimpses of the other house staff I saw. They had much to put up with.

After breakfast I was amazed to find that my luggage, such as it was, a single battered leather holdall case, was waiting in the entrance hall with Lomax beside it and Andrews outside with the Bentley ready to take me to Lytham Station.

As I strode outside and looked back at the hall, I could see Daffodil standing on the far lawn and Michael, the impossibly tall thirteen year-old roaring about in his ridiculous mechanical car. "tearing mad" I muttered to myself.

"I beg you pardon, sir," Lomax said having not quite heard me, "did you want something?"

"No," I said cheerily, holding out my hand, "but thank you for everything." I shook his hand rather clumsily and he smiled.

"My pleasure, sir. Have a safe journey."

Andrews held the door open and I climbed in. I took one last look as I was not sure I would ever see the place again. Daffodil waved as we set off and I waved back, then the car was on the drive and it was gone from view. I felt a little sad but wasn't quite sure why. It was the house I decided, the house had had a bigger effect on me than any of its occupants had. I thought that with some sense of respect. At least I hadn't had to pretend to see the White Goddess as she had stayed back at the Ritz thank God!

Little did I know as I watched the ancient trees pass by that it would be several years before I would see Harry again. I kept myself informed but his life became even more of a circus. A very expensive one too, by all accounts!

Chapter Thirteen

We're In The Money!
The Ghost of Hollywood

Harry Clifton:

My trip to America and Hollywood was a roaring success on a spiritual level. I met a wonderful mystic there, Violet Greener of the Agabeg Occult Temple who, along with my own White Goddess, became a trusted advisor for all things financial and spiritual. She could see into the future you see and conduct exceptional séances. She suggested to me that I would have a "great success" in the film world and that my literary hero Edgar Alan Poe would have a bearing on this success. Well, as you can imagine, I was overwhelmed with this insight and guidance from the spirit world. People called her The Ghost of Hollywood and not always kindly, it was their way of making fun of her and about something they just did not understand. To me she was a divine inspiration par excellence!

One of the actions I immediately took on hearing this spirit guided news was to send a telegram to Brian Desmond Hurst back in London to say that I would like to discuss with him plans to form a film production company for a project that inspired me. It would be perfect to turn Poe's 'The Tell-Tale Heart' into a new talking picture! As I wrote the telegram I could hear my own heart beating in my chest with excitement.

Violet also saved me from an extortion racket that, to me was miraculous, and convinced me beyond doubt she had amazing powers. I had been invited by two rather attractive ladies to a private club near Los Angeles, once there we were showered with the best champagne and I was asked if I wanted to join in a card game, poker, which I enjoyed but was not terribly good at, and eventually they developed it to cash stakes, and I ended up losing a large sum of money, $150,000 which was about £30,000 all told. I duly honoured my debt and wrote a cheque to cover my losses. In spite of the promises of the young ladies I felt rather downcast and left.

Rather than go back to my hotel I went to see Violet and as soon as she saw me she said: "I know what happened." I was amazed at this, how could she I thought, and then she went on. "Who is this George Lewis?"

"My God, how did you know it was George Lewis?" I said – as this was one of the men who I had lost the money to. Her insight and voices relayed it to her as she closed her eyes and shuddered violently; her hoop earrings seeming to vibrate and jangle mystically, "how did you know anything about it at all?"

"The voice," she muttered almost incoherently as she floated in her trance, "the voice…and another man was there, Lew?" She stuttered in her trance.

She swooned and shuddered some more and then sat bolt upright and opened her eyes wide then said "Fanny Brice!" She then slumped back into her chair adding, "no…no…it's Brice but not Fanny…its…its Lew." She opened her eyes again and said directly to me "Who is Lew Brice?"

"He organised the poker game," I said amazed, "and he is Fanny Brice's brother."

"I can hear them laughing, I can hear them saying horrible things…"

"Like what" I gasped still unbelieving, "what are they saying?"

"They are laughing and saying, "we conned 'The Millionaire Squire of Lancashire'…we conned him…"

These words made me suddenly realise I had been set up and taken advantage of. Why would anyone do that to me I thought somewhat forlornly.

"What was the name of the game…the 'voice' is insistent…what is the name…" she cried out whilst still shaking so much the table we sat at even trembled with her violent vibrations.

"Poker," I said, "the game was poker…"

"No…no!" She cried out alarmingly and I worried she might tumble from her chair. Her eyes closed again. "What kind of poker?" She said this again quite aggressively and it made me think hard what she could mean and then I remembered.

"They called it Stud Poker," I said with a shaky voice so moved was I by this, "Yes, Stud Poker."

"This is illegal to play in California," she cried, "illegal. Only Draw Poker is legal…"

"How are you doing this?" I asked with my mouth wide open, "How?"

She shuddered and vibrated again and then said: "It's a God given gift and I am wonderful…the 'voice' guides me through God."

From this I learnt that Draw Poker was legal and Stud Poker was not – so I learnt something that day to my advantage – and that I had indeed been conned. Thank heavens for Violet and her powers, I thought admiringly.

"Stop all the payments," she suddenly cried out, "stop the cheque…"

"I will, I will," I cried out, "and you deserve, and shall have, a big reward for this" I said almost in tears, "a big reward!"

Suddenly she stood, very calmly and serenely, like a ghost, smiled at me and then floated off to her room to rest.

Darlings isn't she amazing? Having cancelled the cheques, though I did receive some death threats unless I paid up, but the police gave me some protection officers until I managed to leave Hollywood and go back to New York.

Once I arrived in New York the 'Daily News' headlines screamed 'Hunt for Two Queens Who Held Hands of Poker Loser'.

This related to the two girls who had coerced me into going to the club as they allegedly worked for Brice and had been paid to 'catch' me for the poker game. Lew Brice, Fanny's brother, was a notorious gambler like her ex husband and had form with the law.

I also discovered, after giving her $40,000 dollars for saving me with her gifts, and some expensive jewellery, that Lew Brice had been arrested at her home. They were friends. So she had known all along and was in on the deception.

All this set my head swimming because they seemed so nice and genuine and friendly. How could you not like people like that? Violet Greener built her temple at my expense but what a gift she had!

It pleased me greatly to hear from William the estate manager at Lytham that the dreaded death duties were almost paid off and I could start to benefit heartily from my birth right. The estates were proving lucrative and thus the incomes were increasing.

My travels to America and then Aisa and Saigon were a splendid distraction but Brian Desmond Hurst and our film project was waiting, so in many ways I couldn't wait to get back to London to start. Hurst had telegraphed me and suggested 'Clifton-Hurst Productions' which was fine by me and promised to send details for the budget of a musical film he wanted to make called 'Nora O'Neale'? That was certainly not Edgar Alan Poe, or 'The Tell-Tale Heart', so I telegraphed him back and told him so!

The 1930s were marching on and all anyone wanted to talk about was a possible new war. I closed my ears to it as it was unthinkable. Instead I focused on positive thoughts and read Poe's 'The Happiest Day' to spur me onwards.

The happiest day-the happiest hour
My seared and blighted heart hath known,
The highest hope of pride and power,
I feel hath flown.

Of power! said I? Yes! such I ween
But they have vanished long, alas!
The visions of my youth have been
But let them pass.

And pride, what have I now with thee?
Another brow may ev'n inherit
The venom thou hast poured on me
Be still my spirit!

The happiest day-the happiest hour
Mine eyes shall see-have ever seen
The brightest glance of pride and power
I feel have been:

But were that hope of pride and power
Now offered with the pain
Ev'n then I felt-that brightest hour
I would not live again:

For on its wings was dark alloy
And as it fluttered-fell
An essence-powerful to destroy
A soul that knew it well.

[E.A. Poe]

Whenever I read Poe, especially his poems, it awoke in me again the desire to make my literary mark on the world and write more poetry. That was lasting and would remain long after I was gone – at least it would if it was of a standard I felt sure I could attain. I decided to abandon singing lessons and focus on that until we could get the film company up and running with The Tell-Tale Heart. How very excited I felt at the thought of working on a film set and being part of that world – a world I knew little of apart from what I had seen at the fringes – but it was a world that could make another fortune for me. As Poe points out in the poem, a line that always resonates with me, is a stark fact that 'I shall not live again' and I shall not, so must make haste and live!

Once back in London I was settling in to my suite at the Ritz and catching up with my guide The White Goddess. She was so very pleased to see me and was beside herself with excitement when she heard the plans for the film. I had arranged to meet Hurst at the hotel and whilst waiting for him and his friend to arrive I was enjoying a few spins of the roulette wheel in the casino.

The casino at the Ritz was a dark, cosy environment, decorated in deep reds and gold, where every need was catered for by the impeccable staff that made sure my champagne was always chilled to perfection. It was never throbbing busy, always just the amount of people to feel cosseted and relaxed – the perfect atmosphere for a casino – one that ensured customers like me could lose money in supreme comfort. It was worth losing though; having an account and good credit meant I hardly noticed what I lost. I was fascinated by the feel and colour of the chips too – they had their own allure as you flipped and turned them in your hand. Like a cooling reassurance from your nanny.

It was very unlike the casinos in Monte Carlo where the whole idea was to be recognised and seen and to revel in the vulgarity of it all; of course this also meant that everyone got to see how fantastically you lost and with what good grace you brushed it off. The Ritz casino was perfect for secretive Catholics, perfect!

As I placed my bet, I noticed Brian enter with his young male companion. He was a strange, stocky looking man, slightly balding, but with oodles of charm and could talk the talk; especially when he wanted to convince anyone to invest money in his films. I played the game as one does, purely to comply with societal expectations. His younger male companion was a typical handsome Ivor Novello matinee idol type – sleek black hair and pretty with an impeccable profile and beautifully dressed in his evening wear. His eyes were particularly striking being an azure blue. I could imagine he made Brian an excellent lover – for they were both obviously exclusive in their homosexuality. That young man would, had I been interested in that life, been my ideal too, I thought, but the charms of ladies were too alluring for me. Sometimes I wondered where these thoughts came from, I shall have to ask the White Goddess tomorrow, I decided. Sitting at a table they nodded an acknowledgment and smiled in my direction, and waited for me to join them - all eyes and fascination for what was going on in the room. I suspected this was their first visit here.

Once I had watched my lovely chips being swept away by the croupier with such indifference to the two thousand I had lost, I sighed, and then made my way to join them. I sat and smiled at them both. The waiter brought my champagne and filled our glasses.

"Good evening, Harry," Hurst said cordially and smiled, "can I introduce you to Horace? Horace this is Mr Harry Clifton."

"Good evening, sir," he said with a twinkle in his eye but I remained untempted by his charms, "I am pleased to meet you, Brian has told me so much about you and the film."

"Yes, pleased to meet you too," I replied and then looked at Brian, "About the film? Shall we get down to business for Clifton-Hurst Productions next venture?"

"The Tell-Tale Heart by Poe is great material for a horror film – but I want it to be really psychologically scaring too. The small success we had with the musical has also helped establish our company name."

"Oh, that," I said waving my hand dismissingly, "Nora or Nelly was it? I can't remember…"

Horace very delightfully found this rather amusing and laughed out loud which made the other gamblers in this hushed church like casino turn and stare. Brian gave him a look that silenced him immediately but it appealed to my sense of fun so I winked at him and stage whispered in support, "Best not to frighten the gamblers, darling."

From this point on his eyes warmed to me and mine to him. Brian did his best to keep things business like and formal and I knew why of course – he wanted to discuss money. I had seen the budget he had sent over and knew that it was substantial. I enjoyed making him work for it.

"Do you have a cast confirmed or a shooting schedule yet?" I asked being serious. "You know how much I liked that young actor – he should certainly be the lead." I turned to Horace and said a bit witheringly, "sadly not a role Mr. Novello would consider taking on alas – considers himself too big a star."

"Norman Dryden," Brian said with so much self-satisfaction I thought he might burst, "he signed the contract for me today to play the murderer."

"That's very good news indeed, well done," I said rather patronisingly which made Horace suppress a laugh again, "More champagne everyone?" I could have sworn that Brian harrumphed a little but he nodded and smiled to try and conceal it had happened. I filled their glasses.

"My mystic," I said seriously to Henry, "The Ghost of Hollywood, predicted I would make this film and it would be a great success. Isn't that fascinating?"

Unfortunately for Horace he was just taking a sip of his champagne as I said this and his eyes widened in disbelief and, due to a momentary lapse in concentration, he missed his lips and it dribbled down his chin. "Ah," I said gleefully, "that reminds me of an old saying my grandmother used to make 'many a slip between cup and lip,' I hope that doesn't mean this film is perhaps a mistake?"

Brian nearly swallowed his teeth and he poked Horace in the thigh as a warning to behave and pay attention. It all amused me and I did take advantage but it was such fun I couldn't resist.

"This film will be a sure fire hit, Harry," said Brian enthusiastically, "we can get distribution here and in America."

"No such thing as a sure fire hit, Brian," I said seriously, "but with this film I am willing to take the chance that it might be."

"I've had to increase the budget though, since the one I sent you," Brian said warily, "but we have to make sure this is quality and being under an hour long it's good for playing as first feature in cinemas before the main feature. We get this right we will be making features full time."

He handed me the new budget documents and I looked at them quickly. This news made me smile and I let him wallow in his absurdity unsure as to whether I would agree or not to this increased budget.

"What do you think, Horace," I asked the startled young man, who looked at Brian for help, "do you think it's worth an extra five thousand pounds?"

"Well, I imagine so, sir, Brian is very sure it will be a breakthrough film for your company."

He said this quite sincerely if not a little nervously. I looked at them both for a few seconds and then reached into my jacket pocket to get my cheque book. They watched me intently as I wrote out the cheque and I was aware of Brian's neck craning to see the amount I was putting.

"There," I said handing him a cheque for six thousand pounds, "I expect a full and detailed account of spending, then added, "let me know as soon as you have a filming schedule in place so it can go in my diary. I want to be there." Brian folded the cheque and put it in his jacket pocket. I looked at the young Horace again, "Do you know what the Tell-Tale Heart is about?" he looked flummoxed immediately which told me he didn't without having to say anything. I held up my hand, they both looked at me.

"Thank you for the cheque," Brian said to try and alleviate the situation, "he means no harm he just listens to my ramblings and he looks after me…"

"Well," I said looking Horace in the eye, "I shall tell you. It's about a young handsome man, not unlike you, who is driven demented then mad, by the repulsive diseased eye of the older man who looks after him. One night he murders the older man and drains the blood from his body in a bucket and pours it down the drain. He then cuts up the body and hides in under the floorboards in the house they shared. When the police arrive after neighbours reported the old man's screams, all seems well until the young man driven mad, hears the old man's heart beating under the floor boards and he confesses to the murder as the sound of the heart beat drives him madder." I could see the look of horror on Horace's face and laughed.

"That…that is gross," he stammered, "really gross, like a real horror film. That bucket of blood too…"

"Be careful and keep your eyes healthy, Brian, I said with a wink, you being the older man." I looked across the room and saw a young man I had spoken with the previous week. He nodded an acknowledgment and I did the same with a smile. Brian had noticed this man too and then turned to me and said with concern.

"Do you know him?"

"Yes, a little," I replied, "I invested a couple of thousand pounds in his film project last week."

"You know he's a con artist, and has done time for fraud."

"Of course I do," I said warmly and looked at Brian directly, "but he's so charming and really rather nice. Everyone deserves another chance in life."

"Don't say I didn't warn you," Brian said a little patronisingly, then added, "We are having a party at my Mayfair flat on Saturday week, you must come."

"Yes, I must," I said with a wink to Horace. They got up to leave and I called out to Brian, "People warned me about investing money in your films too, but it didn't stop me did it? Goodnight." Horace smiled and Brian saluted and then they left hurriedly.

I enjoyed myself immensely investing money in these projects as they distracted me and now the death duties were paid I had free rein to do as I pleased. Mother was always berating me for cutting household expenses at Lytham Hall and for not keeping Kildalton Castle on Islay in a good state. Lytham I didn't mind so much, although I tried to avoid it as much as I could, but Islay was only useful for the income from renting the house out with the shooting and hunting income it brought. Rich Americans loved nothing better. I had no emotional attachment to the place, in fact the opposite as it reminded me of my father, that ever present cloud hanging over me and his damn disapproval - even in death I could feel his eyes on me always. I'd show him.

William had written to me from the estate office in alarmed tones that amused me. I had decided to purchase some wild animals from Chapman's, the wild animal dealers, as I thought a menagerie or zoo at Lytham would be fun and give mother something to organise. I sent William the letter with an inventory of animals purchased: 2 Bengal Tigers, 4 African Lions, Elephants, Giraffes, Zebras and 50 assorted monkeys.

"God bless the King, where are we going to put them," William replied, "the parklands are no good the public will get eaten!"

"Oh, I don't know," I replied, "can't you get something knocked up? Not too expensive you know."

This gave me much amusement as I could imagine them scuttling about in a panic wondering what on earth to do, and probably cursing me under their collective breaths for being the squire at all.

I liked being rich. Money could buy you anything. Anything!

Chapter Fourteen

Lilian Lowell Griswold

Evelyn Waugh:

Harry's lavish spending spree I watched from afar as his excesses kept popping up in the press for all to see. He seemed more delighted than embarrassed by the attention. All this was but the tip of the financial iceberg. Harry knew exactly what he was doing and cared even less. Talk had it that he was known as an easy touch for any con artist or crook in London. They formed an orderly queue.

So it went on, he spent money, gave it away and other times was literally robbed of it, but he carried on regardless and always tried to see the good in people or give them another chance. He never pressed charges against anyone. It was, I thought, like he was on a mission to destroy himself and his family. Was he happy? I'm not convinced he even knew what happiness was.

It was Daffodil who wrote to me to tell me about Lilian.

"Darling Evelyn,

I trust you are well? I'm frightfully worried about Harry and fear he is making an ass of himself, not that that is hard for him, but he seems oblivious to the scandals he creates and the money he wastes on ridiculous projects. We, however, live on a pittance he allows us. We have fewer and fewer staff. Mother just wails in despair! There is no consoling her alas.

I hear now some American cabaret singer or actress has got her claws into him. Where will it end? I wish you could help but I know you can't, none of us can, but it makes me feel better to write to you about it.

If you do see him, try and talk some sense into him!

Love Daffodil,"

What could I do but reply and commiserate? It was pointless me trying to talk to him as I knew he would listen to nobody. His film company with Desmond Hurst had collapsed after the 'Tell-Tale Heart' was released and was a massive flop. He lost buckets of money on that venture and its release in America under the title 'Bucket Of Blood' fared little better.

Everything he tried seemed to fail – if only he could have a success maybe that would make him focus and be sensible – but I wouldn't hold my breath. As much as I realised that Lilian may not be his family's idea of an ideal marriage partner, maybe she would bring some stability to his life and make him calm down? We could only hope.

Harry Clifton:

Lilian was an actress and singer of average talent but abundant charm and wit. She also had the ability to drink, have fun and hang the world and all its problems. I liked her instantly but ironically not on the first meeting.

Brian had invited me to one of his parties at his Mayfair flat. It was the usual kind of crowd with lots of pretty boys flirting with Brian, who was convinced they were attracted to his good looks and charm rather than the money (usually mine!) he flashed about. There's no fool like an old fool as they say. The beautiful drag queens played hostess and revelled in their role as here, in the confines of the private flat, they would shrug off the pin stripe suits and ties that constricted them by day, and slip on the lingerie they felt more at home in. In most cases they looked far more glamorous than glamorous women. Ladies dressed as men in black tie and tails smoking cigars with their feminine partners canoodling at every opportunity. The world was full of people who desperately wanted to be someone else. I understood that more than most. My father's glaring eyes looking at me disapprovingly were never but a heart beat away and haunted me – as he always would. Death though, had rendered him impotent to stop me.

Brian played piano and all the hit standards from America from Gershwin, Irving Berlin to Cole Porter, as those fawning round the piano sang along with various levels of proficiency. I preferred to watch others rather than join in. I had always been an observer of life at occasions like this and it took me a lot of years to be comfortable with that. I had no desire to dance on table tops. A beautiful hostess sidled up to me and put her hand on my bottom whilst she filled my champagne glass. She kissed me on the cheek and winked with her long eyelashes. The smell of Chanel perfume wafted about me and lingered after she walked away.

As I took the scene in standing by the window I noticed an elegant woman cross the room and go to the piano and stand beside Brian. She began to sing Cole Porter's hit song 'Anything Goes', quite an appropriate choice for the occasion and one I fully approved of. She sang the lyrics with great warmth and wit and soon had the crowd, even me, laughing at the quips and double entendres specifically aimed at the current company. The pretty boys loved her and were soon swooning and hanging on her every note.

I looked out of the window and into Mayfair and watched the people walking past the tree lined street. The impressive white stucco houses with their black railings and grand porticos were once large grand houses full of servants and families of mostly notable and always rich families. Now they were mostly converted into rather luxurious flats, maybe six within each house, which although the height of luxury, were still at odds with the original intentions of the buildings.

The rear mews that once housed the stables and carriages were now used for motor cars or sold off to be converted into private dwellings. Everything changes, nothing remains the same, in that moment I wondered what would become of Lytham Hall and Kildalton Castle and if they would still be there in a hundred years – would they have a similar fate and contain lost of flats. What a thought.

With that I heard laughter and applause and turned back into the room. The crowd were showing their appreciation to Lilian and she was smiling and bowing dramatically. She caught my eye and smiled. I smiled back and she began to cross the room towards me. The drag boys were kissing her and praising her with excitable laughter. I sipped my champagne and watched her deal effortlessly with the adulation.

"You are so tall," she said a little breathlessly as she stood next to me waving a cigarette between her fingers, "do you have a light?"

I pulled a lighter from my pocket and snapped it open and lit it. "You sing very well," I said never taking my eyes off her as she lit, drew in and then puffed out a cloud of smoke, "but smoking will not help your voice." She laughed and puffed her cigarette again not taking her eyes off me which was a little disconcerting. "I'm pleased to meet you, I'm Harry…" She cut me off with a laugh.

"I know who you are," she said, her eyes sparkling, "Henry Talbot de vere Clifton but you like the more informal Harry. Actually, we have met before but you don't remember me. Do you?" She laughed again at my puzzled look.

"Have we," I said lamely, "where?"

"At a party in New York, as I recall. I'm a Boston girl but I was in New York trying out for a Broadway show I didn't get."

"I'm sorry, I don't recall but cannot understand why as you are charming."

"That, Harry," she said laughing again, "was the right answer." She looked at me again quite intensely, "do you want more champagne?"

Without waiting for an answer she grabbed a bottle from the hostess's tray and a glass for herself. She then filled my glass and then her own. "Are you always this efficient?" I asked, rather amused by her.

"Of course, darling, especially where champagne is concerned," she looked at the bottle and added, "Wow! Especially this vintage, must have cost a bomb."

"No doubt," I said, knowing how lavish Brian could be with my money, "do you have a name?" I realised immediately that hadn't sounded terribly gallant, but she laughed anyway.

"Lilian, with just the one L, so, not like hell!" This amused her and her laugh was infectious so I joined in."

My mother would hate Lilian, I thought wickedly, she was everything she just didn't understand in the brittle young things that now dominated society – we had all been bright once, but had faded somewhat.

"I don't do anything seriously, apart from live day to day, and I never had what you would call a proper job of any kind. I'm not a very good actress," this she whispered loudly, "and an okay singer, but only at parties when drunk." She paused to look at me again scanning my face for a reaction. "How about you?"

I liked her honesty and desire for hedonistic pleasures with no sense of responsibility, which I could relate to. "Never mind me," I said, "what do you live on?"

"My wits mainly, but thankfully I did have a small allowance from my father…"

"Did?"

"Yes, it ended when he realised I was not doing anything serious with my life," she sipped her champagne and puffed her cigarette, "I guess he thought it'd shock me out of my frivolous ways but he was disappointed. Boy," she added, "you ask a lot of questions for an English guy."

"I understand the effects of having a domineering and demanding father. Mine is dead but he still watches me I'm sure. I feel his eyes on me constantly."

"Gee, that sounds kind of creepy!" She shuddered at the thought and sipped her champagne. She held her hand out, "pleased to meet you again, Harry." She shook my hand and her skin was soft to touch and she felt sensitive. She tilted her head back and laughed heartily. "You're a find!"

"What's so funny?"

"You and all of your questions," she said, "most men just ask if I wanna fuck!"

This made me laugh out loud and I somehow felt I had found a kindred spirit and she was the only person that made me want to dance on the table top with her. We drank and danced that night until the dawn and it all became a blur of pleasure.

Evelyn Waugh:

Harry and Lilian became inseparable after that night. They went on a drunken bender for some weeks and it was widely reported in the gossip columns of the press. Photographs of them drunk in bars and clubs; falling out of taxis into the street; being helped discreetly by staff at the Ritz to their suite via the service lift so none of the guests would see them in their debauched state.

One morning they found them selves stirring from sleep, in their Ritz suite that looked like a bomb had hit it, with drunken debris scattered everywhere along with clothes and their respective self respect. In those moments they first stirred from sleep, along with their long absent sobriety, they were amazed to find the other was still there. Lilian no doubt stared in amazement at Harry, and he at her, and wondered what on earth they had done. The ring on Lilian's finger sparkled in the morning sunlight that streaked through the windows with its unforgiving glare; exposing all the harsh reality they now faced.

The accompanying wedding ring sealed their fate. In some ways I am being flippant in this analysis but it is not far off the mark, the public knew more of their romance and exploits and eventual marriage than they did. Excess drinking does that. They hadn't been remotely sober for weeks.

Harry's worst nightmare was to suddenly realise he had become a hypocrite, just like me, and had conformed like everyone else. But now it was too late, he had made his bed and must make the best of it. For Harry that was almost impossible – nobody had ever showed him how to!

He consoled himself with being married to Lilian with the thought that he could spend money to forget and that his mother would abhor everything Lilian stood for; or didn't as she had nothing, and worse, cared little because of it now she had a rich husband.

The first indication that Harry was once again making headlines with his extravagant spending was newspaper reports of him purchasing the famous Renaissance Egg by Faberge at Christie's Auction rooms on Bond Street – this as a love token for his new wife. This accompanied a photograph of them, looking less than sober, outside the auction house. He was quoted as saying:

"We were just out for a walk along Bond Street and noticed the auction was on that day so I went in and Lilian fell in love with the Faberge Egg - so I just bought it. It was only £40,000!"

They then, it was reported, left the auction house to thunderous rounds of applause to which Lilian responded by waving imperiously at the crowd and hung on to Harry's arm as he made his way to write a cheque for the purchase. She was quoted as gushing:

"Harry's a darling husband and he would do anything for me; buy anything I wanted. Who could ask for anything more?" She then burst into a couple of bars of the song for the delighted crowd.

Spending so much money on a whim was so typical of Harry. His mother was incandescent with rage when she found out and seemed determined to do everything she could to save the family and its reputation from Harry.

To add to his family's woes they decided to also take up residence at Lytham Hall with the rest of the family. I couldn't help thinking that this was a deliberate move by Harry to cause as much discomfort and distress as he could. He enjoyed watching the turmoil he created and found it amusing.

William the estate manager still hadn't quite forgiven him for the Menagerie affair. Having gone to the trouble of securing a site for the animal park and having pens and cages erected to house the wild animals Harry had purchased from Chaplins. Harry arrived one day by car, to be shown the fruits of all William's, and the estate staff's efforts, to look at the construction after winding down the car window he just said "No, I don't think it would do: let's forget about it," and promptly drove off. That however didn't end the matter. Chaplins still insisted on having their invoice for many thousands of pounds paid as the animals had been secured and delivery was in hand.

During this flying visit he also made sure the hated billiard table was gone. He didn't chop it up and burn it as he had threatened as revenge. William managed to appease him by saying the new St Annes-on-theSea Conservative Club would be pleased to have it. Harry agreed and it enjoyed its new home far more than its old one.

Chapter 15

Insanity!

Violet Clifton:

Having spent sleepless nights wondering if half the Serengeti would be arriving at the Lytham Hall park land, imagining staff being eaten by lions and tigers or trampled by herds of wilderbeast; or attacked by hordes of wild monkeys, I then had to also contend with Harry being reported in the newspapers for squandering money in eye-watering amounts elsewhere. Some nights I went to bed and prayed; but then some nights my only consolation was to shed floods of tears to relieve the pressure of my anger at what he was doing to the family and our reputations.

I did my utmost to carry on with dignity and remained tight lipped in regard to any criticism of my errant son. Dutifully I

attended local functions and cut ribbons on behalf of the
Clifton Estate; presented rose bowls to the annual Rose
Queen, who usually looked less like a rose than one could
imagine, and waved past the various floats on the parade day;
having to smile until my face literally ached in agony.
The farms also had their award days and agricultural shows
that required me to trudge about in mud looking at ferocious
looking bulls and cows and get barked at by awful dogs that
were impossible for their owners to control. It took its toll but
I did it as it was my duty. Harry rarely put in an appearance
and if he did he never wanted to have to deal with these kind
of events. He behaved terribly imperiously towards everyone.

This marriage of his to the American woman appalled me
because I could see no good coming of it; they both seemed to
be two spoilt and irresponsible children, although they were
adults in years, who had no sense of responsibility and what
their place in this life ought to be. It was a disgraceful and
vulgar display of impropriety and squandering of money. I
had decided that Harry's mental health was at the very least
suspicious and at worst in need of having him locked up! The
Faberge Egg was the final straw for me and I took matters into
my own hands.

I consulted the family solicitors that had dealt with my
husband so as not to cause any conflict and asked if it would
be possible to pass the estate to Michael before it was too late.
Their answer was blunt. Now Harry had inherited the simple
answer was no, unless there were extenuating circumstances
like he became mentally incapable or incapacitated. Then a
court order could be applied for to manage his affairs on his
behalf. This gave me hope so I made an appointment with a
Harley Street doctor.

As I emerged from my appointment with the doctor and stepped back onto Harley Street I suddenly heard a voice calling me. It was Evelyn Waugh! Of all the people to meet on a day like this, I thought, but then smiled at him.

"Violet," he said rather impertinently, as I preferred a more formal address, "how lovely to see you."

"Mr, Waugh," I said in a business like way, "It seems I was wrong and another war is looming!" His face was a picture and I could see he was unsure what to make of this remark – and my sarcasm. "How odd bumping in to you. I'm referring of course to Mr. Hitler's rise in Germany."

"Oh, yes," he said, "I see," then laughed a little uncomfortably and insincerely, "I hope all is well with you?" he said looking at the doctor's brass plaque, "Are you ill?"

"It is not my sanity I fear for," I said waspishly, "but that of my son."

"Oh, dear, Harry again," he said with an amused tone. I failed to see what was amusing about it. "Twice I have tried to get a doctor to commit him, before there is nothing left," I said rather coldly, "The Faberge Egg was the last straw."

"Yes, I heard about that, in all the papers," he said, then asked, "Committed?"

"Do not judge me Mr. Waugh," I said to him witheringly, "I do this out of love for the family and our heritage."

With that I walked away from him determined that he not see my anguish over the whole sorry business.

Evelyn Waugh:

She looked at me with an expression that would wither most plant life instantly. It struck me as slightly chilling and I stepped back from her slightly. As I did a car whooshed past behind me and I nearly stumbled on the curb. "That's a bit drastic," I blurted out before I could stop myself.

"Drastic? He's obviously insane," she spat out, "and needs locking up. I had hoped the control of the estates would then pass to Michael, who is much more suited to the role."

Suddenly I had visions of the ridiculously tall thirteen year old child roaring about in his ridiculous toy car when I was at Lytham Hall. He hadn't struck me as the model of common sense at the time. She was staring at me and I said "poor Harry" without thinking…

"What rot, Mr Waugh," she was close to apoplectic, "your sympathy is wasted on the scoundrel and his awful wife. The only ones ending up poor are the rest of the family." She gathered herself together and then said as she walked off, "I'll bid you a good day!"

I watched as she marched off down Harley Street, she was tall and frightfully haughty and the other pedestrians instinctively moved aside to let her pass. I could hear the clip, clip of her sensible shoes and her cape wafted and flapped in her wake like wings on a demon, I thought.

I was aghast at the ice in her tone. Not a spark of maternal concern escaped through her fury. To attempt to have her son

committed as insane horrified me. I began to realise how lucky I had been to have such a loving childhood and home life. It hadn't been perfect by any measure but nirvana in comparison. It was obvious that this being her second attempt, and failure, stoked her outrage that she hadn't succeeded in having him declared insane.

However, a seed had been sown in my mind for a new novel. I wanted to immortalise my Oxford years, and those I had encountered from different classes in society, for posterity. Capture a sense of those halcyon days and preserve them for future generations; a romantic and tragic story about a lost world. A world that was changing rapidly and with a sinking heart I felt strongly that Hitler would sweep away all we had known – if another war came - and maybe all of us with it.

Landed gentry like Violet Clifton and the aristocracy would be part of that lost world, and would be the first to be swept away. That made her plight to preserve the family heritage from Harry's squandering more poignant – and futile.

Chapter Sixteen

2023 – Kildalton Castle
Islay

Islay is rather bleak and chilly even on a July day. The wind comes in from the Atlantic and catches you unawares making you shiver and pull your coat tighter about you. It is a beautiful and bracing place and has a haunting quality about it – in more ways than one as it turned out! The cottages and houses that hone into view as the ferry approaches Port Ellen seem to cling to their granite foundations like limpets, determined the harsh winter winds will not dislodge them. The sun suddenly breaking from the clouds seems to change the season from winter to summer in a heartbeat, with its golden rays illuminating magnificently what moments earlier looked bleak. The whitewashed houses and cottages suddenly alive and welcoming until the sun, hiding behind more clouds, changes the mood again. The wind creates an audible sigh of despair and then whips you with laughter like it is playing with you.

The sea is grey and constantly swirling as it contemplates and thrashes the harbour walls in a never ending swell and embraces the small fishing boats and the ferries as they come and go - and gathers behind in their wake as if reluctant to release them. The abyss below seems dark and forbidding but it is all part of the mystery and allure of Islay. It tempts you in and wants to welcome you to explore its boundless beauties; like some ancient sirens calling, the gulls and birds screech and scream at each other and the sound of the wind caresses the rise of the land and the wings of the birds as they constantly swoop and glide above.

Leaving the village along the road to Kildalton Castle the shore is rough and no doubt hardy souls live here in the beauty of its bleakness. The old Clifton estate and lands are all around and I can see why John Talbot Clifton, that hardy Victorian adventurer, the Laird of this place, was inspired by its roughness and its demands to be conquered – for that was his passion, to conquer all before him. I could imagine him marching through the woods and the heather clad pathways and over the fields with his beloved dogs following happily, alert to his commands. He loved this place and it is obvious why. Here you are miles from the intrusion of life – a hundred years ago it would have seemed even more remote than it does today. You would have been cut off in the bleak harshness of winter as the wind howled like a coven of angry witches set for revenge but he would have loved this challenge and would have strode forth in spite of it.

The island's website recalls an experience that suggests the place is haunted and reported how: "Two women were walking in what was once the Laird's property, Carigmore Forest. From nowhere the two women saw a man walking towards them dressed in clothes from another era. Walking his dog, a terrier, the man passed the ladies without any sound and disappeared into the bushes." Could this have been the ghost of John Talbot Clifton, still roaming his beloved lands a hundred years after his death? Or perhaps his loyal factor, the estate manager, waiting for his Laird's return?

Climbing Fairy Hill, known locally by its Celtic name Cnoc Rhaonastie, I could see his grave coming into view along with the panoramic sweep of the vast landscape that were once his estate lands. He would have stood here often and this view would have changed not at all in the hundred years that have passed. This was a perfect resting place for him, chosen by Violet in spite of Harry's complaints as to the cost of returning her husband's, and his father's, body from Tenerife. Reaching the pile of carefully placed stones, topped with a Celtic cross, which marked his grave, it seemed almost too humble for such a giant of a man. A simple plaque tells us his name and how loved he was. The wind caught me and came blustering hard and in that moment I thought I could hear the wails of the piper and Violet as she wept here for the man she loved and had lost. On that day of his internment in 1928 she recalled:

"The men of the isle had resolved on a Highland funeral. Twelve of them offered themselves as carriers of the coffin when it should leave the cart to be carried the steepest part of the way. About a hundred men followed. The women of Islay are never present at the burial of the dead, but today, because they knew that I would follow the dead, some of them had gone to a knoll over the grave and there waited the coming of us mourners. The piper, who had come from far away, also waited among the short trees, piping the lament, 'The Flowers of the Forest', whilst fell the soft Scots mist.

Once again, just as after Talbot's death, but now for the last time, I felt an enveloping beatitude, an invading sweetness…suddenly there fell a winged shadow over the grave. And we looked up and saw a golden eagle that twice soared, and twice stooped, and then swung away out of sight. I thought 'is this to tell me that his youth is renewed like an eagle's? …I then kissed the foot of his coffin for the last time before it was lowered into the ground."

Such drama that had happened here nearly a hundred years ago still seemed to stir the air and echo hauntingly. The ghostly shrill of the piper seemed everywhere and the spirits from that past seemed to whirl about me and cause a chill to run through me. My breathing was sharp and the sudden cold exacerbated the difficulty of catching my next breath. Suddenly the air was oddly calm and the sun burst through the clouds, the golden rays streaking across the leaden sky and catching the spot where this man rested for eternity. It felt like a brief welcome and a reassurance that no harm was intended by any restless spirits about me. As happened then, it happened now, a golden eagle swooped across the sky, circling over me, and caught the sun's rays with its wings and then was gone, leaving the mournful wailing of the wind in my ears.

Looking about me I glanced down and there it was, the ruins of Kildalton Castle. It was in fact more a giant Victorian mansion house than a castle, but in its day it had been beautiful and magnificent in its proportions. Built by a whisky distiller and MP for his family's use in 1870, John Talbot Clifton had purchased it, and the estate, in 1922 when he had been run out of his lands in Ireland by the IRA. It added to his considerable estates in Lancashire and his other home Lytham Hall.

I could see that the many sharp gabled roofs were in disrepair and some sections had no roof at all; gaping holes where there were once windows. Nature was creeping nearer and nearer and would soon consume the now abandoned house. It made the whole story seem impossibly poignant and if only I could have seen this place a hundred years before, when it was maintained and cared for by an army of staff and estate managers, the family living here for long periods so the sound of the children screeching and running through the heather and bracken. A great flock of sea birds swooped above me and seemed to echo that sound of happily playing children making the hairs on the back of my neck stand on end.

As I descended Fairy Hill and the ruins got closer, its spirit still seemed vibrant and the whole place had a look of something enchanted. It was calling out to be taken in hand and loved again. The sadness of the place elevated by the sheer grandeur and scale of it, the need to be embraced again and lived in. Looking into some of the rooms you could still see remnants of what they once were, forlornly they sat open to the elements and nature's creep had sadly passed the thresholds – I imagined John Talbot Clifton's favourite room to retire to with his wife – a cosy study towards the back of the castle with its double doors that opened onto the lawns. Its current state so aptly described by a local on the island's tourist website:

"Kildalton castle now looks the perfect spot for a ghost story. The windows are dark and filled with shadows that play tricks on your eyes. In the morning, the pale mist leaks from the cracked panels. Travelling on the breeze with a swirling vapour, it gives the impression that the house is breathing deeply."

The spirit of this place and those who had lived here remain, like ghostly guardians, and the castle, although abandoned, lives on and waits. With the wind whipping at my ears, the ever screeching birds calling their lament, I left this place reluctantly. It has been an honour to have such a close inspection, as the public are not allowed onto the estate or near the ruin for safety reasons. At least, I thought, the ghost of John Talbot Clifton can haunt in peace and undisturbed by our modern world. My hope is that he can still see Kildalton Castle as it was in his lifetime.

Harry tolerated coming here but hated it. Once he inherited when his father died, and death duties paid, he treated it shabbily by refusing to allow money to be spent maintaining it. The lands and farms were also neglected and he was interested only in what money he could get for renting it out to rich Americans for shooting holidays. His family had to leave this place and move permanently back to Lytham Hall. His mother, horrified, when Harry suggested that if she wanted to remain, she would have to share the castle with paying guests. That was the last straw for her. So she had to leave their beloved Kildalton Castle, and the grave of her husband, and would never return to live there because her son's squandering of his inheritance meant that money was difficult for everyone but Harry.

For Harry, the eyes of his dead father looking at him disapprovingly were nowhere more vivid and haunting than here on Islay. I could imagine John Talbot reciting a poem by Shakespeare or Poe, as he did in life, a passion for literature he had passed to his son:

"A dark unfathom'd tide
Of interminable pride –
A mystery, and a dream,
Should my early life seem;
I say that dream was fraught
With a wild, and waking thought
Of beings that have been,
Which my spirit hath not seen,
Had I let them pass me by,
With a dreaming eye!
Let none of earth inherit
That vision on my spirit;
Those thoughts I would control
As a spell upon his soul:
For that bright hope at last
And that light time have past,
And my worldy rest hath gone
With a sigh as it pass'd on
I care not tho' it perish
With a thought I then did cherish."

[E.A. Poe]

Chapter Seventeen

Storm Clouds

Easter Daffodil Clifton:

As I looked from the window sitting at the drawing room writing desk, I could see one of the gardeners tidying a flower bed in the foreground, and standing majestically in the parkland beyond was a beautiful Oak tree said to be over a hundred years old. If only we could be as firmly rooted, stable and secure in life I pondered. With these philosophical thoughts I became quite transfixed in my reverie. This was sharply broken by a loud thudding noise from above and the sound of a door being slammed; suddenly accompanied by a dog in the grounds barking furiously. Welcome back to Lytham Hall, I thought rather glumly.

The noise above I thought might be the precursor to another flaming row betwixt Harry and his new wife, Lilian, with whom I had hardly bonded in the normal sister-in-law fashion; mainly because she was such hard work, to me anyway, seeing me as a minor irritation to be endured. This thought made me laugh out loud because I had no relevant place in this family and never had really; a child and sibling of no importance. Gosh, I sounded like some odd title for an Oscar Wilde play – the main character being, like me, at least as a child, nothing but an amusement, a distraction, someone to parade in front of friends as the "little sister" or "darling Daffodil," like I was in want of a vase, which was an irony as I had never been remotely little or flowery either. To be fair my other two names were perhaps more useable for some but the charms of 'Muriel' and 'Therese' held no appeal for me either. We were all, due to our parents' genes, vertiginous of stature too; a cross we bore, staring down at people mostly!

The withering looks of the family came crashing down on me when I set my heart on marrying Gerald Fortray Baird. He had been a ridiculously handsome young factor at Kildalton Castle and I had first clapped eyes on him when he was 22 and I was just 11. I was always attracted to handsome and interesting men – never their titles or their breeding; that kind of snobbery I left for the other members of the family. I suppose I was always older than my years until I caught up. We married in Edinburgh in 1936 against my family's wishes, only my sister Avia attended, and I had been pretty much ostracised since then. Harry marrying Lilian (that didn't suit mother and had eclipsed anything I did wrong in the marriage department) and his financial recklessness had created a thaw and I was here to support mater – or at least try to. They still refused to see Gerald so he was working in Scotland at another estate and happy to not have to endure the madness of Lytham Hall and a clutch of hysterical Cliftons all in one place. I bit my tongue for the sake of peace and was glad to not make him suffer – although I missed him terribly.

I chided myself for being dreamy when I was trying to write a letter of such utter importance. I then found myself envying that beautiful oak tree and wondering if it remembered somehow all it witnessed. I liked to think so. I set about the task in hand and smiled as I recalled my terrible flirting when I first met him here at the hall. We had kept in touch ever since and I blushed at the thoughts I once had about him.

"Dearest Evelyn,

It seems an age since we last met and of course I am now happily married to my darling Gerald, although he spends a lot of time in Scotland in the Highlands or abroad working. He's an estate manager, or factor as they call it in Scotland, and once worked for my father. What that entails I have no idea if I am honest, but he does keep me in a financial manner I wasn't accustomed to under my brother's patronage. If war comes, as they say it will, all will change and he will be whisked off in some uniform or other to goodness knows where.

I am so excited to hear you are coming to Lytham Hall again and cannot wait to see you – and I know Harry is looking forward to it too. His wife is, as you may know, American, from Boston, and a bore, which you may not know, and they have frightful rows! How I wish he could have found a wife with a personality as enchanting as yours.

Staying with mater, after she wouldn't speak to me because I married Gerald, has been trying but I wanted to make an effort, and sometimes I think she gets rather lonely. My two elder sisters are off living their own lives having washed their hands of Harry. Michael is starting university unless war comes sooner than later and he is whisked off to the services. Anyway, I am impatient to see you and to hear all your news – I read all your deliciously naughty books. They are a riot and I still hoot laughing just thinking of them.

Love Daffodil"

Just as I scribbled my signature, and right on queue, mater marched in and went to her favourite chair by the fireplace. She seemed, for once, in a brighter mood. "You seem very jolly today," she said whilst glancing at her newspaper, it's about time the mood was lightened in this house. The atmosphere is terrible for the staff," she looked at me curiously, "Who are you writing to?"

"Evelyn…"

"I don't trust him or his cheap novels," she said rather disdainfully, "just be careful what you say to him. We don't want family gossip emerging in those awful books of his."

"Don't be absurd, mater," I said admonishing her, since I married I found I was no longer afraid of her, "and please don't keep talking to me like I am still a child. His novels are not cheap, they are very funny actually."

"Maybe so," she said sadly, "just be careful…"

"Anyway," I said rather haughtily, "as a family we are hardly the paragon, are we?"

"I'm sorry, darling. My nerves are just so on edge with one thing and another," she said whilst pointing at the ceiling to where Harry and Lilian's rooms were, "It's torture listening to them."

"Is Harry paying the estate office, staff and tradesmen's invoices?"

"Yes," she said with, I thought, some hesitation, making me think she wasn't telling the whole truth, "but not always on time or in full. Several of the staff we had to let go as we simply cannot afford them anymore. The suppliers usually champ at the bit for payment. It's very demeaning; sometimes I'm afraid to show my face in the town."

As I listened to this tale of woe, I sealed the letter to Evelyn and wrote the address on the envelope. I then rang the bell for Lomax. "Oh, mater," I said sadly, "just rise above it – at least we can do that without much effort!" She laughed at this reference to our height, and it was nice to see her smile a little. "You must speak to Harry seriously before Evelyn arrives – it wouldn't do to make a scene with guests here. He must be more responsible with money and if he can afford Faberge Eggs then there is no excuse. He always finds money by the cart load for what he wants."

"I will speak to him," she answered half-heartedly, as if she already knew it was pointless, "Anyway, what do you mean Faberge Eggs? I know he purchased one…"

"Didn't he tell you?" I said rubbing home the point, "He spent thousands and thousands on another one – the Rosebud Egg" I looked at her horrified expression, "It really is bad form!"

"Oh, dear, I hope the greengrocer doesn't hear about this. He will want his invoice for the last six months paid immediately."

I looked at her aghast and shook my head at the mess Harry made of things and the unnecessary worry he caused mater. "Try and catch him sober if you can – they are both functioning alcoholics if you ask me."

"Nobody is asking you, darling…"

Before I could tell her off for being so head-in the-sand about such things there was a knock at the door and the ever suffering but fabulous Lomax entered with his usual cool grace and charm. We could learn a lot about how to behave from him.

"You rang, ma'am," he said to mater.

"It was me, Lomax," I said brightly, "be a dear and post this for me pronto." I handed him the letter.

"Of course, ma'am, will there be anything else?"

"Can you make sure a guest room is made up, Lomax," mater said, "I hear Mr. Evelyn Waugh will be arriving in the next day or two."

"Yes, ma'am."

Lomax left us and again I looked from the window to the parkland and the oak tree's leaves were gently rippling in the breeze. "Things are in a pickle, mater, try speaking to the estate manager William about the bills." I said smiling at her, "try and think what father would do if he were here." At the mention of father's name I could see a ripple of sadness flash across her face.

"If your dear father were here," she said with real melancholy, "we shouldn't be in this predicament. He would possibly shoot Harry and be damned with the consequences."

This made me laugh for some reason, mater was hardly ever witty, and I am not sure that was her intention, but it hit the spot and even she chuckled at the irreverence of what she had said. "Yes, I think you are right," I added jollying her along, "just a shame the Harley Street quacks wouldn't have him committed. It would have saved a lot of trouble for everyone."

"Yes," she gasped, clutching her pearls involuntarily, "but we are where we are. In a mess!"

We then both stared at the portrait of my father glaring down at us in his inimitable way. He would be so cross at the way his children had let the side down. I still think that he would have supported my marriage to Gerald, he knew him and liked him when he worked for the family at Islay, they respected each other. My father would not have shown the snobbery and disdain for him that mater had - of that I was sure!

Suddenly there was a crash above us and the sound of muffled voices raised in anger. Mater looked at me and we both sighed. "Here we go again!" She said sadly, "What did he ever see in that woman, the language is atrocious. What the servants must think is beyond my comprehension."

"The trouble is," I said with a resigned shrug, "they sobered up and saw each other for the first time. American women stand up for themselves, Harry didn't reckon on that. He met his match."

The shouting and screaming above continued followed by a loud crash of something smashing. She was a good shot so I hope she didn't hit him with whatever came to her hand, I thought.

"Dear God," mater exclaimed in horror, "forgive them!"

"God can't help them now, mater," I said sadly, "He can't help them now."

Evelyn Waugh:

Rather than drive up to Lancashire alone I had decided to take the train to Preston and then change onto the branch line for Lytham. Harry had arranged that Andrews would pick me up at the station and drive me to Lytham Hall.

I had started working on my new novel, the central character was called Sebastian Flyte, a rather beautiful, troubled and indulged young man from an ancient landed family who arrives at Oxford to bewitch everyone he meets. Christ Church would feature as he would have rooms there.

I was looking forward to seeing Harry again and meeting his wife Lilian. The flighty American! I had seen images of them so frequently in the press reporting their exploits that I felt I knew her already. Seeing the delightful, unabashed Daffodil again would be a joy as always, and make this trip bearable, but seeing his mother Violet I was not relishing at all. Since the Harley Street encounter I had taken to referring to her as Violent! Her blindness to the reality of her family and their problems, and her snobbery over Daffodil's marriage to Gerald, baffled me.

I had decided this was probably the last time I would see Harry and Lytham Hall. The world was imploding and war was inevitable now thanks to Hitler. Aside from that I no longer wanted to endure the exhaustion the Cliftons brought to all who knew them. They really were all tearing mad! - More so than I ever imagined at first sight.

They would be surprised at my news, certainly Daffodil, as I had recently married Laura Herbert, a good Catholic girl for an appalling Catholic boy like me. I wanted children and would damn well have them, aside from that I wanted the peace and security a good wife would bring me. I needed looking after like never before.

Bertie came to my mind and made me smile as he always did, and I laughed to think that out of all us hypocrites and conformers he was the only one who stood firm. It cost him his life, taken by his own hand, but he had the guts to do that. I knew I was too much of a coward to be able to commit suicide – not that it had ever occurred to me thankfully. I cannot imagine what terror it is to see that as a last resort. I wished for a time in the future where the Berties of the world could live in peace and be and love who they wanted; sadly that kind of life was not recognised or tolerated in the world. If the world survived the war that was coming, maybe change would happen in that regard. Bertie would always be with me as a beacon of what to fight for.

Once I had changed trains at Preston and settled down the train juddered from its normal rhythms and then went back to its soothing clickety-click, clickety-click and the motion rocked me to sleep. It has been a long journey.

Before I knew it I was arriving at Lytham Station and as I emerged from the carriage the trusty chauffeur, Andrews, was waiting patiently for me. "Good evening," I said cheerily, wondering if he remembered or recognised me, "Nice to see you again, Andrews."

"Had a good trip sir?" He said smiling, "nice to welcome you back to Lytham Hall, sir." With that he picked up my small case and started to walk to the car and I followed obediently. The other train passengers I noticed peering at me, probably to see if I was anyone of note - obviously not by their dismissal, as they quickly resumed their own journey and jostled past impatiently. Human nature can be so rude at times.

Once in the car we started on our short journey to Lytham Hall. Through the main gates we proceeded along the long driveway to reach the secondary, less formal, gates. I had decided on a big aristocratic house as the seat for Lord and Lady Marchamain. Lytham Hall was a fine Georgian mansion but it needed to be something grander, more excessive in size to represent what had already been swept away. Blenheim Palace was too regally pretentious but Castle Howard in Yorkshire was, in my mind, perfect for Brideshead.
That is what I had decided I would call the house and the novel. Feeling very pleased with myself I said it out loud without realising.

"Brideshead!"

"Is everything alright, sir?" Andrews asked looking at me through his rear view mirror.

Yes, perfectly," I replied, "thank you, Andrews."

Harry Clifton:

Ensconced in this house with Lilian was making me ill and her behaviour was insufferable. She drank too much, actually we both drank too much, as it was the only way we could tolerate being in the same room together. Looking at her in her shabby dressing gown with her hair all disheveled wearing those ridiculous, impractical slippers with fur on made me despair at my stupidity for marrying her at all. Why couldn't she just leave me alone?

"Don't," she said pointedly, "dare to accuse me of using you!" I had a happy life until I met you. You only married me to prove to the world you could but no, sorry to say, you are still a spoilt, petulant child who needs to grow up!"

"God, you have a nerve," I spat out angrily, "I can't tell you the shock and trauma I suffered when I sobered up and realised I'd married you. I must have been insane!"

"You," she sneered and actually bared her teeth, and moved in front of the door to block my path "are an up-tight stupid Englishman with your entitlement and demands. You get taken in and conned all the time and couldn't run anything with success." She swigged her drink back and added, "You make me sick! Your mother had the right idea when she tried to have you sectioned – you are insane!"

"Take a look in the mirror," I shouted, "take a look at what you really are and don't you dare criticise me."

I went to leave but she blocked my way and I tried to move her but she grappled with me and it turned into a ludicrous jostling with neither of us prepared to give in. "Get out of my way," I cried, "for God's sake what is wrong with you?"

"Make me…" She grabbed my jacket and held on determined to get the better of the situation. In the struggle I knocked over a priceless Chinese vase and it smashed in pieces in the floor.

"It suits you when you can spend money though, doesn't it?" I shouted, "look at that ridiculous bathroom you paid all that money for. I hate the colour – it's a cold blue – just like you! A cold and heartless bitch."

I managed to get past her and out the door but she was soon following, determined to win this argument and berate me further, "That's right," she yelled after me, "you coward. Run away and go and hide in your room like a pathetic man child."

I suddenly stopped and rounded on her furiously. It surprised her and she stopped in her tracks and we glared at each other a few feet apart. "Don't push me, Lilian, or I'll…I'll…"

She laughed at me. "You'll what?"

I ran into my bedroom and managed to slam the door before she could follow. I worried that we would actually kill each other one day, so decided to let the whole thing calm down and let her sober up. She wasn't letting go and she started to hammer on the door.

"Let me in you son of a bitch!"

The hammering was making my head ache. I grabbed a drink and sat on the bed as she continued to scream and berate me through the door. I felt trapped and in a nightmare with nowhere to escape.

"I'll make you pay for this!" She shrieked like a common fish wife, "you just watch me!"

After a few moments the hammering stopped and I relaxed back onto the bed. What had I done, what had we done, this was never going to work. It seemed such fun at first but it had turned into a disaster.

I listened carefully but all was quiet, I gathered she had gone back to her room and was calming down. Far from it. I suddenly heard banging and then the sound of a window sash being opened. After a few moments I heard Lilian shouting but it seemed to be coming from outside. I was disorientated at first and then with horror I realised what she had done. She had climbed out of the window onto the ledge and was making her way to my window.

"You won't run away from me," she screamed, "I'll, get you if I have to drag you out of there."

Easter Daffodil Clifton:

Mater and I were listening to all this with horror in the drawing room below. At one point I was going to intervene but mater stopped me and said it wasn't worth the trouble, they would calm down. But they didn't and then we heard the loud crash and I decided another priceless vase had seen its end.

"She's stopped hammering the door," mater said whispering, "at least that might be a good sign?"

"Shhhh," I hissed, "I wouldn't count on it…"

"My head is throbbing," mater said collapsing exhausted into a chair, "what did I do to deserve this."

"I'm sure I heard a window opening," I said straining to hear, "it's quiet again…"

"Maybe," said mater, "they've gone to sleep?"

"Passed out drunk again, more like."

With that there was a sharp knocking on the door and Lomax, a little breathless came in looking unusually flustered. Mother looked pale and ready to faint and I thought that at this moment I would give anything to be back home in Edinburgh with my lovely Gerald.

"What is it, Lomax," mater asked wearily, "it's not a good time."

"The master's wife," he said with trepidation in his voice, "is on the first floor ledge ma'am. She climbed out of the window."

"Good God!" I said in a normal voice, "why are we all whispering? We do all live here."

"Oh, my goodness, Daffodil," mater cried, "She might fall and kill herself."

"Every cloud!" I said naughtily, and I am sure I saw Lomax smile.

We rushed outside to see what was going on and sure enough there was Lilian wobbling along the ledge towards Harry's bedroom window. On reaching it she started banging on the glass and screeching his name.

"Let me in," she screamed, "let me in you son of a bitch!"

"Excuse me!" Said mater indignantly, which completely baffled me and amused me at the same time, "there is no need to be personal."

"Mater," I said laughing, "it's just an expression, a saying, nothing personal I'm sure."

Lilian must have heard this through her hammering and shouting at Harry and responded by looking down and nearly losing her balance in the process: "Don't be so fucking sure, lady!"

This made her wobble and teeter on the ledge and we all held our breath as I was certain she would fall but miraculously, as drunks often do, she managed to catch her balance and teetered no more. With that a distant rumble of thunder rolled across the parkland and the sky had darkened and looked more threatening. Nature, it seemed, decided to join in the drama with a thunderstorm.

"God dammit, Harry, open this God damn window now! Harry?!"

With each mention of God's name my mother genuflected and caught her breath. Once a Catholic, I thought, as it was all adding to the drama and amusement for me. Lilian continued banging on the glass and in that moment I saw the car heading towards the house. Super, I thought, Evelyn has arrived just in time – it would save me having to explain it all later on.

Suddenly we all looked up as Harry's bedroom light went on and he was at the window. He yanked up the lower sash window with such force and with such speed that Lilian suddenly yelped and started to wobble on the ledge.

"Why can't you leave, me, alone," he screamed rather ungallantly at her, "I just want some peace!" He then saw us all standing below and seemed at first as if he was trying to think why we were there. "What?" he shouted down at us, "What are you all looking at?"

Lilian wobbled and teetered again and went to grab Harry but he ducked back into the room and as if in slow motion we watched helpless as she began to fall backwards flailing her arms like some demented, injured bird. As she was in mid air, Evelyn emerged from the car with a look of disbelief on his face, and we all cried out in horror but knowing the inevitable crunch would come as she hit the floor.

Harry was watching her fall and his face was grimacing. "Leave me to my misery," he cried, rather inappropriately I thought, "This is your own entire fault."

On the word "fault" she hit the ground with a rather sickening thud. We all stood motionless looking at her crumpled body on the ground for a few seconds that felt like an eternity. In that time Harry must have seen Evelyn.

"Oh, hello Evelyn," Harry said from his window, jolly as a jolly thing, "I hadn't realised you'd arrived."

We all looked up at him in silence as he withdrew into the room and slid the sash down. We all then looked at the heap that was Lilian still on the ground.

"Is she dead?" asked Evelyn aghast, "shouldn't someone check…"

"Hello darling Evelyn," I replied, "Just in time, you might have missed all the fun."

By this time Lomax was kneeling beside Lilian and assuring us that she was very much alive, just stunned. He put her into a more comfortable position and began to check for any broken bones.

With that a huge rumble of thunder sounded across the parkland followed swiftly by a crack and flash of fork lightening. Some large globs of rain started so we all made our way inside. Lomax and Andrews carried Lilian.

"Lomax," said mater, having regained some composure, "call the doctor to come immediately."

"Yes, ma'am," he said breathlessly as he carried Lilian's limp body with Andrews, "right away, ma'am."

We all followed them in and watched at the bottom of the stairs as they heaved Lilian up to her room. She must have been a dead weight to them as they were sweating and struggling to carry her. How undignified, I thought, typical American to cause all this fuss. Once they had disappeared we trudged into the drawing room.

I wondered if the thunder was my dead father's way of showing his anger at the mess Harry had wrought on us all. Thus assembled in the drawing room with tea and anxiety, nobody knew what to say, small talk seemed frivolous, we all waited to hear the verdict about Lilian. Harry was nowhere to be seen, which was rather rude of him as Evelyn had arrived. The thunder and lightening continued out side but the rain was holding off for now. Mother stood by the window looking quite frail. We waited like this for nearly an hour.

"No rain yet," she said, like a prophet of doom, "but it's coming."

Lomax appeared and looked quite flustered for once – his cool calm reserve vanished.

"How is she," I said with as much concern as I could muster, "what did the doctor say?"

"He said mistress Lilain will be fine with rest. Just bruising, but nothing broken, a sprained ankle and perhaps mild concussion. He has given her something to make her sleep.

With that he crossed to put a log on the fire.

"It probably helped that she was drunk," I said, adding, "When she fell."

"What a night to arrive!" Evelyn said rather cautiously, "That thunder is biblical too…"

"The Gods aren't too happy by the sound of it," I said to him with a wink.

"Daffodil," snapped mater, "there is only one God. Isn't that right Mr. Waugh?"

"Yes Violet," he replied.

"I have taken your case to your room, sir," Lomax said to Evelyn, "is there anything else you need?"

"No thank you," Evelyn replied, "Is Harry joining us? I mean Mr. Clifton?"

"He went out a few minutes ago, sir."

Mother suddenly turned to look at Lomax having heard this. She seemed rather perplexed again. "Out?" she said, "Where?"

"He's probably gone to cool off," I said, "and sober up. Can't face Evelyn after all that drama."

With that a crack of thunder shook the house to the point it made things vibrate which shocked and silenced us all. We looked at each other and seemed to have all gone rather pale. The fork lightening then crashed and flashed and lit up the room sending us all a weird bluish colour.

"I must try and find him," mater said concerned, "he shouldn't be out there in this weather."

With that she followed Lomax out of the room leaving Evelyn and I alone. Another loud crash of thunder shook the house and I grabbed his hand almost unconsciously. He pulled me to sit beside him on the sofa.

"Are you all right," he asked kindly and smiled, "it's a horror of a storm."

"Perfectly, thank you," I said smiling and feeling better, "Funny isn't it? The first time we met you were an adult and I a child with a crush on you."

"Goodness," he said looking rather embarrassed, "you'll make me blush. I did like you too," he added kindly, "very much, but had to be sensible and mature."

"Funny," I said laughing, "that's what my husband Gerald told me when I was eleven. He was twenty two at the time but I made it clear I would marry him when I grew up. And I did."

"Where did you meet him?"

"He worked for my father as a factor at Kildalton – a factor is an estate manager or game keeper. That's why my family don't approve of my marriage and shun him."

"Darling, very Lady Chatterley," he said laughing, " D.H. Lawrence would be proud of you…"

"Well, I say 'shun' but actually they just pretend that Gerald doesn't exist at all. As if that will make him disappear altogether."

"They were probably just looking out for you…"

"That," I said sarcastically, "is the most boring thing I have ever heard you say, Evelyn. There is a little part of me still in love with you, of course, but not in the way I imagined."

"Are you letting me down gently?"

He said this with a twinkle in his eye I found adorable. "No," I laughed, "with a big thud! Besides you are married too, she is a lucky girl." I nudged him in the ribs and he laughed, "Now we are equals, in an emotional sense, I see how hopeless it would be. We would be the ones throwing ourselves off ledges in the middle of a storm and having terrible rows."

"You are right of course," he laughed, "we would drive each other mad!"

"As hatters, darling, but even madder! We are already terminally insane with little prospect of ever changing."

"Tough as old boots! That's you, Daffodil. Your husband is a very lucky chap."

"Oh, yes, I love him desperately."

I hugged him tightly and in that moment imagined all that might have been had things been different for us both. But in a way this thing we had was, and would always, remain untainted by reality. That was the beauty of it, life and drudge could never destroy it. That made me smile and hug him a little tighter.

"It was a nice dream," he said, that made me realise he had had similar thoughts, "I shall find a way to immortalise you."

"In your new novel?"

"Brideshead."

"Funny title," I said smiling at him," I was hoping for something rather racier." Looking at him I wallowed in his beautiful eyes for a moment, then added delightedly to lighten the mood, "Anyway, mater will be furious if I make it into one of your "cheap novels" so I couldn't be happier!" Suddenly another loud bang of thunder reverberated through the house and made me shiver. The lightning made an awful cracking noise and I was sure a tree in the parkland had been hit. Evelyn looked concerned which made me more uneasy.

"There is terrible trouble brewing," he said with an uneasy voice, "this storm is far from over."

I stood and crossed to the window and he followed me. We stood there watching the storm and knew it was a metaphor for the mess the family was in. Mater came back into the room and flopped into her chair exhausted by it all. We remained by the window.

"We can't find Harry," she said wearily, "I do hope he will be alright …"

I'm not sure I cared much anymore. One thing I was sure of was that Harry cared even less for us!

Epilogue

Parting

Harry ran across the parkland towards a clump of trees near the stable block and looked back at the house. He was sweating in the humidity caused by the storm. The clouds lowered menacingly and seemed to get blacker and blacker and swirl in anger above him. Fork lightening suddenly streaked down from the blackness above and struck a tree with a loud crack – a sound that reminded him of his father's shotgun exploding. This made him run into the open as he remembered that being under trees during a storm was dangerous. He reached open ground and felt a pain in his chest and couldn't get his breath. His energy drained away as he gasped for air. He felt the occasional glob of rain hit his face but this only foretold of the deluge yet to come once the heavens opened.

A huge roll of thunder shook the ground and reverberated through his body. It was like the Gods were angry with him. Looking up at Lytham Hall at the very moment the lightning flashed again and streaked its blue shards across the dark sky to the ground, in the eerie light it created he was shocked to see the ghost of his father standing at the window staring down at him. His eyes glaring in anger and disapproval.

Harry tried to run but was still breathless and couldn't get away. His father's eyes burning into him. As the lightning dissolved into the ground and gave way to the blackness of the clouds his father's ghost melted away. His heart started beating erratically and panicking he fell to his knees and began to crawl along the grass. Looking towards the house he could see the silhouettes of Daffodil and Evelyn in the drawing room window looking out towards him. They seemed unmoved and were motionless so he knew they could not see him. He lay there for a moment turning onto his back and looking at the darkness above.

The fork lightning streaked down again at the same time the thunder roared its anger so the storm was right above him. He sat up and looked back at the house and there again in the eerie blue electrical light was the ghost of his father staring down at him

"Noooooo!" he screamed in fear and dread at his father's ghostly apparition, but his words were swallowed up and unheard. "Leave me alone, you will not beat me. I will destroy you and everything you ever stood for" he cried almost childlike. Harry stood now and stared back defiantly at his father's form, his confidence growing, the fear he felt finally ebbing away. "Stop haunting me," he screamed as another flash and roll of thunder came along with more frequent globs of rain. "Do you hear me? I hate you and how you treated me!" He then started to move closer to the house, the ghost of John Talbot Clifton stared down defiant from the window. Harry screamed at him, "I just want to be me!" Suddenly the rain came and a torrent washed down over him in a great spattering deluge. As this happened his father's ghost slowly dissolved and Harry began to laugh hysterically as he fell to his knees. He had stood up to his father for the first time.

He looked back at the house and there in the doorway he could see someone standing looking at him. He tried to focus his eyes but the rain had made them sting and his vision was blurred with the tears. He wiped his eyes with the back of his hand and he could make out Daffodil and Evelyn still silhouetted in the drawing room window but in the doorway he saw Bertie standing there smiling at him and waving, and in his arms he was holding Aloysius the teddy bear. Harry

cried out his name but it was eaten up by another, more distant rumble of thunder and the patter of the rain. Suddenly the White Goddess appeared behind Bertie and placed her hand on his shoulder. He gave one last wave and they slowly dissolved away.

Harry lay there in the rain feeling full of joy and liberated from the staring eyes of his father. Bertie was watching over him and that made his heart nearly burst with happiness. Life was to be lived, life was for the living. Nothing would hold him back now, nothing.

Evelyn Waugh:

I decided after this visit to part ways with Harry. It was better, I thought, to remember him as young and charming, full of love and laughter - the man that had enchanted me when I first glimpsed him on his arrival at Oxford. That was, I decided, the Harry I wanted to immortalise somehow. This haunted, drunken husk he had become was too much for me to bear. It is hard enough fighting the living, impossible to fight the dead. Love, as they say, really is the sweetest thing – but it can also turn ugly and be unforgiving too.

Evelyn Waugh

Chapter Eighteen

Aftermath.

*"Making his blood flow,
And his cheque-book to open
More lavishly then ever heretofore,
That all he loves, the good opinion
Of posterity; his own free conscience
May prompt his of all wrong absolve
In this great new struggle
For freedom and right…"*

[Harry Clifton]

Once World War 2 was declared, Harry had the notion to join the Royal Air Force as he saw himself as a 'Lawrence of Arabia' type character. The R.A.F. saw him otherwise and he was not accepted. Instead he decided to concentrate on farming as there were demands from the government for landowners to start growing food so the country could be as self sufficient as possible.

He decided to purchase other farms in the country as far away as Hertfordshire and Essex, and also demanded that the Lytham home farm be brought up to scratch and start producing more crops; and thus the same with the estate on Islay. He set up a company called Clifton Agricultural Company with a head office address of 40 Buckingham Road, London. This would be his mission for the war years as it stopped any travels abroad – that said, it didn't stop him spending money like water, and he certainly had plenty of it. The other major change was that, unlike Evelyn Waugh who converted to Catholicism, Harry denounced it in 1941 and joined the Church of England. Lytham Hall, or the upper floor, was also used as military hospital during the war with Harry's blessing. Sadness too for the family as his sister Avia passed away in 1942.

In the late 1930s he had ordered his estate manager William to sell all the ground rents he owned in the towns of Lytham, Ansdell and St Annes-on-theSea, this comprised about half the ground rents owned by the family that had been "carefully built up over the last hundred years." William was no doubt hoping that the proceeds from the sale, that amounted to a handsome sum of £700,000, this in addition to the land sold to create Blackpool Airport that brought another £175,000 for his disposal, would mean he would not be receiving any more telegrams like this:

"Close Lytham Hall; sell horses; dismiss all staff. Stop. Absolute order. Stop. Cancel sisters allowances. Stop. Raise mortage ten thousand pounds in case I need capital; cable Royal Hawaiian Hotel five hundred pounds. Stop. Cancel subscriptions all my clubs. Advise me orders carried out. Clifton. SS Lurline."

Harry was wont to issue this kind of directive via telegram and William knew that the trustees would never allow him to carry them out. He cabled back to say the money had been cabled to the hotel in Hawaii and that orders would be carried out. When Harry arrived in London a few weeks later he never mentioned these instructions again.

From the mid 1930s to 1940 Harry had sold off land worth more than a million pounds. That was not all at his disposal as he had to pay off mortgages he'd raised to the tune of £400,000. So the financial merry-go-round continued but Harry's recklessness would start the final decline in the family's estates and fortunes.

Once Lilian had recovered from her fall from the ledge outside Harry's bedroom, in the event she suffered "chest injuries, a damaged spine and fractured her right arm in two places, according to an account in the Clifton Chronicles, by the estate's chief surveyor, she:

"Lay for several weeks in the principal bedroom attended by nurses and visited by eminent doctors and surgeons. Here she held court, received friends and took a keen interest in all that went on. I – then chief surveyor of the estate – was one day summoned to her bedside to take a glass of sherry and have a chat. During the conversation she said, 'I guess you're wondering what all those crates are.' Down one side of the room were about twenty stoutly made wooden boxes, which could not fail to attract attention in such surroundings.

'Yeah, we've cornered the world emerald market,' she said with a slight note of sarcasm in her voice. 'Go on, bring one over and dump it out on the bed.'

Her instructions being complied with, out came a quantity of pale cloudy green fragments, somewhat like the green chippings used for filling inside the kerbs round a grave.

'That's dross from a South American emerald mine; if you can find a clear bit, that's an emerald. You have a look!'

An anxious search through the dross not revealing any pieces of the required transparency she said: 'We can't find any either. I guess we've been done again.'

This kind of sums up the way people took Harry for a fool and royally fleeced him time and time again. They separated and their divorce eventually came through in 1943, she admitted adultery with a naval officer. Lilian tried to cite cruelty over the fall from the ledge, but the judge threw it out saying:

"As to the window incident the husband said he was in no way responsible for it, and had no part or lot in it. There was no corroboration of the wife's allegation that her husband pushed her."

Several years later she wrote to Harry after hearing some story that he missed her. It seems clear that she believed there was another woman involved and she seems to have never got passed that. That was more likely to have been one of Harry's games to try and manipulate her and see how she reacted – as he was capable of doing to all those who knew him personally or through business dealings. She also claimed that his mother Violet was working with Harry's estate manager, William, to try and get him certified as insane. She wrote:

"Why you ever married me and fell in love, while [she], giving you the royal run around, still fascinated you. No doubt you thought you could outsmart her. You should know that those women have lived an entire life of mean paltry greed and their entire mentality is given to improving their technique in separating the male from his wallet. Any man who thinks he can outsmart a woman at her job of more and more security is not thinking…believe me, had I been after money, I'd have demanded more pay for playing nursemaid to a brat who had his candy and broken his chains…"

Who this woman was, if she ever existed, is a mystery as no name is given. Lilian declares she still loves Harry even though they were divorced. She went on:

"I know I could have controlled the ghastly mess but I didn't want to then. There was no happiness in it for me and if you were so insistent on destroying your happiness and your possessions I'd be darned if I was any old school teacher to a stubborn mule who thought he was a hell of a smart guy who could out-clever professional crooks. The only way you'd ever learn was when your cheque bounced and there was no more land to sell and the art collection swindled out of you.

To tell the truth you didn't care. A nasty little boy can be spanked but a grown man who has no more self respect than a lot of cheap vanity is just a plain nuisance. I was bored with a silly pest who was so sure he was God's original genius...I know you were acting like a nut from hurt pride, but I had nothing to do with it and I got the brunt of your entire thirty-four unhappy years...I can enjoy you while you don't have me in your collection, but when once bought, quickly forgotten. That wasn't a nice experience.

As friends we might be happy in each other's company, but not as one of your possessions. I just wanted to make sure you understood why I asked you to visit. I want to see a very dear friend of whom I'm terribly fond. Please come over Harry. I can think of nothing which would so please me.

Affectionately yours,
Lilian"

By the end of the war Harry had in his inimitable way managed to get involved with businessmen and ideas that cost him dearly. From land purchases to works of art and precious antiques – mostly all proved to be forgeries - he was conned and robbed mercilessly but, oddly, seemed to brush it off as bad luck. It was as though he really believed he was a clever man and that all the schemes were good but rotten chance intervened along the way. It was self-delusion on a grand scale.

When Waugh published Brideshead Revisited in 1945 it is recorded that Violet Clifton, Harry's mother, never spoke to him again as she was convinced that Lady Marchmain was based on her and Sebastian Flyte on Harry – and that it also echoed other members of the family. That said, half the aristocracy in England had the same thoughts after supposedly recognising themselves in the book. Surely that is a testament to Evelyn Waugh's skill in portraying believable characters that reflected their world back at them...

Lilian Clifton, Harry's wife, outside Lytham Hall circa. 1938

Harry Clifton

The Last Squire of Lytham

Chapter Nineteen

Decline & Fall
The Last Squire of Lytham

"Our revels are now ended. These our actors,
As I foretold you, were all spirits and
Are melted into air, into thin air:
And, like the baseless fabric of this vision,
The cloud-capp'd towers, the gorgeous palaces,
The solemn temples, the great globe itself,
Yea, all which it inherit, shall dissolve
And, like this insubstantial pageant faded,
Leave not a rack behind. We are such stuff
As dreams are made on, and our little life
Is rounded with a sleep."

[William Shakespeare]
The Tempest

In 1957 the London Evening Standard mentioned Harry in a newsletter by Sam White. Harry had been living in Ireland and France for tax reasons and was a 'non resident' in the U.K. It was a 'news from abroad' type article:

"Of the many eccentrics who pass through the gilded salons of the Monte Carlo casino, the most notable, as befits tradition, is an Englishman. He is fifty-year-old Harry Talbot de vere Clifton, Squire of Lytham in Lancashire. Clifton has the reputation of being a mystic and a poet. He looks the part.

Tall, bearded, always dressed in heavy tweeds with a heavy brown scarf wrapped around his neck, he wanders around gambling tables as though in a trance.

His abstracted air is something of a legend in the casino. He sometimes speaks to complete strangers under the impression that they are old friends, and ignores old friends under the impression that they are strangers. He is a bachelor and describes his family as 'The Royal Commoners' who can never accept a title because of their royal descent.

Clifton is the author of several little-known volumes of poetry. In the casino, apart from his trance-like air, he is notable for heavy gambling carried out with the appearance of complete unconcern, and sudden outbursts of indiscriminate generosity.

Recently he fished two pieces of jewellery out of his pocket and distributed them to two complete strangers. Clifton [claims] he has lived a great deal of his life in India and it is to this that he attributes his apparent sensitivity to the slightest chill in the air. During a spell of cold weather he will not leave his hotel suite for several days on end.

India has also given him an interest in mysticism and a friendship with Nehru and his sister. He plies Nehru and other Asiatic politicians with letters and cables advising them on the conduct of affairs.

But the oddest thing about Clifton is that, despite his mysticism he retains a lively interest in the world of business. Outwardly a recluse, he confers constantly with a circle of international business men. They stand [Harry states] in considerable awe of him, and it is an interesting sight to see them agitatedly waiting a summons to his suite. Clifton's current business preoccupation is the establishment of a tanning industry in India."

By this time Harry was living in a dream world, and his delusions had greatly increased with every failure, and none of this bears any relation to the reality apart from his gambling and wasting money. He had visited India briefly but hardly lived a great deal of his life there, and the so called "businessmen" desperate to see him were no doubt crooks and con artists who had heard what an easy touch he was. It is very sad and nobody seemed able to do anything about it.

His mother, Violet, died in 1961, and had lived at Lytham Hall to prevent it being repossessed my the mortgage company. By 1963 Harry was desperate to find things left to sell and it was perhaps inevitable that the Lytham Hall and its estate would be next. It was finally taken over and purchased, to repay the heavy mortgages, by Guardian Royal Exchange. John Kennedy, the last estate manager, recalls:

"Although I was employed by Guardian from May 1963, I continued to look after Lytham Hall until the company bought the house in 1966. After the sale there remained on the premises family portraits and a few pieces of furniture.

One day, one of Harry's henchmen arrived at the estate office and informed me that 'Mr. Clifton had sent him to Lytham to see if there was anything left in the hall or office that could be sold, as he was in need of money.'

Suddenly I felt a surge of anger amounting almost to fury at the prodigal and stupid waste of a magnificent estate. I pulled open the strong room door and said:

'Look! Here are his father's guns; the furniture, Sotheby's say, should be sold on the premises. Let's put the lot together and have an auction sale at Lytham Hall! My God! The end of Cliftons of Lytham!'

A picture fell to the floor of the office. I picked it up and turned it over. It was the engagement photograph of John Talbot Clifton and Violet Mary Beauclerk.

By 1979 Harry was living in the rather seedy Emerys Hotel in Brighton owned by a friend. It was renowned as a dive in the town. He was taken ill at the hotel and died in the Royal Sussex County Hospital. The cause of death was cardio-respiratory failure, bronchopneumonia, debilitation and ischemic heart disease. He was 72.

He left just under £30,000 in his will. In his lifetime he managed to spend over 3.5 million pounds by ravaging the Clifton estates until there was literally nothing left. That is worth about 70 million pounds in today's money.

He outlived all his brothers and sisters.

His Obituary stated:

"Mr. Harry Clifton, Fylde's most famous landowner, former Squire of Lytham, traveller, gambler and friend of kings has died in Brighton aged 72.

The white-bearded, nomadic recluse, once one of the richest landowners in the country and until 1937 owner of most of Lytham St. Annes died in hospital yesterday, virtually penniless.

He had taken ill with a heart attack, the second in a short time, at the Brighton home of his close friend for the last twenty years, Mrs. Margaret Kilner, a soothsayer.

Mortem aut Triumphum!

Grand Duke Michael
Brother of Tsar Nicholas II
Visitor to Lytham Hall in 1908

Easter Daffodil Clifton and her husband Gerald Baird

Violet Clifton – Harry's Mother

John Talbot Clifton – Harry's Father

Avia Clifton and Easter Daffodil Clifton at Lytham Hall 1935

*They both met Evelyn Waugh during his visit that year where he described the
Cliftons as "all tearing mad" to Lady Asquith.*

Parents:
John Talbot de vere Clifton. 1868 – 1928
Viloet Mary de vere Clifton (nee Beauclerk) 1883 - 1961

Children:
Henry [Harry] Talbot de vere Clifton. 1907 - 1979
Yseult Hermione Aurea Alathea de vere Clifton . 1908 – 1952
Avia Lena Elmira de vere Clifton. 1909 – 1942
Muriel Easter Daffodil Therese de vere Clifton. 1914 – 1978
Michael Richard Alleye de vere Clifton. 1917 – 1974?

References:

Books:
1. The Clifton Chronicles by John Kennedy. Carnegie Publishing Ltd. 1990.
2. The Book of Talbot by Violet Clifton. Harcourt, Brace & Co. New York 1933
3. Gleams Britain's Day. Poems by Harry Clifton. Duckworth. London. 1942.

Poems:

1. Eldorado / chapter one / E.A. Poe
2. The City In The Sea / chapter 8 / E.A. Poe
3. The Raven / chapter 8 / E.A. Poe
4. To One In Paradise / chapter 8 / E.A. Poe
5. Autumn / chapter 10 / A.L. Rowse
6. Song / chapter 11 / E.A. Poe
7. The Happiest Day / chapter 13 / E.A. Poe
8. Imitation / chapter 16 / E.A. Poe
9. Prospero's speech from the Tempest, Act 4, scene 1, by William Shakespeare

Further Reading / Evelyn Waugh (1903-1966) :

1. Decline & Fall by Evelyn Waugh. Chapman & Hall, London. 1928.
2. Vile Bodies by Evelyn Waugh. Chapman & Hall. 1931.
3. Brideshead Revisited by Evelyn Waugh. Chapman & Hall. 1945.

Quotes from the Islay Tourism Website: Pages 249 & 251

The Ritz Hotel Restaurant – Perhaps Harry Clifton and The White Goddess still dine there every week in spirit, a table always ready for them…

Faberge's Renaissance Egg – 1894
Owned by **Henry Talbot de vere Clifton**: 1937-1947.

Original purchase price: 4,750 rubles in 1894

Alexander III commissioned Carl Faberge to create the Renaissance Egg for his wife the Empress Maria Feodorovna. It was crafted in the Faberge workshop by Michael Perchin. The contents of the agate, jeweled Easter Egg remain a mystery but it has been speculated that pearls were the surprise. Others believe that Faberge's Resurrection Egg was the surprise inside as its form perfectly fits the curvature of the Renaissance Egg.

The egg was purchased at a London auction house by Henry Talbot de vere Clifton in 1937. It was in his ownership for ten years until he sold it at a New York auction house in 1947.

It is now in the collection of the Faberge Museum, St. Petersburg.

https://fabergemuseum.ru/ru/collection/item/26

Faberge's Rosebud Egg – 1895

Owned by **Henry Talbot de vere Clifton**: 1937-1941.

The original purchase price: 3,250 rubles in 1895

The Rosebud Egg was commissioned by Nicholas II for his wife Alexandra Feodorovna in 1895 as a love token for her first Easter in Russia after their marriage. The yellow rose symbolized her love for the flower and its rarity in her native Germany. It was made by Michael Perchin under the supervision of Carl Faberge. The surprise was the rosebud along with a cabochon ruby pendant and a miniature of the golden imperial crown with diamonds and rubies. The latter two surprises are lost.

The Egg was purchased by Henry Talbot de vere Clifton at a London auction house in 1937. He sold it at an auction in New York in 1941 – the same year he divorced his wife, Lilian, so it may well have been part of her settlement.

It was rumoured that the egg was damaged due to a marital dispute in the 1930s. One can speculate that perhaps this damage occurred during the stormy relationship between Henry Talbot de vere Clifton and his wife Lilian

It is now in the collection of the Faberge Museum, St. Petersburg

https://fabergemuseum.ru/ru/collection/item/28

Flyte of Fancy
Short Film

Screenplay by David Slattery-Christy
Filmed on Location at Lytham Hall
With: Mathew Rajat Bose (Harry Clifton), Ann Bougett (Violet Clifton),
Martyn Coyne (Lomax the Butler).

Directed & Filmed by Gillian Wood
Sound by Ed Christiano
Original Music by Adam Simpson

1930s Austin Car (Image above) with thanks to D Hollowell & Sons

Full length screenplay 'Flyte or Fancy' based on this book
in development 2023

Milton Keynes UK
Ingram Content Group UK Ltd.
UKHW011813231023
431195UK00003B/62/J